PRAISE FOR RICHARD B. SCHWARTZ

Proof of Purchase

It's like this guy is just channeling Raymond Chandler on every page. . . . The ending . . . would make Mike Hammer proud.
— Jochem Steen, *Sons of Spade*

In this engaging hard-boiled mystery, one of three in Schwartz's Jack Grant series (Frozen Stare; The Last Voice You Hear), the seasoned California PI looks into the disappearance of an ex-girlfriend at the request of the woman's husband. When her mutilated body turns up in the woods, Grant makes it his mission to track down her murderer. With the assistance of Lt. Diana Craig, an attractive fast-riser in the San Bernardino police department, Grant follows leads that point to his client, as well as to a consortium of underworld bosses who are branching out into a mega-real estate project. The pair find time, between car chases and gun battles, to begin a relationship. . . . Fans of Robert Parker will enjoy encountering Grant . . . .
— *Publishers Weekly*

The Last Voice You Hear

It's not often that an author's second book is as good as the first, and even less frequent are the instances when an author . . . top[s] it with an extraordinary second . . . deliver[ing] a walloping good tale as well. Richard B. Schwartz has done just that. In *The Last Voice You Hear*, Mr. Schwartz places himself on par with our finest contemporary murder-mystery writers. This is a book you won't want to miss. . . .
— Alan Paul Curtis in *Who Dunnit*

The author . . . writes vividly, putting the reader right into the scene. Schwartz explores the meaning of right and wrong, crime and justice.
— Mary Helen Becker in *Mystery News*

The story rockets along . . . a fast-moving, well-told story with a surprising conclusion that blurs the line between crime and justice.
— Joseph Scarpato, Jr. in *Mystery Scene*

Jack Grant, the Vietnam vet and Pasadena-based PI who debuted in Frozen Stare (1989), returns in this engrossing sequel by Schwartz, author of several scholarly studies of Samuel Johnson. Schwartz knows his London, but surprisingly he evokes California with equal ease, mainly with vividly etched strokes. An apparently maniacal killer is on the loose in London, someone strong and very practiced at impalement. So far, so nasty. But when a victim is dispatched in similar fashion in Disneyland, of all places, Jack Grant is called in. He discovers the killer's identity, but there's a problem: there's a method to the killer's madness. Moreover, Grant has an ethical problem of his own: he's plagued by his conscience, since he understands and even sympathizes with the murderer's cause. The cinematic climax takes place high above the floor of the California desert, and Schwartz squeezes every last drop of suspense from his setting. . . . The result is a high-tension thriller awash in sanguinary detail. Paper towels, anyone?
— *Publishers Weekly*

Frozen Stare

I welcome Richard Schwartz to the club. It's been a long time since I've seen two more engaging characters entering the series scene.
— Sandra Scoppettone

Grant and White play nicely off each other and the switch-on-a-switch works well.
— *Kirkus Reviews*

This tale, in the California private eye tradition, has a rousing finish and is an enjoyable read.
— *Publishers Weekly*

A new author devoted to the hard-boiled tradition. . . . Schwartz has the hard-boiled formula down pat. . . . Schwartz does not break any rules in Frozen Stare. . . . He writes crisply. The narrative moves at a slam-bang pace as bodies pile up. . . . As a dedicated student of the hard-boiled school of detective fiction [Schwartz] has learned his lessons well.
— *The Washington Post Book World*

Gives a whole new meaning to the phrase 'cold-blooded murder'. . . . This is a quick read with plenty of action. Schwartz's first novel is a winner!
— *Sarasota, FL Herald Tribune*

This is a delightful tale, full of amusing touches, and the relationship between Grant and his good cop friend, black Frank White, is a joy. I hope that Schwartz can keep this standard up for a long time to come.
— *The Armchair Detective*

Nice and Noir: Contemporary American Crime Fiction

Opinionated but always fascinating, shrewd and smart, but always readable. . . .
— *The Thrilling Detective*

BOOKS BY RICHARD B. SCHWARTZ

FICTION

The Jack Grant Novels

Frozen Stare
The Last Voice You Hear
Proof of Purchase

The Gwen Harrison Novels

No Exit
Red City

The Tom Deaton Novels

Into the Dark
The Survivor's Song
Nightmare Man
Death Whispers
Poison Touch

Short Stories

Townhouse and Other Stories

CRITICISM

Samuel Johnson and the New Science
Samuel Johnson and the Problem of Evil
Boswell's Johnson: A Preface to the Life
Daily Life in Johnson's London
After the Death of Literature
Nice and Noir: Contemporary American Crime Fiction
The Wounds that Heal: Heroism and Human Development
(with Judith A. Schwartz)
ed. *The Plays of Arthur Murphy, 4 vols.*
ed. *Theory and Tradition in Eighteenth-Century Studies*

MEMOIRS

The Biggest City in America: A Fifties Boyhood in Ohio
Accidental Soldier: A Reserve Officer at West Point in the Vietnam Era
Postwar Higher Education in America: Just Yesterday

EBOOK

Is a College Education Still Worth the Price? A Dean's Sobering Perspective

TOWNHOUSE
AND OTHER STORIES

RICHARD B. SCHWARTZ

TOWNHOUSE AND OTHER STORIES

Published by Dark Harbor Books
First Edition 2024

Cover design: Jana Rade

ISBN: 979-8-9899271-0-4 Paperback Edition
         979-8-9899271-1-1 Hardcover Edition
         979-8-9899271-2-8 Digital Edition

Library of Congress Control Number: 2024900866

Author services by Pedernales Publishing, LLC
www.pedernalespublishing.com

10 9 8 7 6 5 4 3 2 1

Printed in the United States of America

v5

*For Steve, Norbie and all of
the Good Guys who Strengthen
our Hearts and Lift our Spirits*

CONTENTS

PREFACE

After completing a study of contemporary crime writers and their novelistic fiction entitled *Nice and Noir* I felt a certain frustration at the fact that I could not continue on, knowing that new, excellent novels would appear on bookshop shelves the moment I was finished. That has proven to be the case, of course, and while every person who writes on anything 'contemporary' does so with full knowledge that the work will be immediately dated, the feeling is particularly intense with regard to crime fiction, which continues to grow in quality and influence in the American, British and, indeed, world markets. Most of my favorite writers have published exceptional books in the months and years since I relinquished my grasp on the (provisionally) final manuscript. I have satisfied my desire to record my responses to a large number of those titles by reviewing them for Amazon.com, but I wanted to do more.

The only alternative which I could find was to reinforce my admiration for those who work this ground by doing some stories of my own that reflect a number, but by no means all, of the dominant themes and modes of this most popular of forms. With one exception the stories are not designed to imitate specific crime writers, but rather to reflect, in a very modest way, the vast breadth of practice within the broad parameters of the genre. I have even strayed into the previously-unexplored world of the *cozy*, the more English, more east coast branch of the genre that attracts a vast number of readers (though I set the story in northern California). The impulse to attempt ambidexterity is not unique, given the fact that many writers have developed multiple crime and mystery series so that they themselves might move among the different modes that constitute contemporary practice. Ruth Rendell, to take a notable example, even changes authorial titles (to Barbara Vine) when she explores the darker side of life.

I have now broadened my own work to three novelistic series, focusing on more investigative elements in one, more procedural elements in the others (and expanding the setting to the east coast with greater frequency). In the process I learned several things about myself. First, my novels' subjects tend to be very different in nature, even though they might share the same ensemble casts. That is because I tend to write on issues that are either of current interest or ones that are of special interest to me. I also learned that I have a warm spot in my heart for revenge stories, mainly because they seem to work so well and provide satisfying endings. I must confess, however, that fifty years of experience in academic settings have also provided some stimulus for the practice. The late Henry Kissinger (revising a statement made by Samuel Johnson with regard to commentators on Shakespeare) once said that the battles within academe are so fierce because the stakes are so low. An Oxford friend of mine once said that the Morse series was very unrealistic because actual murder (with the exception of the mortal assaults on personal reputations) was very rare in Oxford. Writing crime fiction has enabled me to expand my reach beyond the passive aggression of the faculty meeting into the more lethal (though sometimes less violent) 'real' world. Finally, I learned that one of my favorite forms of physical reprisal is the breaking and flattening of noses against cheeks, probably because the blood flows freely and the antagonist's popped eyes instantly announce the fact that his attention has been secured. I make no apologies for this repeating image, nor for the frequent plays on the antagonists' surnames.

I have enjoyed the opportunity to write short stories in multiple subgenres with very different casts of characters because it has provided me a holiday from the constraints of writing within a novelistic series, even though astute and faithful readers will note that several of the stories here were, in effect, earlier takes on aspects of one of my favorite Tom Deaton novels. It is also the case that my prized legal creation—Donald Fell—appears in one of these stories. (It is a little known fact, unknown, e.g., to Erle Stanley Gardner, that Donald's grandfather, John 'Black Jack' Fell was once a partner in the premier L.A. defense counsel firm of Mason & Fell.)

The general subject of the stories—crime in its many facets—remains the single constant. I will leave to others the question of whether one can branch out in multiple directions without sacrificing one's personal 'voice'—a subject that turns, of course, on the definition of that term. Keats's concept of negative capability has always struck me as an appropriate and wise one, but genre writers who follow it aggressively are in a decided though select minority. I can only say that it felt natural to me to write stories as putatively different as those that follow here.

While the stories reflect a number of my personal interests I hope that those interests are broad enough to attract other compulsive crime readers. There is some classic noir with grifters of both genders, Leonard/Runyonesque thickies, a mini- mob saga, the discovery of the horrid in unlikely places, revenge schemes, frames, black humor under the bright sun, odd, historic crimes, memoir noir, and a reasonable assortment of lawyers, shamuses and vigilantes, users, abusers, killers and justice seekers.

One of the stories ("Still Got It") has few contemporary precedents, but good characters are often adaptable in interesting ways and I could not resist the temptation to use them for somewhat unexpected purposes. The result is a piece of homage that will require the reader to remember one of the more striking recurring images associated with the original. Another ("The Bishop's Gambit") is far from contemporary America in its time and setting, but historical crime writing has long been of great interest to American readers and as Englishmen like Jim Grant ('Lee Child') and Tim Willocks explore the cultural landscape of America, that of England remains of great interest to readers on the western side of the Atlantic. For that matter, the story's protagonist has long been the successful subject of historical mysteries as well as a figure with whom I have had a long and loving association. The stories "Freelancer" and "Townhouse" originally appeared in *NEFARIOUS—Tales of Mystery* and "Freelancer" was reprinted in *HandHeldCrime*. I am grateful to readers of those stories who encouraged me to try my hand at others.

I

FREELANCER

Sometimes you catch a break and sometimes your luck takes a turn and you catch three or four. A year and a half ago I was ready to settle in behind a few square feet of polished walnut, flick memos at other peoples' problems, and court out-of-town clients over lobster and sirloin. Maybe even commandeer some A-space on the twenty-ninth floor and look out toward the Pacific rather than at a parking garage, a cheapo Chinese place called Hot Wok, and a steady line of cars waiting to get on the Harbor freeway.

It never happened. When I missed the bonus trip to Cabo by 120K's worth of second-quarter sales the suits sat up and took notice. They took a quick meeting, checked the numbers, and concluded that the best action all around would be for them to have a nice lunch and me to have two months' pay and two weeks' notice.

The competition started to make some halfhearted overtures, but I knew they'd take whatever I knew, wring whatever they could from it and then cut me loose without a single twinge or a moment's hesitation. I put them on hold as a fallback, told them I was taking some time to "explore other opportunities" and lined up a piecework job in the Valley installing computer equipment for small businesses.

It was strictly autopilot stuff: open the boxes, put the manuals on a vacant shelf, plug in the cords, draw down the software, and set up the units. I knew the real money would come from some freelancing on the side and I figured it wouldn't take any major brainpower. All you need to do is smile a little, act polite, help when you can, drop a few words and execute a few keystrokes. By the second day you're the resident guru. By the third you're a consultant.

I still can't believe how easy it was. I'd go into an office with some external drives, or a box of toner cartridges or surge protectors, wait till a head turned, hit a key or two, turn a screen into screaming chaos, and then piously volunteer to help. By the end of the client's coffee break I'd solved the problem. By the end of the next afternoon I'd drummed up some additional business, helped myself to some goodies from a safe or open desk drawer, and stripped whatever software I could use from the company system. The next week I was installing free product at just-below-market rates to my next customer. My mother always told me to buy low and sell high.

But that was only part of the game. The real fun came after I polished the act and started to get into the rhythm of it. I'd start with a little drama--sit down uneasily, lean in, click the mouse, and stare at the blue genie. I'd freeze my expression in a mask of deadly-serious deep concentration and then I'd start to listen.

Amazing what I learned. At the AutoFoto at the top of the Glen the junior desk clerk is dating the senior photo processor. By mid-afternoon they're usually ready for a trip to the plywood portrait studio in the back of the store. They settle in on the shag-upholstered platform in front of the Waikiki sunset and make like they're in paradise.

Over at Mr. Security, a credit checker on the north end of the boulevard, half the employees are checking on their relatives and boyfriends rather than on their clients' customers. "Look at this," a woman named Myrna keeps saying, "he still owes money on the truck and the Bayliner and now he's trying to buy a hybrid sedan from some guy in El Monte. No wonder he never takes me anywhere but the discount matinee and the North Hollywood Big Boy."

Lesson One: most of the people riding a desk are spending their days bitching to friends, gossiping with their coworkers, thinking about lunch, or calling somebody to help them figure out why their computers won't work. Lesson Two: if you pay a little attention and figure out how to bleed the system you'll never need to look for the offramp to Easy Street. You're already there.

I file away every word, not knowing when I might need it. In the meantime I troll for more easy business. Yesterday morning I hit the mother lode. I set up a network of Macs for a guy named Al Greene, a Toyota dealer over on Moorpark. First we agreed on a preliminary price. It came out to about $350 an hour. I told him I'd get the system up and running, come back the next day, make sure everything's copacetic, then check back from time to time--even give him a discount on the service calls. When I came in this morning he took me aside to show me his pride and joy. It was sitting on a table next to his desk: a powerhouse with more RAM than a New Zealand sheep ranch. His twelve year-old recommended it. He went for the top-of-the-line to impress the kid and now he wants to know how to turn it on.

I load him up with a set of security software on permanent loan from Mr. Security and some clip art I lifted from Design-a-Mug and ReadyPrint. I show him how to print up some handmade letterhead. I throw in some games to amuse the kid on the days when Al has to play daddy and I show him how to play a couple. Then I ask him if he'd like to record his own alert sound, maybe put in something the kid would like, only I don't call him the kid. He rehearses a few samples and settles on the long "duh-h-h-h" that the kid gives him whenever the old man boofs. Then we record. I hit the sample box, he hears his own voice and he lights up like a Pacific islander in a loincloth who's never seen himself on a polaroid.

"Here," I tell him, "go to the end of that line of text and icons and start hitting the space bar." *Duh-h-h-h, Duh-h-h-h, Duh-h-h-h,* the computer responds, and he can't get enough of it. He offers to buy me lunch and I tell him thanks but I've got too much work to do.

A couple hours later I'm sitting at his computer table with the screen turned away from the showroom door. I'm drinking somebody else's iced Starbucks from the office refrigerator and playing *League*. Suddenly she walks past the open door: very tall and very soft, with green eyes, chestnut-brown hair, 3-inch heels, legs from here to San Berdoo, and a short skirt which swings back and forth when she walks as if it knows that it's waving to a man in serious need. She looks at me for a second and I lower my eyes.

Her suit is all business, but so are her hips, and her chest is pushing her jacket buttons so hard that they're practically parallel to the showroom floor. I shut down the computer game, put the coffee under some papers in the basket next to the desk, and think about moving in for a closer look.

Her desk is the third on the right, toward the front of the showroom, next to the red Supra with the special wheel rims and the black leather seats. You can look right across the top of it and not miss a bit of her. She's going over some forms, filling in boxes. She puts her pencil down, makes a phone call, and turns toward the desk calculator, punching in a series of numbers.

By now I'm standing at the water cooler, sipping a second cup of Lake Arrowhead's best, and trying to appear invisible. I put the cup in the basket, take a pen from my pocket, and walk across the showroom to the empty desk on the opposite wall from hers. The pen is my insurance. I'm trying to look like William F. Buckley, Jr. making a house call rather than Leisure Suit Larry leering at the help. I put the pen in my shirt pocket, sit down on the edge of the seat, and turn on the computer.

For a moment I catch a glimpse of her. She's still working the phone and the calculator. I'm checking out her posture, admiring how everything turns in just the right direction. I change position, checking connections at the back of the computer, moving to the floor to check the surge protector and the phone line. Each time I move I catch another angle. She looks better every time. I can see her ankles and calves. Her legs are smooth, her toenails meticulously groomed. She's talking more intently now. As she pushes the calculator to the edge of the desk her hair falls across the side of her face. She slips it back over her left ear with two fingertips and the bright red polish gleams in the midday sun.

Suddenly this windowshopper comes in, looking for a way to kill some time. He stands next to the Supra and when I turn again he's blocking my view. I move to the next desk. It's occupied by a guy in a cheap suit with a Tag Heuer watch. "How's your computer working?" I ask. "Never use it," he answers. "I let the accounting types worry about things like that. If I sat here all day playing with toys I'd never move any product. And pal . . . I move a lot of product. Try this--how about seventeen units last month?"

I smile meekly and start to walk away. He leans toward me, as if he's really interested. "What are you driving now?" he asks.

"A Tiguan," I answer. "Plus the van, of course." There's no reason he has to know about the Beemer.

"A Tiguan?" he says, his lips twisting as if he just tasted some spoiled yogurt.

"It gets me around," I say, as I smile and start to move on. The next desk is vacant and there's no computer there. I'm two desks away from hers. Progress. The next is occupied by a salesman with a mark. He's explaining the true meaning of the numbers on the dealer's sheet and the sucker is lapping up every word of it. "This is our price, this number here," he says. "As a consumer you should know that." I pause for a moment and listen. I love to hear a pro at work.

The next desk is occupied by a young guy in a dual-breast, beige linen suit. He's wearing a white tee shirt and chunky gold ring, trying to look like Mr. Hollywood. He blows it by saying "Swell" and playing with a quarter while he talks. He probably calls it his lucky piece. I don't want to hear its complete history so I look knowingly at his computer screen, give him a wide berth and a thin smile and move on.

In the few moments before I get to her desk I try to hear part of her conversation. She says "Sure," then she says, "No problem," but she says it like she's agreeing to something interesting. Not routine office stuff, maybe something involving cool drinks and soft lights.

By now she's off the phone and looking over some more forms. I check some wall ports, look at the connections behind her machine, give her my meekest smile, and in a quiet voice ask, "How's your computer working? Is there anything I can help you with?"

"It's great," she answers. Her eyes are as deep as mountain pools and I want to stare forever, but I don't. Then she gives me a smile and says it was nice of me to ask. She's still using the soft-lights voice.

I tell her that it's my job to help and that she should give me a call whenever she needs anything. I say it in a businesslike tone but I add some soft edges. Nothing threatening, but maybe just a slight invitation, opening the door wide enough to let in a little light.

"There is one thing…" she answers.

So there really is a God. I try not to jump too fast. "Sure. How can I help?"

"Well," she says, "it's probably not complicated at all for somebody like you, but it's giving me fits."

I lean down, look at her screen as if I'm checking for symptoms, and catch the smell of her hair. She lets me come in close for a second but then stops, checks her watch, makes a frustration sound with her lips and the tip of her tongue, and tells me she's sorry for wasting my time. "I've got to go out on the lot for awhile," she says, "and then I've got to drop off some of these forms and meet with some people in Thousand Oaks. I'm not going to be back until around 8:00."

"I should still be here then," I answer. "Otherwise, I can check it out tomorrow." I feel a little jolt of pride. I'm telling her that I'm available but not overanxious. This is all strictly business. I'm a nice guy. Helpful, decent, not some drooler who's planning to cozy up to her in a dark showroom after everyone else has packed it in and left.

When the clear-glass door closes behind her her hair is swinging from side to side in parallel with her hips; the back of her looks a whole lot better than the rear of the used Corolla that eventually blocks my view. Instantly bored, I check the refrigerator but there's no more Starbucks. I think about springing for something from the service department waiting room, but finally go for some free, fresh coffee from the sales staff's kitchenette.

Since I'm planning on a little overtime I help myself to a second cup of coffee and recalculate Al's bill. Then I return to her desk and try to find some note or form that lists her name. I figure someone is watching, so I rest my right hand on the keyboard of her computer and stare thoughtfully (yes, the doctor is in). Meanwhile I slide open her center drawer slowly with my left hand and cast my eyes down every few seconds to see what I can see. Maybe I'll get lucky, I think, maybe find something personal.

I check the contents of the metal dividers in the front tray, but the most promising discoveries are a packet of matches from a swish restaurant on Robertson called Kalamata and the business card of a couch salesman from Leather Life. Just behind them are a couple of paper clips--the plastic, triangular type--and a rusty staple remover whose points are covered with something that looks like old pocket lint.

When the guy with the bad suit and the good watch comes by I ease the drawer closed. He looks down at me and forces a smile. "A Tiguan, huh? I thought computer jocks made big bucks. I figured you for a Supra or something with a little more jazz."

"I couldn't afford a Supra," I say meekly, "but it's a very nice car. Maybe some day…"

"Whenever you're ready," he says, "give me a jingle. I could even run some numbers now if you'd like me to."

"Thanks," I answer, "but not now."

He gives me a little two-fingered salute, checks his watch, and strolls across the showroom floor, whispering promises in the browsers' ears and offering his business card to whoever will take it. I return to the center drawer of her desk but begin to come up empty. There's even less in the side drawers, not even a stray paper clip or dried rubberband.

By now it's 4:35 and I'm starting to check my watch every six or seven minutes. I decide to go out to my van for a little personal happy hour. I've got a bottle of Stoli on ice in the cooler and I figure a couple of scooters will add some glow to a slow afternoon. I open the front seat windows and ease back behind the driver's seat, leaning against the side panel and listening in on the outside world.

A couple of silk shirts from West Hollywood are arguing about a leather package for their new Camry and a Consumers Report thumper from the north Valley is arguing trunk space and acceleration with the guy with the Tag Heuer. He promises the mark that the car he has in mind will hold more than a moving van and get to 60 in less time than it takes him to ask his next question. The mark is undaunted and asks him whether or not both airbags are the same size and shape when they inflate.

On the other side of the van is a beach boy who wants to put his board in the back of a Corolla hatchback to check the fit. I take another hit from the Stoli and wonder whatever happened to the human interest stuff--the guys putting the moves on perfect strangers or the girls reporting on their boyfriends' performances and statistics. So far I haven't even heard a good argument or a clean joke. I pick up the Stoli bottle and slide to the rear of the van, checking the back window for better game.

And suddenly there she is. Back early. I return the Stoli to the cooler and check the glove compartment for some mints. They say you can't smell vodka but that's bullshit. Especially Stoli. There's always that little hint. I find some tic tacs, pop a handful, check myself in the mirror, straighten my collar, close the front windows, pick up a couple of cables, and make my way back to the showroom.

I'm moving slowly, Mr. Cool with the tools of his trade, but just before I get to the door she's on her way back out. She flashes me a smile, says she forgot something, that she has to go back out, but that she'll return at 8:00 and hopes I'll still be here. I tell her I'll do my best, wave good-bye with one of the cables, and return to the showroom.

Al returns a few minutes later. He's wearing a new gold necklace. Getting ready to hit the lounges on Van Nuys. He walks past the guy with the Tag Heuer, pats him on the shoulder, hears the sound of the cash falling into the register in the back of his head, and walks toward me.

I tell him the system is purring like a tomcat and he refers me to a parts dealer in Northridge who might also be in need of my services. Says they had lunch together today. I give him gratitude and a little grovel as he checks out his necklace in the mirror above the water cooler.

At 6:10 I take off for a little dinner. I go for protein and caffeine and when I return I remove the tic tacs from the glove compartment and take a few for insurance, just in case she comes back early.

My luck holds. At 7:52 she walks into the showroom, looking as fresh as she did the first time she crossed my radar. She's even carrying a gift-wrapped, oblong package in royal purple, maybe 8" x 20". I can see it sticking out of this boutique bag with plastic handles. I'm sitting in Al's office, looking out through the doorway, checking out the red satin bow and the broad ribbon, thinking maybe negligées or garter belts, a little gift to herself. Something she might like to share. I stay in my seat and give her a 'whenever you're ready' wave. She walks over to the door and stands there, silhouetted against a sky that is suddenly all yellow with streaks of reddish orange. She tells me she's ready and I nod that I am too. "This is really very nice of you," she says.

"I'll be right there," I say, popping an extra tic tac for backup as she walks toward her desk. I follow her like a loyal retriever. "It's the printer," she says. "It always worked fine before, but now there's some kind of problem. Something happened when you put in the network."

"Probably a TCP/IP problem," I answer. "I'm sorry. I should have caught it earlier." Giving her vulnerable. "It's all yours," she says, standing back so I can sit down at her desk. "I'll get out of your way for awhile."

She picks up the scissors from the front of her desk and walks off with her package. I think of the possibilities--cutting off the tags and those damn little plastic connectors with the t-shaped ends. I hate those things. They're like worms in farm apples; you always get one half but then you have to worry about the rest. They scratch the back of your neck all day or fall out on your date's bed or carpet that night. Lets her know you put on a new shirt just for the occasion. Gives her ideas.

I diddle for a few minutes longer than I need to. Raise her appreciation level a little. After awhile I look around. She's not there, so I diddle some more. Five minutes later she's back and she's thanking me as if I just saved her life.

"It was a simple problem," I answer. "It should be fine now. If you need any more help, just let me know."

"I'm sorry you had to wait around for me like this," she answers. "Let me treat you to dinner. Nothing fancy, just a little thank you."

"I had a sandwich before," I answer, "but that's very nice of you."

"Then how about a drink?" she says.

Like I said: sometimes the breaks just keep coming.

"I'll tell you what," she says. "Give me a few minutes' lead time to make a stop and change my clothes and then meet me at my apartment. It's just a couple miles away, in Studio City. There's an Italian place down the street that's got a nice lounge. Here…"

She jots down her address on a card and hands it to me. Then she asks me to promise her that I'll be there. I tell her not to worry, that I'll follow her in forty-five minutes. "Make it forty," she says and I'm suddenly feeling like a sixteen year-old walking through the lingerie displays at Macy's.

When I get in my van I notice that my good blazer is hanging from the hook above the side door. As I drive out of the lot I'm thinking it's like some convergence of the planets. Normally I'd turn on KFI and listen to callers spill their guts to strangers lost on the freeways, but tonight I figure I'll leave the radio off and just sit back and enjoy the anticipation.

I figure her for a classy name, not something bubblegum like Brenda or Debbie. Maybe Sarah. Or Caroline. And no nickname. Something formal and adult…add some spice when the hair comes down and the buttons are undone.

Along the way I stop off at a Ralph's, make a pass through the family planning center, just in case she's picky. That phrase always kills me. I'm not planning on creating any family. While I'm there I pick up a bottle of California champagne. Pretty good stuff. Besides, it's on sale. Twelve minutes later I'm back in the car.

It's hard to keep my mind off those eyes and that hair, but then my mind turns toward the basics. I pick up the card she gave me, which is sitting on the passenger seat. I hold it up to my nose, try to catch some scent. Maybe she used her fingertip to dab on some perfume.

I'm thinking now of her voice, how I want to listen to every word she speaks, to every syllable. I want to hear her voice in different rooms and in different positions--across the table, across the couch, from above me and from below.

Enough of that. I'm starting to drift. A guy in an old Dodge Dart cuts in on me and I nearly drive up the back of his bumper. Idiot. I don't need anything like that now. I've got to concentrate. I'm only a few minutes from her house. I want to be on time and in one piece.

I check the card again. Mountain View at Grove Lane, apartment 4-C. Probably upstairs. Maybe it will actually have a view of the mountain. We'll go back there after we have some drinks. Check it out.

My mind starts wandering again. I'm back to the smell of her hair against her neck. I turn on the radio for distraction. There's some guy talking about his job, how he can't make ends meet. I feel sorry for him. He needs a deal like mine and some clients like Al Greene. Deep pockets and small brains. Al can tell stories and sell cars; he just can't do long division without a calculator or figure out which icon takes him to his streaming services. I love guys like Al; they make guys like me possible.

The guy with the scut job finally hangs up. He's followed by a woman who says she can't say no to men. I jump in before the radio shrink has a chance to answer. "That's not a problem, babe, it's a career choice." I hear a slight bump in the back of the van. The ice is melting in the cooler and the Stoli bottle is washing around. I don't need it anymore anyway. The sign for Grove comes into my field of vision. I turn, heading south toward Mountain View. I'm moving the wheel with the heel of my hand. Cool, relaxed, anticipating.

The apartment is in the last building on the west end of the development. The entry is lined with miniature fan palms in beds of dark wood chips and the balconies are draped with bougainvillea and framed by banana trees. All very neatly trimmed. No brown fronds or trash stuffed among the greenery. Upscale all the way. Just what I expected.

I park the van, check my collar, run my comb through my hair once or twice, and put on my blazer. I slip the champagne into the cooler, saving it for later. I'm walking toward the steps, thinking about that package again. I always like surprises, especially those involving women with long legs and all that goes with them.

The lights are dark in the adjoining apartments. Fine. When I get to the door and knock there's no response. I reach for the knob, think that maybe I should have stopped to pick up some flowers--nothing fancy, just a gesture--and then figure, no, no reason to look overanxious. Let her make the gesture. Better that way.

The knob turns and I walk in. The lights are low and there's music playing. Something old with a lot of violins. The sound is faint. Maybe it's coming from downstairs. I step inside, say "Hello," and a light comes on in the corner of the room. There's a guy sitting there in a bad suit, smoking a cigarette. There's another one behind me. He's in shirtsleeves, picking at the ridges of his left thumb with the point of a penknife. Except for the smoker's chair the room has no furniture.

The one in the corner stands up, takes a few steps toward me, and asks me to identify myself. "What is this?" I ask.

"Just answer the question," he says. I do and then he starts in with this "You have the right to remain silent…" shit.

"Wait a minute," I say, interrupting him. "What's the charge?"

He keeps reading from his card while the guy behind me moves in a little closer. When he finishes he says, "The charge is grand theft. You hacked into Mr. Greene's corporate account and transferred out eighty-five grand. We don't know where yet, but we'll find out."

"That's bullshit," I say. "I haven't stolen a penny from Mr. Greene. Where is he? I want to talk to him. He'll clear this up."

"He's back at the dealership, waiting for us," the guy behind me says.

"Fine, let's go there," I say. "This is one hell of a misunderstanding. I hope you guys have some good lawyers, because I guarantee you I do."

"Let's go," the guy from the corner says, slipping the Miranda card into his coat pocket as the guy behind me takes out a pair of cuffs.

Al Greene is sitting in his office and he doesn't look happy. The gold necklace is gone and he's dropping the remains of a cigar into a cup of dead coffee. His kid is sitting in the corner of his office, listening to something through ear buds, in his own world. I tell Al I'm glad to see him and he stares at me and says, "Really? After you ripped me off?"

"What do you mean?" I ask. "I never touched a penny of your money."

"Yeah?" he answers. "I've got something you oughta see." He picks up the phone and talks to some guy named Harry in Security. A couple minutes later Harry comes in, carrying a tiny TV with a built-in VCR, the kind you see in the stores playing advertising loops. He's an old guy with a wrinkled uniform and a wrinkled face. When he sets down the TV you can see his hands shake. Jesus, I'm thinking to myself, this is their witness?

He plugs the set into the wall and we wait for the picture to come up. It's Wheel of Fortune and everybody's laughing their asses off and applauding like hell. He reaches over with a twitchy finger and hits the play button. Suddenly everything's in black and white. I'm sitting at her desk, working the keyboard. The time is blinking in the lower right hand corner of the screen: 8:00, then 8:01. The security camera pans. All of the other screens are shut down, the desks empty. Harry fast forwards. At 8:08 I'm still sitting at her desk, working away.

"The money was transferred out at 8:06," Al says. "Do you see anybody else in the movie?"

"It was the woman," I answer.

"What woman?"

"The saleswoman. That was her desk where I was sitting. I was fixing her computer."

"I don't have any women selling cars for me," Al says.

"She must have been in your office," I say, "transferring the money. She set me up."

"Bullshit," Al says. "The techs were already here to check the fingerprints on the keyboards. Those on mine look the same as the ones on the computer at the showroom desk. You were there last, buddy boy. The camera doesn't lie."

"What about the camera in your office? Let's see what's on that tape."

"I don't have any camera in there. Why should I? I don't have to worry about myself. It's my goddamned dealership."

Then it hits me like a steel beam across the bridge of my nose. "She carried in a separate keyboard. She had it wrapped up in a box. She unplugged your keyboard and temporarily plugged in the substitute. That's why you found my fingerprints when she replaced the substitute with yours. I'm telling you, she set me up."

"That was a gift for my kid," he answers. "She picked it up for me. Damn nice of her too after the way she was treated."

"In a purple box with red ribbon?" I ask.

"Yes. She had it wrapped for me. I asked her what she thought my kid would like and she said that "music is always a good idea". The complete collection of some band he likes. I thought that was a pretty good idea. She bought the set and put 'em on a zip drive for him to download. Not big money, but after all it's the thought that counts. She included some pictures of the album art."

"She used the gift box to distract me," I tell him. "She must have had the keyboard in there too. She cut the ribbon, took out the keyboard, transferred the money, and then taped the package back together. She wrapped up the keyboard in her shopping bag and slipped out when I wasn't looking, probably went out the side door to her car. I'm telling you, she set me up."

The two cops are looking at each other as if they just heard the lie of the century. "Look," I tell them, "she gave me the address of the apartment and told me to meet her there. How did you know about it? She tipped you off. She had to."

"The address was right here," Al says, pointing at a piece of paper next to his computer. "You recalculated my bill and printed your address on the bottom, so I'd know where to send the check."

"I didn't do that. She did," I tell him. "What were you doing here anyway? How did you know that your money had been transferred?"

"I come back every night at 8:30 with the kid," Al says. "He transfers the money for me. When it was already transferred he noticed right away. That's why I got the new computer. He operates it all the time so I got him the kind he wanted. I figured I'd also get him a present. He's gonna be thirteen years old next week."

"I don't believe this," I say. "I'm telling you the truth and you're believing her."

"And I'm telling you she was straight arrow," Al answers. "The best accountant I've ever had. Freelancing for me, checking on my people. I'll tell you this much--she was a hell of a lot cheaper than you and she gave me better service. She used to work for a big-eight firm. Plus, she was more than happy to run the errand for my kid's present. But now she's not coming back. You know why? You know what happened? Talk about a chickenshit organization with some pissant employees. She put a can of Starbucks in our refrigerator and somebody in the office stole it. She told me she could work under just about any conditions, but she couldn't work with thieves. Can you believe anybody would be that cheap…steal a damned can of coffee? Anyway, she thanked me, left the present in my office, and told me to please call somebody else the next time I need an accountant."

I look around the room and they're all staring at me in disbelief, all except the kid, whose eyes are closed as he plays the drums on his knees. I start to respond and the cop in the bad suit takes my arm and starts walking me to the door. "That's enough," he says. "We got other stuff we got to do tonight besides listening to you."

"But you don't understand!" I yell.

"We understand, buddy," he says. "We understand it all."

II

TOWNHOUSE

"I've never heard of such a thing," he said, measuring out the final sips as if they were his last.

"What, a guy disappears? That happens all the time."

"No, a beer for nine dollars."

"Eight ninety-five."

"OK. Eight ninety-five. For you that's a big difference?"

"You're not just paying for the beer, Billy. You're paying for the leather seats without any cuts or holes and the shiny walnut bar and the chilled mugs and the gold design on the wall paper and the fancy art work and the men's room that don't smell bad and the hot snacks, and… and all that stuff. Especially the hot snacks. The fact that you don't eat 'em means that you're not taking full advantage of the situation…you're not gettin' your money's worth, but that don't mean that the price is too high."

"Where else in the world is eight ninety-five for a beer a good deal?"

"Lotsa places."

"Like…?"

"Like at Harry's Bar."

"What Harry? Harry Billings? Harry Kahlmeier?"

"No, just Harry."

"Harry who?"

"The Harry in Harry's Bar, the Harry in Venice. How should I know his last name?"

"Venice? You mean like in L.A., with the rollerbladers with the shorts climbing up their ass and the sweaty muscle boys and the guy who juggles chainsaws?"

"Venice, Europe, Billy. Harry's Bar. It's famous…and it's pricey."

"And how often do we drink there, Larry?"

"It was just an example, Billy. I saw it in this magazine at the barber shop. If you'd read you'd know these things."

"I wouldn't know about that Venice, Europe shit, since my barber don't have real magazines any more, just those plastic folders with the pictures of the pretty boys with the perfect beards and the gooey shit all over their hair. The ones with the names of the haircuts underneath. The Princeton. The Rugged. The Windswept. The Grease-Ass."

"Forget it; we're here, we're thirsty and the food is free. They've even got those scallops with the half-cooked bacon wrapped around 'em."

"You think those are scallops, Larry? I hear that most of what passes for scallops are really pieces of shark. They scoop 'em out, kinda like those little melon balls. They're practically the same size. Maybe they use the same tool."

"And can you tell the difference, Billy?"

"No, 'cause I wouldn't eat 'em anyway. That's not the point. The point is that the eight ninety-five is not that good of deal, even if you eat the hot snacks. Not when the snacks are some phony-ass kind of shark and not real scallops--not that anybody would want to eat scallops anyway, especially when they're wrapped up in greasy pieces of bacon."

"Well, I'm gonna eat 'em." He walked over to the silver-plated steam tray, reached for a scallop, paused, thought better of it and then picked up some miniature drumsticks from the adjoining tray.

"Not in the mood for shark, huh?"

"That's not it; the chicken just looked better."

"Enjoy it."

"And I'd appreciate your not saying that it's actually pigeon…or worse."

"Pigeon is very big in Europe, Larry."

"Yeah, and down on the square with the big fountain in the center."

The bartender nodded and Larry said, "Yeah, hit me again…and one for my partner."

"Very generous, Larry," Billy said. "So what did you think of that house?"

"The townhouse?"

"Yeah, the townhouse."

"Very strange. I mean, who builds an expensive place like that in an expensive neighborhood like this and doesn't put any friggin' cupboards in it?"

"Larry, I explained that to you. How many of those beers have you had? I think your mind's goin'."

"Oh yeah, I forgot. Don't you ever forget anything, Billy? Jesus, I can't believe you'd say something like that to me. It wouldn't hurt you all that much to try to be a little more sensitive. I mean, not every day or anything—I don't want your head to explode—but maybe once in awhile. Lemme see…the house was originally for the guy's kid, who's going to the toney private college down the street. He doesn't want him to become too, what did they say—materialistic? So he doesn't leave him any place to put anything. This guy must be really rich, 'cause who's gonna buy a house without any cupboards. I mean, he's not worried about resale; he's only worried about his kid and about how he grows up."

"Probably too late by then anyway," Billy said. "I mean, you know there must have been cupboards at home. The kid must of had a mother, right? What kind of woman would live in a house without cupboards? The kid must of grown up with cupboards full of shit…and he must of gone home for vacations and stuff. By that point he took 'em for granted. And he filled 'em all up."

"The resale doesn't matter anyway," Larry answered. "The kid graduated and the old man sold the house to the college, probably made a shitload of money on it. Then they could use it for a buncha kids, put up some of those standup cupboards…what do they call 'em?"

"Standup cupboards."

"No, there's a term for them. Wardrobes."

"The wardrobe is the shit you put in the standup cupboard," Billy said.

"It's the same word for both, Billy. You put your wardrobe in the wardrobe. If you'd study you'd know that kinda shit."

"Whatever. Besides, it don't matter anyway, since the college gave it to the guy who disappeared, and anyway, since it's burned down now there won't be any students or wardrobes or wardrobes in wardrobes or any of that shit."

"So why do they give a house without cupboards to a guy in the first place?"

"It's a townhouse, not a house," Billy said. "You figure the guy has a real house someplace else. This is for when he was in town. It's like a cabin or a fuckpad; you don't live there."

"But the guy did live there," Larry said.

"I know, I know, but you're missin' the point," Billy said. "That's the concept of a townhouse. This neighborhood is filled with 'em. I know… it's the only place some people got, but other people don't know that. They think it's like some kind of toy. Think about it this way, Larry. It's like a boat. They don't have a lot of space, even the big ones, but they're still expensive and only the rich people have 'em. So it makes you look like King Shit to live there. For this particular guy it was like a major bennie. I mean, other people get hired but they don't get a house, especially a townhouse in a neighborhood full of rich pricks."

"Without any fucking cupboards."

"Jesus," Billy said. "I'd draw you a picture, but it wouldn't do any fuckin' good."

"Maybe they were trying to punish the guy," Larry said. "I mean,

I hear he was a first class asshole. So they hired him and gave him a free house and gave him this big desk and title and told him he could fuck over everybody, and he buys into the deal and then suddenly realizes, 'Hey, this fuckin' house they gave me ain't got any fuckin' cupboards.' So, where he thinks he's the top dog, playing kiss-up-and-shit-down, he's actually takin' it up the ass too. That's the theory, at least."

"If you want to believe that," Billy said, "it's fine with me." He signalled to the bartender. "Yes, thank you, me and my pal here would like another round."

"Her name's Sarah."

"Whose?"

"The bartender's. Pretty fancy name for a bartender," Larry said. "But then, this is a pretty fancy place."

"There's a student place downstairs," Billy said. "Burgers and pizza and cheap beer and shit. Upstairs here it's fancy. This is where the parents eat."

"It's like Cheers."

"You mean on TV?"

"Yeah. The bar is in the basement and then there's the pricey place upstairs, with the bald-headed prick owner."

"I think the same guy owns all of this," Billy said.

"It's probably not some guy; it's probably some chain," Larry said.

"That's the most intelligent thing you've said since we walked in here," Billy answered.

"Yeah? Well here's another one. I don't understand them hiring this guy and giving him the townhouse."

"What do you mean? What don't you understand?"

"Well, this college costs a fucking fortune to get into, right?"

"Right."

"So you get a lot of rich people, right?"

"Right."

"So these rich people…they got, like, expectations, right?"

"Yeah."

"They want to be taken care of. They want service. They don't want to make their friggin' beds and wait in friggin' lines. They want their computers and shit to work 24/7. They want to be able to throw their shit on the ground and have somebody else pick it up. They want it to be just like at home, with maids and shit and gardeners."

"Right."

"So this asshole with the townhouse with no cupboards comes in here and he starts slashin' and burnin'; he's downsizin' and rightsizin' and outsizin' and firing people right and left…"

"Outsourcing, not outsizing."

"Whatever."

"That's modern business, Larry."

"Listen. This is what you call a service operation, Billy. They ain't making things or emptying things or cleaning things. It's part of what you call your information industry."

"Yeah, OK. So?"

"So how can you cheapen the product and still bring in the business? If this asshole's job is to fire everybody, then what's left? Who in the hell is gonna pay big money for some kind of bargain basement shit?"

"What am I, some kind of economic genius? Maybe they were chargin' too little; maybe they give the client somethin' new instead. Video games. That's it. That's what the kids want anyway. You let 'em kill dragons or invaders from Mars or something. No, wrestling. That's big now. You get the WWF games. Let 'em piledrive each other, throw their ass on boards covered with tacks or throw shit in their faces."

"They already got those, Billy."

"Where?"

"I don't know, but they've got to have 'em somewhere; that's what's making the money these days."

"Fine, they already got 'em. You know what? This bullshit of yours is giving me a helluva thirst. Sarah…"

"Two more, gentlemen?"

"Yes, and have one for yourself, on us," Billy said.

"Thank you sir, but I'm not permitted to drink while I'm working."

"OK. Classy place. I'm sorry."

"That's quite all right, sir," the bartender said, as she handed them new beers in fresh frosted mugs.

"So Billy, let me have it again. Who was this guy?"

"He was a lawyer, Larry; I told you that. The college was on the ropes because they got a president who couldn't find his dick in the dark. The money's goin' down the tubes and they bring in the lawyer to stop the bleeding."

"You mean fix the plumbing," Larry said, smiling and tipping his glass.

"Whatever. They bring him in to bail out the dickhead and keep the place from goin' under. Which he tries to do by cutting costs. Which means firing people. Only he fired a few too many. Plus he pissed too many people off. He's takin' away their fringies, freezin' their salaries, and jackin' up parking fees--makin' people ride the fucking bus. Meanwhile, he's sitting in a fucking townhouse a block from campus."

"Which..."

"I know. Which don't have any fucking cupboards, but the people on the bus don't know that and they're still pissed off."

"So finally they can't take it anymore and...he disappears."

"Yeah, he's gone. Sure as hell. He's gone."

"And they gave us twenty-five large to make sure he never comes back."

"That's right. Which I finished up personally, so they don't have to leave the fuckin' porchlight on, waiting for him."

"And we torched the townhouse too."

"That was part of the deal. It really pissed 'em off and they didn't want to see it anymore either."

"So isn't this a little risky, returning to the scene and all that?"

"Not in the least," Billy said. "I did the oily rags thing in the garage, right next to the gas can and the lawn mower. Totally kosher. Nothing suspicious. Nothing."

"OK, so the townhouse is gone, everybody can see that, but what about him? When he don't show up for work won't people start to get a little suspicious?"

"I don't think so."

"Why not?"

"Because they'll think he ripped off the college and took off with the money."

"But why burn down the house, excuse me, the fucking townhouse. Won't that be a little too much of a coincidence?"

"If they don't think it's an accident, they'll think maybe he did it out of spite. But they won't be able to prove it. Like I said, it was strictly according to Hoyle. My best work, Larry."

"Wait a minute, I get it," Larry said. "People will like it, because they'll figure he took off when his boss screwed him somehow. The guy hired to screw everybody else gets screwed himself. Plus, he may have torched the townhouse too, just to get even with the boss who was behind the whole deal anyway, so the dickhead boss—who nobody likes either—is left with his mouth open and his thumb up his ass. So what we got here, Billy, is what they call a fucking 'win-win-win'."

"I don't know about that; you may have one too many fucking wins in there, but I think they're all gonna like it."

"So who bought the hit and the torch job, Billy?"

"I can't tell you that, Larry. For your own protection. I can tell you this much; it wasn't the dickhead boss. I mean, this lawyer guy was becomin' a bigger and bigger liability, but it still wouldn't help the dickhead that much. Now he don't have anybody to blame for all the shit that goes wrong except himself. Plus he's got to do the job alone, instead of hanging around back stage, lettin' the lawyer take the hits for all the nasty stuff he was doin'."

Larry smiled. "But there is some bright side for the dickhead. At least he don't have to pay the bastard anymore. If he don't show up for work he ain't gonna draw no paycheck. And the dickhead'll get the insurance payoff on the townhouse so he can rebuild the sonofabitch and put in some proper fucking cupboards. All thanks to you, because you, like, take so much pride in your work, and did the full greasy rags number."

"It's what they call a subsidiary benefit," Billy said.

"So you still haven't answered my question. What are we doin' here?"

"Come on, I'll show you," Billy said.

Leaving the spine-chilling air conditioning they stepped into warm, humid air. The joints of the red brick sidewalk had been freshly topped and the footsteps of countless walkers had formed the dense wet sand into waffled layers or pushed it toward the gutters in tiny waves. The smell of the taxis' exhaust outside the restaurant mingled with the kitchen smells drifting in from the alleyway. Except for the façade of the upscale restaurant the rest of the street consisted of functional shops, most now closed. A beggar sat in a storefront on a foldup chair, balancing a portable television on his knees. When the two men passed him he extended a can wrapped in white paper. He didn't look up.

"He don't wanna miss nothin' on his favorite show," Billy said.

"So what are we gonna do?" Larry asked.

"We're gonna take a little walk," Billy answered, "just down to the townhouse."

"I don't think that's a very good idea," Larry said.

"It'll be fine," Billy answered. "Just two guys out for a stroll. Happens all the time. Especially in this town. If anybody says anything, just hold my hand, like as if we're on a date."

"I don't think so," Larry said.

Billy smiled. "Relax," he said. "Just follow my lead."

They walked another block, past a row of buildings that were owned by the university, but now sat vacant. ("He downsized *their* ass," Larry said.) When they came to the corner Billy turned left and Larry followed.

The scent in the air changed as a breeze came in from the southwest. It carried the harsh smell of wet charcoal.

A minute and a half later they stood in front of the townhouse. The brickwork had survived the fire, but the metal roof was twisted and scorched, the windows were shattered, the woodwork reduced to rows of black chunks. There were pools of water everywhere, each filled with nondescript pieces of rubble and twisted metal. The doorway was covered with a piece of makeshift plywood and a yellow notice with a black border had been stapled to it at eye level.

"No police tape," Larry said.

"Nah. They don't suspect anything," Billy answered. "Come here a second. I wanna do something."

The side of the townhouse had a parking space for a second car; the paving then narrowed to a passageway between the burned townhouse and the adjoining building.

"Where are you going?" Larry said, growing more and more nervous.

"Relax, come on."

Behind the house was a small porch and a garden area, no more than eleven or twelve feet wide and about twenty deep. Some rattan furniture on the porch had been scorched when the back door blew out. Except for some blackened muck scattered around the back of the house the garden had been spared.

"Have a seat," Billy said, pointing to a stone bench in a rose arbor.

Larry sat down, uneasily. "Maybe just for a minute or two," he said. "I think we should get the hell out of here."

"Relax," Billy said. "I've got to do something." He reached into each of his jacket pockets and pulled out two clear plastic bags. "Sort of like saddlebags," he said. "I needed to be balanced out." He put the two bags on the stone bench next to Larry and reached into his pants pocket.

"What's in those?" Larry asked.

"Let's say…fertilizer," Billy answered. He removed a knife from his pocket, opened it, picked up one of the bags, and gently slit open the top.

"Fertilizer? What the hell do you need fertilizer for?"

"I like roses, Larry. Don't you? You have to take care of 'em if you want to see 'em bloom right."

"Sure, but this ain't your place," Larry said.

"No, but it's nice to bring a little color into the world. You see, Larry, I'm one of those guys who practices random acts of beauty or kindness, or whatever the fuck it is. I'm like, civic-minded." Taking the first bag he sprinkled the contents on the bedding beneath the west row of roses. The fertilizer was gray and dusty. Then he opened the second bag, closed the knife and put it back in his pocket, and sprinkled the contents on the bedding of the opposite row. "There, isn't that nice?" he said.

"Jesus, it's him, isn't it?" Larry asked.

"I think I'd say *was* rather than *is*, Larry. Kinda completes the circle, doesn't it? This was his place; nobody thought he shoulda had it; the only thing nice about the whole deal is the flowers. He's gone, the house is shot to shit, and the flowers are still here. So we put the sonofabitch to good use. He's able to sorta stick around, but not so's he can do any damage. This time he only does good. Kinda pretty when you think about it."

"Let's get outta here," Larry said.

"No, let's just sort of enjoy the moment," Billy said. "Here..." He reached into his inside jacket pocket and pulled out a half pint of Johnny Walker black. "Let's toast the bastard. First we roast, then we toast, what do you think?"

Larry took the bottle, unscrewed the cap, and took a deep drink. "I don't like this," he said.

"What's the matter? You don't like graveyards? Here, gimme..."

Larry handed him the bottle and Billy took a drink. Suddenly Larry heard some movement on the sidewalk. He put the palm of his hand in front of his mouth. The sound increased; someone was coming through the passageway on the side of the charred townhouse.

"Relax," Billy whispered, slipping the bottle into his jacket pocket.

"Gentlemen?" a voice said. A figure emerged and stood in the shadows. He was dressed in a dark uniform. There was a slight gleam from the silver badge over his shirt pocket.

"Evening, officer," Billy said. "We was just sorta taking our leisure."

"Odd place," the officer said, "what with the fire and all."

"We figured it would be quiet," Billy said. "How 'bout a drink? We was just sorta toasting the evening." He reached for the bottle but the officer held up his hand.

"Not while I'm on duty," he said. "Besides, you're not supposed to have an open bottle on the street like this. You could if this was your backyard, but I'm thinking that that's probably not the case."

"Oh no," Billy said. "This ain't my place. Nor his…" His eyes turned toward Larry, but Larry kept looking down at the ground.

"Besides, I hear this place never even had cupboards. A fancy place like that in a nice neighborhood like this. What were they thinking?"

Larry shifted his weight. Jesus, Billy, he was thinking, shut your goddamned mouth. How are we supposed to have known that the fucking townhouse didn't have any cupboards?

"Yes, it was sort of famous for that," the officer said. Larry relaxed, but only a bit.

"The guy who built it had it built for his son, who was a student at the University. He wanted him to be able to live in a safe part of town, but he didn't want him to get too comfortable, if you know what I mean. Kids now…they want fancy clothes and fancy cars…all that stuff. Apparently the old man wanted the kid to live simply. Kind of a good idea, when you think about it."

"So he wouldn't get, what would you call it, too materialistic," Billy said.

"Yes, exactly," the officer replied. "Then the old man sold the place to the University and it sat open for a few months until the President hired this new Vice President, who got the townhouse as part of his appointment deal."

"Pretty nice bennie," Billy said, "even if it didn't have any cupboards. I mean, you could always put in—what do you call those things—wardrobes."

"Right," the officer said. He slid a long flashlight out of the case on his Sam Browne belt. "Look here…" He turned on the light and shined the beam into a second floor window. "If you look to the right you can just see what's left of one of the wardrobes."

"Oh yeah," Billy said. "So that's where he put his clothes…he put his wardrobe in the wardrobe."

"Right," the officer replied, smiling. "I hadn't thought of it that way." By now the flashlight was pointing toward the ground, at the base of the rose arbor. Larry scooted to the left of the bench, trying to block the beam.

"You know, that Vice President was never very popular," the officer said.

"Really?" Billy replied.

"No. He was brought in to save money, and I guess he did that, but he sure hurt a lot of people in the process."

"Really?" Billy replied, as Larry started to squirm. Goddamn it, Billy, he thought, let's stop the Sunday Social bullshit and get the hell out of here.

"You know what he used to call himself?" the officer asked.

"No, what?" Billy answered.

"The President's Son-of-a-Bitch."

"And I guess he sort of earned the title--right, officer?" Billy said. The officer nodded approvingly. Billy turned to his left and said, "What do you think of that, Larry?"

(I'm gonna kill you when we get out of here, Billy. That's what I think of that. Why in the fucking world did you have to tell him my name?) "Oh yeah," Larry said. "Quite a title, but it sounds like it fit him."

"It sure did," the officer said. "The only thing anybody ever said good about him was that he took care of his garden. Especially his roses. Aren't they beautiful?"

The officer directed the beam at the blooms and buds and then along the stalks to the bedding beneath. Larry tried to look as if he was listening politely, turning his head and following the light. "Very beautiful," he volunteered. Suddenly he noticed something at the base of one of the stalks. It was white, with some dark shading, about the size of a fingertip. Jesus Christ, Larry thought to himself, it's a piece of bone. He scooted back toward Billy, trying to block the beam.

"I've always loved roses," the officer said. "My mother grew them. Did you fellas know that in ancient times they used roses for medicinal purposes?"

"I didn't know that," Billy said.

"Yes, they did. And you still see rose hips, right?"

"Oh yeah, I guess so," Billy said.

"The Romans loved roses; they thought they were sacred to the goddesses. They ate roses in salads, too. Isn't that interesting?"

"Yes, it sure is," Billy said.

(We've got to get the fuck out of here, Larry thought. What is with all this rose bullshit? Come on, Billy…)

"Of course the English people just love roses," the officer said. It was the East India Company that brought roses from the Orient. I mean, the English had roses before that…sure…but these roses were different. I mean, they were all from the same family, I think, but these particular roses bloomed all the time. You know…like little tea roses and such…"

"You really know your roses," Billy said.

"I don't know that much," the officer said. "My mother did. She knew everything about roses. Grew them herself, of course. Not all of them—that'd be too many for anybody, but she grew a lot. I can't always pronounce their names right, but I can remember some of her best ones: Adam Messerichs, Belle Nanons, La Reine Victorias, Zigeunerbluts, Boule de Neiges, Reveils, Province Panachees; I mean she had rows and rows of them. Something always seemed to be in bloom. Of course, she had to have the greenhouse. It does get cold here, not like in the north or anything, but it does get too cold for roses. Now these roses…"

He directed the beam at the blooms.

(Just don't go down that fucking stalk, Larry thought. He could feel his heart beating faster and felt a set of sweat beads forming on his forehead, just above his left eye.)

"These are just common roses, but you can tell that they've been cared for. See there…that one has been pruned and look at all the flowers now. It's funny—you cut something away and it makes you stronger. That's what that Vice President always said. Of course, he was doing a lot of cutting…"

Billy stood up, slowly. (Finally, Larry thought. Let's get the fuck out of here.)

"It's been great talking to you," Billy said, "but it's getting close to our bedtime. Actually, it's not really that close to our bedtime, but I'm kinda thirsty and I think what we're gonna do is go home and have another drink. I don't want to break any laws or anything here, you see." He was smiling. "You're sure you won't join us?"

(Great, Larry thought. He already said no. What are you gonna do—fucking tempt him again?)

"No thanks. I feel good just looking at these flowers." He shined the light up and down the stalks again, as Larry clenched. "What's this?" he said, reaching down toward the base of one of them.

Larry tightened up. If he tried to leave, the cop would be suspicious and if he ran he might even get shot. If he attacked him and the cop—who was pretty good-sized—won, he'd either be shot or get convicted and face life. His mind jumped to both possibilities and back again as he froze in place.

The officer picked up the piece of bone between his thumb and forefinger, looked at Billy and then at Larry, and suddenly flicked the piece away, over the fence and into a neighbor's yard. Larry exhaled slowly as the officer held the flashlight under his chin, made some notes on something attached to a miniature clipboard and then pressed it into Billy's hand. He patted Larry on the shoulder, and said, "Nice talking to you fellas. I think you'd better go now. This neighborhood can get a little dodgy after dark."

They cleared the passageway and walked east as the officer walked west. They could hear the click of his heels against the sidewalk bricks. Larry turned; he could see him more clearly now as he passed under the streetlight. He wasn't wearing a gun or nightstick.

"What the hell?" he said.

"What?" Billy answered.

"He wasn't wearing a gun. I thought we were dead there for a second, but he was so fucking big I didn't hit him. I just sorta stopped for a second. Then he flicked the bone into the other yard."

"He's a campus cop, Larry. I thought you saw that. Was that what he picked up, a piece of bone?"

"Jesus Christ, Billy. Welcome back to the fucking planet. We're two steps away from a life sentence and you're talking about the fucking roses."

"Here," Billy said, opening his palm and revealing a small money envelope. He opened the top and slid out four thousand-dollar bills. He handed two to Larry.

"What the hell is this?"

"Read what it says. It's a bonus," Billy said. "A bonus for a job well done. You gotta start learning how to trust people, Larry. Jesus, you think everybody's like that asshole lawyer, just trying to screw people so he can live in a fuckin' townhouse and feel important? We did our job and we got our pay. That's the way it's supposed to work. It's not all cutthroat, Larry. It's not all dog eat dog. Thank God," he said, pausing for a moment, "there's still some fuckin' trust left in the world."

III

———

AMBITION

"Gino, isn't it? OK. Gino, you're a good boy and I like you. You work hard. You're always here. I don't see you drunk. I don't see you running around with whores. You always keep your hands in your pockets. Don't get me wrong, your private life is your own business, but when it becomes public it reflects on the family and I want you to know we're all very proud of you for keeping your nose so clean. Some guys… they start drinking too much…they start gambling too much…they let their dicks take over for their brains…sooner or later it's a problem for all of us.

"That's why I wanted to have this little talk. Sorta to let you know how you're doin' and maybe just give you a headsup on things you might wanta avoid. Lemme tell you a story or two.

"Remember Ricky Testa? Smart kid. Tough. A good knife man. Very quiet. Very efficient. What happens to him? He earns his bones on the street, has this very bright future and then ends up throwing it all down the sewer. Why? Well, with Ricky it's very sad and very simple. He's got this thing for redheads, not nice Irish girls with the freckles and all, but the ones who got dye jobs with streaks and dark spots. One he went out with had hair the color of a fuckin' fire truck. The moment he's off the clock he's with the redheads…so one night he's sitting in Lou Terrino's place with one of them--her whore's name is Brett (now what the hell kind of name is that for a young woman?)--and they start arguing over price, and they're getting loud about it, and then louder, and finally Ricky reaches over under the table and grabs her. It's not some kind of sex thing; it's like he wants to humiliate her, show her he can do it if he wants to. So she stands up (and she's wearing something like 4" heels, the kind with the little metal taps that announce her presence very loud and very clear) and looks down at him.

"He says something like 'Get out of here you whore,' (actually it was much worse than that, but why say those words when you don't have to) and she looks at him, spits on him, and comes down on the front of his ankle, just above his instep, with that metal heel. And she does it with a little bounce in her step and a little jump. Rosina Scarlatti's kid is standin' over at the bar--the one who went to Lehigh University--and he takes this all in and later explains to us what he calls the physics of it…how the end result of 120 pounds of weight all coming down on that little heel is more or less like having a fucking Buick Roadmaster dropped on you.

"Anyway, the heel is actually sticking out of Ricky's foot and he's bleedin' all through his sock and screamin' in pain like a sonofabitch. Before this Brett can get away, Ricky grabs her wrist and starts breakin' her fingers. Lou's patrons are startin' to freak out, they're askin' what the hell kind of place is this, and he tries to stop Ricky, who proceeds to break a bottle on Lou's nose. Now Lou's bleedin' like a sonofabitch too and there's wine all over the carpet and all over the people at the next table, so his wife Anna calls the cops, and suddenly it's all over and Ricky's in jail. Only he's so angry at the whore and at Lou and still in so much pain that when the cops come through the door he forgets the notepad he's got in his pocket…which the cops take, and read, and read some more…and suddenly there's a story on the front page of the fuckin' paper and a shitstorm on the street.

"And all because of this jones Ricky Testa's got for redheads. Thank God you don't do that, Gino. And I'm not sayin' you ever would or anything like that, but that don't take us entirely out of the woods.

There's somethin' else I want to warn you about. And again, let me tell you, you're a good kid and I like you. Hell, the street guys are startin' to call you the genie, what with the way you're able to get things done, but maybe, sometime—not now yet, but sometime--that all ain't enough; maybe you decide that you want a little more, and maybe, just sometimes, you might want a little too much. Ambition is not a bad thing, Gino. It's a good thing. It's something we all need, it keeps us goin'; it keeps us young, but let me tell you kid, you want to be ambitious—you gotta do so in moderation.

"The family'll look out for you. They'll take care of you and they'll move you along, but don't try to move too fast, kid. There's a lot of guys here and they all have their own ideas and they all got things they want and we gotta work together on things or there could be…well, let's just say there could be some results that would not be the kind of thing that you'd want to see happen.

"Let me tell you about somebody, kid, somebody before your time, somebody you never knew, OK? Try some of your wine and let me tell you about him. There. Good, huh? OK, first I gotta start with somebody else. His name was Billy Mugavero, but nobody called him that. They called him Billy Moves. And they called him that for two reasons. You see, there were some guys that liked him and some guys that didn't. Those who did used to say that he had all the right moves. He did all the right things. I mean, Billy got his head patted by every guy who mattered on the east coast. He'd do this favor for one and that favor for another. He'd take shit jobs when nobody else would. This guy kissed so many asses that you'd think his lips would of swollen up and fallen off.

"And there's guys that like that. You know, guys that are always bendin' over, waitin' for guys in their crew to pucker. Anyway, Billy chose very carefully and he had this string of guys who said he was aces and that he could do anything. Plus, he was the kind of guy who would do anything. So he had the moves, but he was also very hard to pin down. He's not a guy who was exactly in love with what you'd call the truth.

Like, one day Tommy Carbone's kid Vincent got sick and Tommy's wife Clara tells him to take the kid's temperature, so he's shakin' the shit out of the thermometer and it slips out of his hand, and of course it breaks and of course there's glass and mercury all over the floor and Clara's gettin' progressively more pissed off, because she's worried about Vincent and because she's also worried about her floor, so Tommy—who's a guy who'll beat you to death with a 2 x 4, but won't say shit to his wife, Clara—is trying to pick up the glass and mercury and it keeps slidin' around the floor, and he's yellin' at it, sayin' it's worse than fuckin' Billy Moves, it's WORSE than fuckin' Billy Moves, and Clara says to him, 'Who's Billy Moves?' and Tommy says, 'You know, that's a good fuckin' question. I wish I fuckin' knew,' and then quickly adds: 'darling.'

"Anyway, Billy's also a guy who moves from place to place, I mean, this guy's nickname is really perfect for him. He starts out in Queens and does some good work there and persuades the capo to let him go up to Providence, from which he moves to Boston, and then down to Atlantic City. I mean, this is almost never heard of, but Billy's buildin' this rep for bein' an effective guy and nobody ever stops to ask themselves, maybe he just looks that way since he never spends enough time anywhere to really do anything. He kisses all the asses in sight; these guys punch his card, tell him he's the best, and then suddenly see his cheeks jiggle as he's makin' his way out the friggin' door.

"Anyway, he's finally back in town and he convinces everybody he's in it for real now. He's ready for the big time and they give him half the Brooklyn operation. Why not? This is fuckin' Billy Moves. The only problem is that he's got this guy who handles the numbers action, a guy called Jimmy Frattiani, who everybody calls Jimmy Numbers. Now they don't call him that because he handles the numbers. They call him that because his numbers are always the best. Whatever he touches is suddenly very yellow and very shiny. When Jimmy had the loan operation the income tripled; the slow pays started diggin' deeper and somehow there was always new business. When he handled the escorts everything was aces. The money flowed; the girls were happy; the outsiders and the freelancers suddenly disappeared, and there was so much new action that it was like the whole borough was on Viagra. Now he's got the numbers action and they had to buy some new bill counters to keep up with the daily drop. Jimmy Numbers is fuckin' golden.

"So where's the problem? If I'm Billy Moves I fall down on my knees and I start thankin' St. Dunstan…What? Oh, he's the saint for the goldsmiths, kid. A little joke. I mean, he really is the saint for those guys and believe me, we all should pray to him regularly, 'cause that's our fuckin' business, right? Anyway, Billy should be wearin' holes in the fuckin' kneeler, thankin' everybody up above that he's got Jimmy Frattiani. Plus, it ain't just that Jimmy's so good. He's got this guy workin' for him named Smart Julie Lorenzo who's got brains comin' out his ass and who keeps comin' up with new ideas for Jimmy Numbers. Just when they get one piece hummin' Smart Julie comes up with somethin' different. I mean, this crew is fuckin' tops.

"So if I'm Billy all I got to do is sit back and take some of the credit for this operation, which is strictly quality. And, by the way, it's strictly honest, since Jimmy and Smart Julie are originally out of Kansas City, where they was brought up to work hard and always tell the fuckin' truth. They're makin' more money now than they ever dreamed and they've got the good fuckin' sense to be content with it and not try to steal more. Or let anybody else steal. So their operation ain't plagued with shrinkage. Which means you not only get more money, but you don't have to whack any guys for skimmin', which saves you the money you don't have to put out for the whacks and also builds a kind of operation where everybody's more or less copacetic. I'm tellin' you, this operation was like a fuckin' Jap factory, with everybody showin' up on time, workin' their asses off, and pickin' up fair pay envelopes that they was happy with because the work was steady and they didn't have to look at a buncha guys laying around on the floor whose heads had been used for batting practice.

"So it was golden, but not for Billy Moves. Why? Because Billy

Moves was too fuckin' ambitious. He wants to run it all and there's no fuckin' way that's ever gonna happen because he's workin' for Victor Bennuci…here, kid. Let me fill up your glass. This ain't a long story, but it's a little complicated. Go ahead and put your feet up. That don't bother me. I want you to learn somethin' here.

"Victor took over after his uncle Dominic keeled over with a fuckin' heart attack. Dominic was the best, kid. It was Dominic who brought in Jimmy Frattiani and Smart Julie Lorenzo. It was Dominic who took the whole operation out of the toilet and put it back on fuckin' easy street, and I mean, he did it with style and efficiency. And Jesus were we rich.

"There was only one problem with Dominic; he fuckin' died. That left us with Victor, who was thicker than a fuckin' railroad tie with less fuckin' imagination than a retarded turtle. Plus he had never run anything larger than a fuckin' midget basketball team and had spent most of his time lookin' at himself in the fuckin' mirror.

"The problem, kid, was that he was Sicilian on both sides, plus he was Dominic's nephew. Nobody would go outside the family and everybody wanted a Sicilian. Now if you were in fuckin' Palermo, that'd be fine, but we were in fuckin' Brooklyn. That means that when you get right down to it you don't have jack shit to choose from for the top job and that means you end up with somebody like Victor Benucci. With Dominic we were lucky, kid. We didn't know how fuckin' lucky, but lemme tell you, we quickly found out.

"Now, like I said, Victor is dumb but he's also vain. He wants to be in charge, but he don't know how to do anything. Billy Moves takes one look and thinks, shit, I just died and somehow ended up in fuckin' heaven. This guy'll think I'm some kinda gift. He'll be so fuckin' grateful that he'll treat me like a fuckin' adopted son. I mean, I may have to do a few things, hang around for a few months, kiss an ass or two, but before fuckin' long, this douchebag's job will be mine.

"I know, I know, kid. You're wondering how in the fuckin' world could he ever…and you're fuckin' right. Billy Moves is from fuckin'

Naples. They'll hand over the family to him just about the time that the head fuckin' devil slips on the fuckin' ice in hell and breaks his fuckin' tail in half. But I never said he was smart, kid. I said he had moves. And I said he'd do fuckin' anything.

"So what happens? Billy's in the job for a few days and already Victor's startin' to fuck up big time. It seems like he can never make up his mind but he also can't bring himself to trust anybody. So he won't do anything, but he won't let anybody else do anything either. Meanwhile we're startin' to stand still and in this business you just can't do that. That's why they call 'em loansharks, kid. If you're not movin' and eatin' you're fuckin' starvin' or drownin'. The Tongs are movin' in, the goddam crips are movin' in; people start askin', what is this—a fuckin' goin' out of business sale on New York turf?

"Meanwhile Victor's ordered himself a new car and a cupboard full of new suits, but nothing's happenin' in the fuckin' business. We're gettin' stolen blind and he's tryin' on new alligator shoes and shiny new silk ties. The only thing in the organization that works is Victor's fucking mirror. And suddenly we're havin' all these fuckin' meetings. People are thinkin', what the fuck is this, Blowjob Billy tryin' to learn how to run the fuckin' White House by goin' to some Ramada seminar at the fuckin' beach?

"Anyway, it fast becomes clear that Victor is fuckin' clueless and that he needs some help, so what does he up and do? He brings in a fuckin' Irishman from New Jersey. An Irishman. Can you fuckin' believe it? And we're not even talkin' about somebody with red hair and freckles; this sonofabitch had gray suits, gray hair, gray eyes, and gray skin. In the fuckin' nursery when this sonofabitch was born, you'd see pink diaper pins, blue diaper pins, and fuckin' gray diaper pins just for him. He looks like a fuckin' undertaker with blow-dried eyebrows and the thinnest fuckin' lips I've ever seen in my life. I'm thinkin', 'What happened to his fuckin' lips? Did he swallow the sonofabitches; did he wear 'em out lyin'?' Plus he's a fuckin' accountant. Now I know it ain't that odd to have an accountant in the rackets, but I don't think this sonofabitch knew anything about either activity. Basically he was nothin' more than a fuckin' hatchet man with a pen.

"Victor couldn't fuckin' figure out how to bring in new money, so he decided to save what he already had. Now, as you know kid—at least I hope you know this—we don't have any early retirement plan in the family, particularly for guys that get forced out. We figure this might sour 'em on the operation and give 'em bad ideas, so the Irish fuckin' undertaker (his name was McCarry, by the way) starts havin' guys whacked and starts consolidatin' their territories.

"Victor, meanwhile, is looking at himself in the fuckin' mirror and tellin' everybody to talk to fuckin' Michael (that's McCarry's first name) if they have any questions. He even starts to let this Irish stiff come to the full-city meets; I'm tellin' you, the guys from the other families are lookin' at Victor like he's outta his fuckin' mind. The only thing that saved him was that fuckin' McCarry was so fuckin' gray he faded into the fuckin' wallpaper and you could forget that he was even there.

"So now things start to get really interesting, 'cause guess what— Billy Moves is shittin' his pants like a sonofabitch. Not only is he not gonna be sittin' in the back of the big fuckin' limo in Victor's seat; he may not even be sittin' at all. McCarry (who, by now, everybody is calling Sonny—short for sonofabitch) is suddenly Billy Moves's new boss and this fucker is even more ruthless than Billy.

"So what does Billy do? He starts kissin' Sonny's ass and starts eliminatin' anybody who could be put in his chair. But it ain't that fuckin' easy, because his biggest threat is Jimmy Numbers and Jimmy has always been golden. Plus he's got Smart Julie who's been figurin' out some ways to move farther out onto the island and bring in some fresh cash to stop the fuckin' bleeding. This is the fuckin' goose that always shits the golden eggs. But fuckin' Billy Moves don't think that way; he thinks about little Billy first, then about the family. You see, kid, he's too fuckin' ambitious.

"He's also a fuckin' chickenshit, so what does he do? He finds himself a fuckin' weasel to do in Jimmy and Smart Julie. Which brings me to the subject of my fuckin' story. And did I say, kid, that I appreciate your patience? I think this is somethin' you really need to hear. Let me fill up that glass again…anyway, the weasel's name is Willy Diorio, but everybody calls him Willy J.

"Now they don't call him Willy J for like Jay—you know, like he likes reefer. They call him Willy J because his clothes remind everybody of J. C. fuckin' Penney's. This guy had the cheapest fuckin' clothes I'd ever seen. He had these cotton ties, I swear to God they looked like fuckin' clip-ons. He had Thom fuckin' McAn shoes like some farmer would wear on the big day that he went into town to buy fuckin' seeds. You know the cheap suits they have hangin' out there on the big racks, the ones with the name in 'em that you know is really fuckin' Penney's brand? The ones with the permanent, fuckin' sale sign on 'em? Well, Willy J never wore anything that fuckin' good. He used to shop at this discount place in Jersey City that stocked the shit that was ripped off of hijacked trucks on their way to fuckin' Wal Mart headquarters. Willy J wore whatever shirts were on sale. Sometimes they were three sizes too big and the collars fell down over the top of his fuckin' undershirt; sometimes they were three sizes too small and his face would turn as purple as the top of Ricky Testa's dick when he saw a new redhead on the street.

"But there was one thing you could always say about Willy J: he was fuckin' ambitious and he would do absolutely anything to get ahead. Do you see where this is goin', kid? Stay with me…

"Billy Moves calls in Willy J and tells him he's gotta help him get rid of Jimmy Numbers and Smart Julie. Naturally, the little weasel is flattered, what with a guy like Billy actually talkin' to him and makin' him feel like he ain't such a fuckin' lowlife afterall. Maybe he's even a somebody. Or a lowlife who could become a somebody. Shit, he could even take over Jimmy's fuckin' operation. This starts the wheels turnin'. 'Sure, Billy,' he says, 'what can I do for you?'

"Now Billy says to Willy J that there's a guy in Smart Julie's crew that is pissed at Julie for not givin' him a larger cut of the loan action in

Brighton Beach. The guy is an asshole who shoulda been taken out years ago, but Willy J don't know that and Billy makes Willy think that he's on some kinda mission for Victor and McCarry. Which, of course, is also bullshit, since Billy never even talks to Victor or McCarry 'cause how can you ever talk to a guy when you're busy suckin' his dick?

"Willy J starts makin' calls. He talks to Smart Julie's guy who is pissed at him; then he tries to find somebody else who might be pissed at him; then he tries to find somebody who might be pissed at Jimmy Numbers. He keeps reportin' back to Billy Moves on what he's been able to find and he even tries to make up some things that he thinks Billy might like, but all of this comes to exactly fuckin' nothin', except that some guys who ain't performing have been squeezed by Jimmy and Smart Julie and they're pissed about it. Billy sends him back to the street and tells him to keep scroungin' until he finds somethin'…which eventually he does, though it don't amount to jack shit.

"It seems that Jimmy and Smart Julie have been tryin' to start some action in Westchester, which is something that ain't been done before. Now this don't mean squat, except for the fact that Willy J tells Billy Moves and since Billy Moves is graspin' for anything he could use, he starts askin' Jimmy about it. Then he starts askin' some more. He asks him about the guys who are pissed off. He asks him why they're pissed off and are there any problems with his crew?

"Now unbeknownst to Billy Moves, Jimmy and Smart Julie have pegged him for the asshole that he is from the fuckin' get-go and are already makin' enquiries in Kansas City about how they might come back home. There are like, no hard feelings, and Victor will be told if and when it works out, but the long and the fuckin' short of it is that they're ready to move on.

"Which makes the family in KC very happy, since Jimmy and Smart Julie got the fuckin' numbers and the fuckin' ideas.

"Meanwhile—who would believe it—Clara Carbone throws a wrench into the whole fuckin' works. This is Tommy's wife, now Tommy's widow, since McCarry has had Tommy whacked after Tommy told him to go fuck himself once in front of Victor Benucci. Victor don't know that this was McCarry's idea, but then Victor don't know a whole lot about fuckin' anything.

"Clara plays the good soldier, just like she's supposed to. She goes to the funeral. She smiles through her tears at all the right people, thanks them for comin', tells them how wonderful they've been to her and all that bullshit, collects thick envelopes from all the guys, and then goes home and waits. She waits a coupla weeks, then a coupla months. Finally she tells McCarry that she'd like to see him. He says OK, what the fuck, since he don't know that she's figured out that it was he who had Tommy taken out.

"Clara goes to his office. She's dressed real nice. Her hair is all done up. She's even wearin' new shoes that match her dress and purse. They make small talk and shoot the shit and Sonny asks if Clara would like a drink. 'You know,' she says, 'I think a drink would taste real good.' Whereupon he digs out a bottle of Ballantine's 35 year-old, thinkin' maybe he'll get her sauced and then maybe even get lucky. She takes a sip of the scotch, smiles, and says, 'Hey, that does taste good.' Sonny says, 'I thought it would,' and reaches for his own glass. Whereupon Clara takes an ice pick out of her brand new purse and sticks it in Sonny's eye. 'And how does that taste, you cocksucker?' she says. Now needless to say, it don't taste very good, and while Sonny's flailin' around like a fuckin' string puppet that just had a couple of his lines cut, Clara says to him, 'That one was from Tommy and this one is from me,' whereupon she takes out another ice pick and sticks it in the general area of his dick.

"Now the unfortunate thing about Sonny is that he happens to have a wooden chair in his office, so the pick goes through his goods and into the wood and lodges there, so now he ain't flailin' around so much anymore. He's just makin' a lot of weird sounds and thinkin' to himself that it probably wasn't a very good idea to have fucked with Tommy Carbone.

"Anyway, Victor finds out, he starts shittin' his pants, and Clara goes to see him. She tells him that McCarry had Tommy whacked for no good reason, that Victor's operation smells like a shithouse at a chili competition, and that if he even thinks about fuckin' with her or her boy Vincent she'll send a full fuckin' account of his operation to the heads of all the other families, the New York Police, the FBI, and the New York fuckin' Times, but not necessarily in that order.

"And Victor knows she fuckin' means it and he's smart enough to know that the shit is already written up, addressed, and safely stashed. So he can't do nothin' but get the shit cleaned out of his pants, think about runnin' the fuckin' operation by himself and block out a spot on his fuckin' calendar to attend Vincent's fuckin' confirmation ceremony, where he will greet his mother and wish her all the fuckin' best.

"By now Victor's even more fucked up, 'cause his cash cows, Jimmy and Smart Julie, tell him they're movin' back to KC. Billy Moves is shittin' his pants because the whole show is fuckin' fallin' apart and he had been plannin' to star in the sonofabitch. He starts makin' calls up and down the fuckin' coast and finally persuades this guy in Baltimore to let him run the numbers operation there. It ain't big but it's simple enough that Billy Moves won't be able to fuck it up too bad.

"Do you see where this is goin', kid? No? Have another drink. Now think about it. Victor's got a fuckin' brain you could stick up a gnat's asshole and still have plenty of room left over, but he's a fuckin' Sicilian and he's Dominic's fuckin' nephew. Billy Moves is a guy who would lie about the fuckin' weather to Willard fuckin' Scott while Jimmy Numbers and Smart Julie are good guys. Here's the point: it don't make no difference, kid. They're all made guys. You gotta remember the system; we got human beings involved here and there are people who like to get their asses kissed who will even look out for a scumbag like Billy Moves, so that prick is gonna survive. And there's nothing to worry about with Jimmy and Smart Julie, cause they're back on friggin' Easy Street. Victor is sittin' on a porch somewhere with a blanket over his legs, dribblin' outta the side of his mouth, but he's still drawin' breath. So run the fuckin' numbers. Who's left, kid?

"You don't see it? I'll tell you, kid. Who's left is Willy J. This little sonofabitch fucked with people he shouldn'ta fucked with. Why? Because he was too ambitious, kid. He forgot his limits, kid. Don'tcha see? That's what I want you to learn, kid. I want you to keep doin' a good job. I want you to be patient. I want you to wait your turn. If you keep workin' hard there'll be a place for you, a good place. But, kid, don't try to press it. And don't start suckin' on the dicks of liars like fuckin' Billy Moves, just because you think there might be somethin' in it for you. There ain't anything in it for you, kid. Nothin' but grief.

"You're welcome, kid. I'm happy to tell you these things. What? What happened to Willy J? I don't really think you want to know that, kid…

"OK, then. It ain't no secret. After it was all over, after everybody was killed or gone, the heads of the families took Victor aside and told him it was time to retire. He told 'em he wasn't ready to retire and they asked him what he WAS ready for? He thought about it a second and told 'em he thought he was ready to retire. The oldest Orsini brother was put in charge of the family and everything quieted down. Then one night—it was in June, about ten years ago now—the members of Jimmy and Julie's crew that were still around paid a visit to Willy J. They told him to put on his best suit, that he was goin' someplace special.

"They drove him out on the island, out to the end of the north shore, past Riverhead, out past Southold, just by Plum Island. It was a long ride, kid; the first fifty miles were bad and the rest weren't much better. When they got there they took him down by the beach. By then it was pretty late; nobody was around. They talked to him first. They told him what he was and they told him that he shouldn't have fucked with their boss who also happened to be their friend. He tried to lie and make excuses and somebody backhanded the little sonofabitch across the mouth. Then they went after him with claw hammers, takin' their time.

Finally they threw what was left of him into Plum Gut to feed the fishes and whatever might be crawlin' around on the bottom there.

"Yeah, kid, it wasn't pretty, but we had to do it. If we can't trust the guys in our crew, who can we trust? What are we supposed to do when we're out on the street--wonder who's tellin' the truth and who isn't, act like we're fuckin' IBM or somethin'? We can't afford that luxury, kid.

"Anyway, file it away. Remember it, kid. Sure, anytime. It's honest advice; take it to heart. Yeah, I enjoyed talkin' to you too. Do me a favor… the next kid out there…on your way out…ask him to come in."

IV

STILL GOT IT

Dag was feeling down. Not down down, but a little blue, particularly for a person with a taste for life and a highly-developed sense of the importance of the everyday. Beasley had moved to Nalcrest, the national association of letter carriers' planned community between Tampa and Vero Beach, where the retired postal employees could muse about the old days, bitch about botched zip codes, sliding standards on the supervisors' exam, and the ways in which the desk clerks now seemed to all be weighted down with those damned little enameled pins.

Herb and his wife had moved to the upper peninsula, where they were now buried in snow but still intent upon taking more than their fair share of walleyes and northerns. Unfortunately, Herb was running true to form and had taken Dag's leaf blower with him as well as his carborundum stone that still had its original cardboard box, now scented with years of sweet, light oil. A Christmas card had promised their return, but it was nearly March and neither had yet appeared.

After Blondie had opened her fourth catering site the offer came from a Marriott subsidiary to buy the whole package. The $3,000,000 offer took both of them aback, with Dag on sharp pins and long needles while Blondie exacted a promise, in writing, that her employees' contracts would all be extended and the level of quality which she had attained, continued.

She was still sorting through the arrangements for the transition, working late each night. Cookie and her husband had moved to Seattle the previous spring and Alexander was in graduate school in New York, studying hotel management. Daisy and her last litter of pups were still holding on, but she was moving a little more slowly with the passing years.

The old man was out of town, shoring up relationships with some long-term clients in Columbus and Dag's out-box was brimming with the Thorson, Reeder, and Intercontinental contracts he had just reviewed and approved. He mused about the boss, admiring the old man's tenacity in the face of a new world of junk bonds and hostile takeovers, covert monopolies and incrementally-debased products and services. Dag had read a book about eighteenth-century thieves who clipped the edges of coins, slowly accumulating a trove of precious metal; the old man compared them with his competitors' armies of MBA's.

J.C. never went to business school, but he never stopped to worry about it as he pressed ahead. He still worked harder than anyone at the corporation and he still kicked the occasional backside, as circumstances required. The only significant alteration of his lifestyle came with the installation of a dedicated ventilation system for his office and a new, airtight partition between it and his conference area. This preserved his freedom to indulge in his favored panetellas and robustos, a tradeoff reluctantly agreed to by his internist in return for a forty-pound weight loss and a regimen of water aerobics (after which he continually complained about the chattering of the middle-aged women who were his poolmates).

Over the years Cora had moderated without fully mellowing and the two had settled into a more comfortable, less turbulent relationship. In fact, everyone had. Except for J.C.'s bypass—earned many times over—everyone's health had held. The next generation appeared in proper course; the bill collectors and repossessors stayed at bay and the creeks never rose. Thanks to the Marriott corporation the Bumsteads were even rich. So why did Dag feel the way he did? Why was there a nagging sense of emptiness in mid-mornings and in late afternoons?

Except for the slightest touch of arthritis in his left knee and right ring finger he was as strong as ever. His hair was increasingly gray but still, in the main, intact. With Blondie's tight schedule, he stayed with his exercise routine, running the streets of his neighborhood at regular hours, rather than chasing after buses or carpool sedans. He did three eight-minute miles three days a week, watched the carbs, and took his selenium, saw palmetto, and 81 mg. aspirin-regimen tablet daily. His newest supplement was a mix of glucosamine and chondroitin, which seemed to be helping the left knee and offered the added benefit of a scent which brought back memories of Horlicks' malted milk tablets, a childhood mainstay.

He was the very picture of later middle-age health and he had even blocked out time for some reading he had always planned to do but for which he had never quite found the time. His current interests were English history, cosmology, and genetically-engineered food and he was developing some real expertise (for an amateur) on the physiology of sleep.

But there was still something wrong, something that continued to eat away. Part of it was the lingering memory of a recent experience, part his personal frustration at his inability to shake it and move on. What was eating at him was Davey Kupher, the surname pronounced [ku:per] after a childhood struggle with [ku:fer], which, when paired with [da:vi:], tied his lisping tongue in a single, tight, and embarrassing knot.

Davey was a mercy hire, a sad little puppy dog face atop a diminutive body who charmed the Human Resources women with thank-you notes on personal stationery and urgent expressions of a burning desire to work for J.C.D. The more people got to know him, however, the more the beagle nose and jaw morphed into those of a weasel or Norway brown rat.

They started him in Records, in a room full of women—Katrine

Gortzimer, Mary Sue Hosier, and Virginia Harborough. They each treated him like a pet and he warmed to the role, relying on Mary Sue to navigate the system and troubleshoot problems along the way. Mary Sue, a passive/aggressive with ambitions, had longed to supervise someone, just as Davey had longed for a sucker whose newest role in life would be to cover his backside and do most of his work. He rewarded Mary Sue with appreciative, glistening eyes and maintained a look of grateful dependence whenever their paths crossed. Meanwhile, he settled in behind his computer screen, stared intently, sipped cup after cup of the womens' herbal tea, and surfed adult internet sites.

This all came out later, when the reasons behind the rearranged furniture in his tiny office became clear. Davey had barricaded himself in a corner, with his back (and his computer screen) facing an unreflecting beige wall. Davey's fantasies ran to leggy older women, a fact that would have shocked his wife Debbie, particularly as she was carrying their first child at the time. It was amazing how easily that hard drive gave up its secrets. Very few of his coworkers would ever have accused Davey of overloading his brain, but few suspected he was spending the better part of each day feeding his overactive imagination.

And fewer still would have thought he was spending his nights in bars, nights that sometimes ended in fistfights or worse. The first indication of Davey's darker side came the previous March when he was picked up on I-71 by a highway patrolman named Earl Norris, who put Davey in the drunk tank and charged him with driving under the influence and resisting arrest.

The thing is, he was just so small in both body and spirit. Taking a swing at a stranger or mouthing off to a guy with a nightstick when you stand 5'7" and weigh about 117 is not what most people would consider prudent.

It was the anger. Or at least that's what he pled. He had "issues" with his temper and he had even been referred to a specialist in "anger mitigation." Which meant he was trying to change. Which meant he had good intentions, even if it would be hard. Which made him a victim instead of your basic immature and nasty little punk. Which made Mary Sue Hosier and Katrine Gortzimer and Virginia Harborough all want to take care of him. It didn't hurt that he'd sneak peeks at Mary Sue when she was working the lower files in the workroom cabinet. Davey knew how to turn his head away in shame and then address her in tones of abject politeness. So she continued to think he was a sweet young boy who couldn't help himself, a boy who respected her above all, but suffered those moments in which he couldn't resist a worshipful look at the swells of her female form.

By late April it all started to go south. A job came open in Purchasing. The money was the same, but the title caught Davey's eye. When the job went to a woman named Kathryn Harrison, Davey cried foul and demanded a meeting with the head of the division, a J.C.D. stalwart named Bill Chambers.

Davey promptly accused Chambers of blocking his career and argued that he should have been considered for the job. Chambers informed him that Mrs. Harrison had a master's degree, three years of experience at J.C.D., and a record of accomplishments that (with all due respect) far exceeded his. He also told him that he appreciated the fact that he was ambitious and that he would keep his eye open for appropriate opportunities. Davey thanked him perfunctorily, left, and stormed upstairs, demanding a meeting with Mr. Bumstead.

Mrs. Blanchard informed him that Mr. Bumstead was in Toledo and was unavailable. "When will he be back?" Davey asked, in his most intimidating tone. Mrs. Blanchard, who was twenty-five years his senior and outweighed him by approximately 115 pounds, thought him rude and presumptuous, and inquired concerning his needs.

"Perhaps I could be of help," she said.

"You can't help me," he answered curtly.

"Perhaps someone else in the office…?"

"I want to see Bumstead and I want to see him as soon as he gets back," Davey answered.

"I'll speak with him when he returns and ask if he'll see you," she said, her words now encased in frost.

"You do that," he responded, turning his back on her and storming through the doorway.

When Dag returned and heard the story he was angry. He knew that Gertrude Blanchard would put each encounter in the fairest, most optimistic light. Thus, when she described Davey Kupher as a somewhat nervous young man, anxious to excel, though a little high strung, Dag pegged him as a bratty punk who had gotten by through manipulation and intimidation. "I'll see him on Tuesday afternoon," Dag said, giving himself some time to check the kid's file and have a word with Bill Chambers.

Bill was also doing his best to be fair, but after digging his toe in the dirt for six or seven minutes he finally put his hands on the table and said, "I have to tell you this, Dag; I think the kid's bad news. It's not just the attitude; it's the lack of self-awareness and the fact that he couldn't see that the Harrison woman was clearly better qualified. I can't see him ever supervising anybody else, since he seems to have so much trouble just controlling himself."

Davey arrived early for the meeting, squirming on the bench beside Mrs. Blanchard's desk. He wasn't carrying any papers and didn't have a pad on which he might take notes. He was there to vent. As he picked at his fingers and twisted them compulsively he seemed to be coiling himself, harnessing his anger so that he might release it in a flood of aggression.

"Mr. Kupher?" Dag said, pronouncing it [ku:fer].

"[Ku:per]," Davey replied, deciding to skip the pleasantries.

Before Dag could even offer Davey a chair and sit down himself, Davey hit him with a demand: "I was screwed out of a position by some guy named Chambers and I want to know what you're going to do about it."

J.C. would have thrown the little twerp out of his office, but Dag sat down, offered Davey a glass of water, which he declined, poured one for himself, took a sip, sat back, and began.

"Are you saying that Mr. Chambers consciously and unjustly eliminated you from consideration for the position?"

"The result's the same," Davey answered.

"I've been studying your record here at Dithers as well as Mrs. Harrison's, Mr. Kupher. She has a master's degree, a little more than two-years' additional experience, and a record of strong reviews from her supervisor. I'm not at liberty to discuss a personnel matter such as this in great detail, but I can say that she has accomplished a number of things and solved a number of problems that have collectively brought her work to the attention of upper management. You, as yet, have not. Are there particular skills which you have to offer which are not likely to be reflected in standard personnel records?"

"No, I don't have any skills at all. I'm just here to waste your time. I've never done anything for the company and my branch of the Records department is a mess. Oh yeah, and I'm a white male, so I can't help you out with your quotas."

"Mr. Kupher," Dag said, "we don't have quotas at J.C. Dithers. We have goals. And our highest goal is to advance the success of the organization by encouraging and promoting those individuals who have made and are likely to continue to make the greatest contribution toward that goal. I suggest that you dedicate yourself to the task of expanding your experience and improving your performance; appropriate promotions will then follow."

"Yeah, right," Davey said, and stormed out of Dag's office. He stopped for a moment at Gertrude's desk and said, "What's he got, some kind of card that he reads that crap off of?"

She looked at him politely but held her tongue. Dag followed him through the door. "I heard what he said," Dag said. "I'm sorry that he talked to you that way."

"He is high strung," she said. "Perhaps he'll request a meeting with Mr. Dithers."

"I don't think he'll enjoy the reception he receives there," Dag answered.

But he didn't. Instead he retreated into sullenness, backbiting Kathryn Harrison and kissing up to Mary Sue, Katrine, and Virginia, lining up his references for his next job and plotting his revenge. He filed a grievance within J.C.D., made a formal complaint to the EEOC, and persuaded a lawyer to send a threatening letter to Dag and to Bill Chambers, copying Kathryn Harrison, whose performance was challenged in the letter.

Davey's plan was to so rile Mrs. Harrison that her performance would be affected and his case strengthened. He would then respond that he was simply asserting his rights and that if she folded under the democratic procedures of a democratic society she certainly couldn't be counted on in moments of real stress.

The EEOC told him to exhaust his remedies at J.C.D. The company grievance panel found no grounds for a claim of discrimination and they were sustained by the appeals board. Two days later Bill Chambers informed Dag that Mrs. Harrison's car had been vandalized. That evening her son had tried to repair the damage, thus removing any possibility of finding latent prints or other evidence.

"Why me?" Dag thought. "Why do I have to act like an adult, when that little punk is acting like a spoiled child? What he needs is some swift schoolyard justice."

He skipped lunch, keeping his edge, and called in Davey Kupher. He informed him that Mrs. Harrison's car had been vandalized and he told him that he was not making an accusation. He also told him that he should know that the matter was being turned over to the police and that the company would not tolerate behavior such as that. "Do you understand, Mr. Kupher?"

"Yeah, I understand," Davey answered. "I understand that you're railroading me for something I didn't do just because I exercised my rights."

"There's something else you should know," Dag said. "I've been informed of your incarceration for dwi and resisting arrest. You abused a highway patrolman."

"And?"

"I believe you should either plan to alter your behavior or resign your position at J.C.D."

Dag knew it was coming, but he still winced inside at the words: "So you blame me now. I get screwed out of a job I deserved and you piss all over me when I'm down."

"Young man, there's no reason to use that kind of rude language. I heard what you said to my executive assistant the last time you were here and I let it slide, under the circumstances. Not anymore. Empty your desk. You'll receive two weeks of severance pay within three to five working days. If you haven't left the premises by four o'clock this afternoon I'll ask Security to escort you out."

Davey's mouth broke into a mean smile. "You wanta play that way, Bumstead? That's fine with me."

He walked out of the office slowly, looking around as if he was in search of a weapon. Dag followed him to the door, checking to make sure that he didn't say anything vulgar to Gertrude Blanchard. Then he called Bill, asking him to inform Kathryn Harrison, and then Security, putting them on guard that they might have an incident and asking them to post someone at the south exit to keep an eye on Kupher as he walked through the parking lot to his car.

Nothing happened for the next ten days. Then it started. The first thing to happen was a series of late night phone calls. No words were spoken; there was nothing beyond light breathing, but the calls came at 3:00 and 4:00 a.m. and Blondie was frightened by them.

"What is he trying to do?" she asked.

"I don't know," Dag said. "It's not even clear that it's him. I phoned the caller i.d. numbers this afternoon from the office and no one picked up. They're probably phones in public booths."

"What about the police?" she asked.

"I called them yesterday," he said. "I suggested that they keep an eye on him and see if he makes calls at the times that we receive them. They didn't laugh at me, but I could tell that they thought the request was unreasonable. They've got drug dealers and murderers to deal with. They told me to screen calls with the answering machine during the day and unplug the phones when we want to go to sleep. So far there's been nothing that could be considered threatening or obscene. It could, as they say, just be somebody who works nights and calls the wrong number repeatedly."

"That's no help," Blondie said.

A week later when Dag was leaving work for home he found that his car had a flat. The garage was unable to find a puncture. "Sometimes it works loose around the rim," the mechanic said. "Then it heats up and the added stress on that tire hurries the process along."

"But I would have noticed it, wouldn't I?" Dag asked. "It should have thumped or something. I didn't hear or feel anything. And I look at the tires every time I get into the car."

The mechanic shrugged. "Tires are weird," he said. "Anyway, keep an eye on it; if you have a problem just give us a call."

Dag smiled politely and drove home. As he turned left onto Elm he noticed that he had torn the cuff on his shirt, changing the tire. He had also cut the heel of his left hand and some of the blood had stained his leather watch band. When he turned onto Lincoln Boulevard he thought he saw an old pickup truck turn with him. He turned abruptly onto Bluff Drive and the truck followed. When he turned onto Bluff Terrace the truck stopped. Dag looked over his shoulder, saw the truck turn into a driveway, back around, and then drive off. It was a battered, maroon Dodge from the late 80's. He was unable to get the license number.

A week later Gary Harrison's bike was found in the street outside of their house. The frame and the wheels had been twisted out of shape by the vehicle that had driven over them. There was some maroon paint on two of the bent spokes. The police took the report over the phone. Three days later his dog, an eleven year-old border collie mix, was found dead by the side of the porch. The vet suspected poisoning; the police declined to investigate. Dag called J. C.

"I'm going to need some time off, Boss," he said.

"What for?" the old man responded.

"That kid that I had to let go, the one who abused everyone—Kupher…"

"Yes…"

"I think he's harassing my family and Mrs. Harrison's."

"What do you mean, harassing?"

"Gary Harrison's dog was poisoned."

"What!?!"

"That was the vet's opinion."

"And what do you plan to do?"

"I'm going to investigate it. The police won't do anything…not enough evidence. Someone has to…"

"Don't be a numbskull. You're not going to investigate this alone. What time is it now—nine o'clock? (Mrs. Carter! [holding down the intercom switch] Cancel my afternoon appointments.) Dag, come back up at eleven thirty."

"Yes, sir," Dag said.

J. C. rolled his chair the length of his desk, opened up his outsized humidor and pulled out a Churchill cigar. He clipped the end with the silver cutter Cora had given him two Christmases ago, lit it, and reached for his rolodex. "Kill a kid's dog?" he said aloud. "That punk is mine."

Mrs. Carter showed Dag in at 11:29; J. C. was gathering notes from the edge of his desk blotter. The remains of another cigar were smoldering in the onyx ashtray on the end table at the side of his desk. Dag could hear the whirr of the ventilation fan.

"Did you bring your lunch?" J. C. asked.

"Yes, sir, but I left it downstairs."

"What did you bring?"

"I've got some liverwurst on white and a tin of kipper snacks."

"Leave 'em," J. C. said. "Mrs. Carter…" he said, his finger on the intercom.

"Yes Mr. Dithers?"

"Call that place over on Warren. Tell them we want four roast beef sandwiches on rye and two large coffees. The biggest ones."

"They're called venti, sir."

"That's fine," he said, forcing a polite expression. "We'll pick them up in about ten minutes."

"Very good," she said.

"Come on," J. C. said. "We're going on a stakeout."

Dag checked the positioning of the coffee containers in the big Lincoln's cup holders, wiping away some of the coffee that was oozing out of the cap slits. He then wrapped the damp napkins around the cups to catch any additional spillage.

"Here," J. C. said, handing Dag a handful of slips of paper. One had Davey Kupher's home address as well as the address of his parents. A second had the license number of his truck as well as its registration number. A third contained the address and phone number of the school where Davey's wife Debbie taught second grade.

"I hate to bring her into it," he said to Dag, anticipating his reaction, "but if this guy has any brains at all he'll trade vehicles with her until he can get the scratches on his truck fixed or let the repairs weather a little."

"Then you knew about the Harrison boy's bike."

"Of course I knew," he answered. "Why do you think I have the corner office on the top floor? The wife usually drives an old Civic," he said. "Blue, with a little rust over the rear wheel wells."

Dag's eyebrows rose slightly. "I talked to her mechanic," he said. Dag sat silently.

"Just checked her VISA records, looking for the name of a garage."

"You got access to her credit card records?"

"What planet do you live on, Bumstead? After forty-three years in this game you develop a list of names you can call for such things. Pass me one of those sandwiches. Leave the paper around it. I don't want to spill the contents on the seat and catch hell from Cora."

"They put in some of those little peppers," Dag said.

"I'd be damned disappointed if they hadn't," J. C. responded. "Put 'em on top of the beef. When I was in high school there used to be a place called the Wigwam just down the street from the school. They had these Italian beef sandwiches. They heated up the beef in this spiced oil and then ladeled it onto sub rolls. We'd save up our spare change for a couple weeks and then treat ourselves. Good eating. The best."

Dag took a bite of his sandwich and a sip of coffee just as J. C. hit the brake. "There!" he said. They were at the Warnsley Avenue School already. "There's the truck, right next to the Dempster Dumpster." J. C. parked on the street. "Go check it out," he said. "Don't worry, I won't eat your sandwich."

"Well?" J. C. asked.

"Right behind the right front tire," Dag said. "He covered over the scratch marks with touchup paint. There's an indentation in the metal too. It looks like he spread paint over it, trying to fill it up."

"Let's go find that Civic," J. C. said.

Davey's apartment building was a brick and cinderblock box atop rust-stained cement pillars. Beneath it was a first-come, first-served parking area, a row of communal garbage cans, and a set of shredded wooden steps leading to the main structure. There were no Civics, not even any Hondas, parked below.

"He may have it parked a few blocks away," J. C. said. "Here, let me try something." He reached into his jacket pocket, pulled out his cell phone, checked one of his slips of paper, and punched in the number. A moment or two later he spoke: "Yes, Mr. Kupher, this is Gary Arnold at Hanson Gutter and Siding. How are you today?" When Davey cursed at him he clicked off.

"He used foul language with me," J. C. said, smiling. "That wasn't a very good idea. If he had any brains he would have said that he didn't habla inglés. Now we know he's there and you know what? He's about to be in guano profundo."

"I didn't know you spoke Spanish, boss," Dag said. J. C. just laughed and reached for his sandwich and coffee.

"Save the second one," J.C. said, "we could be here awhile."

"Right, boss," Dag said, catching the scent of the second set of sandwiches but rolling up the paper bag to hold in their warmth.

"You've got to be patient," J.C. said. "That's what this is all about. We're going to wait him out, watch his moves. That could take time, a long time."

Dag looked longingly at the bag of sandwiches between them, but sipped at his coffee and waited patiently. He realized that if J.C. could go for hours without a cigar he could go for a couple hours without that second sandwich.

Two and a half hours later a door opened on the second floor of the building. "Here he comes," J. C. said.

J. C. was right. It was Davey. He descended the steps slowly. When he came into view he was looking to his left and right. Under his arm was a thick, brown parcel. Dag suddenly forgot the hunger pangs that were gnawing at his stomach.

"Look," J. C. said.

"I see it," Dag answered. "I wonder what's in the package."

"Not the package," J. C. said. "Look at his hands. He's wearing rubber gloves."

Dag blinked and started to focus. He saw the difference in tone between Davey's hands and forearms. The old man was staring through thick glasses but he had been right.

"He doesn't want any fingerprints on it," J. C. said. "Probably a dead rat or something. He may be sending it to you."

Dag thought about that for a second. "I'll confront him," Dag said. "If he runs we know he's guilty of something."

"Good idea. Tell him you want to talk to him about an additional severance package, but make it clear that you're trying to read the address on the parcel. That'll flush him out."

Dag opened the door, closed it quickly, and walked toward the building. J. C. started the engine and rolled closer. As Davey saw Dag approaching him he turned the package upside down so that Dag couldn't see the address. "What do you want?" he said.

J. C. reached for his cell phone.

"I want to talk to you about your severance package."

"Forget it," Davey said, "I don't want anything more from you."

"Do you always wear rubber gloves in the summertime?" Dag asked, moving closer.

"That's none of your damned business," Davey answered.

"It's my business if you're harassing our employees," Dag said.

Davey stopped. "Here," he said, "you want to see it?" He raised the box and then suddenly struck Dag in the side of the head with it. The cardboard was soft but the corner point caught him square in the left temple and his head exploded in a starry black flash. Davey started to bolt, but Dag leaped toward him, his head swimming and vision blurred. He reached blindly in the air, catching Davey's belt with two fingers and pulling him to the ground.

Davey started kicking ferociously, catching Dag in the ear and then the cheek. Then he brought the heel of his shoe down across Dag's hand. There was a snap and Dag let go. Davey jumped to his feet, thought about running, but then turned and kicked Dag again, this time in the stomach. Then a second time, in the ribs.

Dag was losing consciousness as his body shuddered in pain. Then, just as he braced himself for another jolt, the kicking stopped. He tried to focus, attempting to see the direction in which Davey had run, but there was no one in sight. He blinked and looked again, the pain in his chest bringing tears to his eyes.

From the corner of his eye he thought he saw something. It was somehow above him, hanging in the air. He put his hand across his chest and tried to shift his position. The hand was throbbing from the heel kick. He rolled to the side and saw Davey in the air, his shirt tight around his throat, his feet dangling. The old man had grabbed him by the back of his neck and lifted him off the ground. Most of what happened next was blurred, but Dag could see clearly enough to realize what happened.

J. C. paused a second and then delivered a kick to Davey's behind that sent him into the air and then into the ground face first. His body was convulsing with pain. The black wingtip had been delivered directly to its soft target and done its work. Davey was screaming and cursing wildly. J. C. gave him a second, this one softer, but he kept the point of his shoe lodged between Davey's butt and groin. "You even think about moving and you'll regret it forever," J. C. said. "And shut your filthy mouth. I'm tired of hearing the sound of your voice."

Then there was a new voice. "Julius?"

J. C. turned and saw a familiar face.

"What did you do, Julius, give him the old size 9?"

"I had to. He was trying to kill my most valued employee. I think if you check that parcel you'll find that he was trying to harass someone. You see the rubber gloves?"

"Trying to avoid fingerprints. Ha, look," the lieutenant said, "he wrote the address in his regular handwriting. You aren't too quick, are you boy?"

Davey didn't answer.

"I told him not to speak," J. C. said. "Who was it addressed to?"

"To somebody named Harrison," the lieutenant said.

J. C. turned to Dag and said, "So you survived this one; it wasn't for you after all."

"It depends on what you mean by survive," Dag said.

"Oh come on, Dag; let's let Lieutenant Carlson do his work. We've each got another sandwich left in the car."

They were five minutes from County General when J. C. told Dag to sit patiently. They'd soon be at the emergency room. "I think I'll be OK," Dag said. "They may have to set a finger and tape my ribs a little, but I'm starting to get my appetite back."

"A hot bath and a few hours on the couch and you'll be fine, my boy," J. C. said.

While Dag was being x-rayed and taped J.C. called Lieutenant Carlson. Then he clicked off the cell phone and walked into the recovery room, pulling the privacy sheet back from the side of Dag's bed. The intern and nurses looked at him as if he was an intruder. "I'm so happy," he said.

"Why, boss?" Dag answered, his voice a little weak.

"Do you know what was in that box?"

"Of course not, boss."

"I know you don't know; it was a rhetorical question."

"Sorry."

"Don't apologize, Dag. Your tackle brought the little punk down. It was a collar and a set of dog pictures. He was trying to break the Harrison boy's heart a second time."

"That's terrible, boss," Dag said. "So why are you so happy?"

"Because the boy didn't see them and because I was able to give that little weasel a second kick. If Carlson hadn't gotten there so quickly I might have had time for a third…"

"I'm not sure that would have been a good idea, boss. He may have trouble walking, as it is."

"I certainly hope so," J.C. answered.

"You did a good job, boss," Dag said.

"You know what, my boy?" J.C. said. "We've got to do this again some time; it's important for me to stay in touch. Besides, I love getting out of the office. The fresh air…the challenges…the chance to do something besides pushing paper…"

"I know what you mean, boss," Dag said. "I don't know why, what with the bruises and all, but I'm feeling younger than ever."

"Ha, ha," J.C. said, "and now here's your reward." As J.C. removed a quadruple-deck sandwich from some waxed paper, Dag noticed the silent face of a sardine peeking between a slice of ham and a slice of swiss cheese. The sardine was resting atop a pair of black, pitted olives. "Heaven," Dag said, as he caught a glimpse of Blondie coming through the door, carrying a sack from a deli and wearing a warm, relieved smile. "Heaven."

V

OOPS

The toddies were perfect. With Carlotta at the stove they could always count on that extra pinch of sugar, which buffed the sharp edges of the Old Grand Dad. It had been unusually cool for November and the stone walls which had offered comfort in July seemed to seep cold air, the draft penetrating capes and winter habits and clinging doggedly to necks and shoulders. In the northeast corner of the parlor the bare branches of a plum tree were scraping against the metal downspout, the wind reminding those fortunate enough to be inside of the onset of winter.

Bernardine and Origen had commandeered the rockers and, with them, the afghans which had hung over the back splats. Augusta and Austin, whose technically-corresponding names had long been a source of amusement, took the wingchairs, counting on the thick backs to provide them the necessary insulation. Rose and Carmelita took the couch, Carmelita first fluffing the throw pillows which sat in her corner. Terence stoked the grate fire and then sat on a three-legged stool, impishly blocking the heat from Virgilia and Roberta who had tarried at chapel and now found themselves on heavy ladder-back chairs with thin seat cushions covering the hard oak.

Carlotta refilled the cups, promising all another round when this one was through. "These are lovely," Carmelita said, taking a deep sip. "You should always make them, Carlotta."

"No one seems to complain when I do," Carlotta replied. "There are cakes as well," she said. "Not quite as fresh as they were yesterday, but they should still do."

When she returned from the kitchen she brought a small porcelain plate with dark squares smelling of something between strong lemon and mild disinfectant. No one reached for them immediately. After a few minutes Terence tried one, nibbling at the corner first and then washing down the remainder with a gulp of toddy.

"Shall we discuss our day?" Austin asked. "Mine wasn't terribly interesting. I ordered household supplies and talked to Mr. Gardner about repairing the broken pane in the garage."

"I was with Mother," Augusta said. "We went over accounts, developed some new policies with regard to the spring promenade, and then put the *Telegraph Registers* in the back of the church."

"I brought in wood, as you can see," Terence said. "We couldn't have a cold parlor now, could we? Are you comfortable, Virgilia?" she asked.

"Yes, quite," Virgilia answered. "We all appreciate your efforts, dear. Those long hours outdoors must have made you particularly uncomfortable. I'm so happy that you now have the opportunity to warm yourself."

"And how did you spend your day?" Terence asked.

"In prayerful meditation," Virgilia responded. "I won't burden you with the details. Suffice to say that I asked Our Lady to intercede with her Son to help reduce the pain and suffering in the world caused by inadvertent acts and petty meanness."

"Very thoughtful," Terence responded.

"The new textbooks came in," Bernardine offered. "I opened the first box this afternoon."

"How nice," Origen said. "Feel free to open mine as well if you wish to."

"Your's hasn't yet arrived," Bernardine said. "I hope it's not lost. That could put you to a great deal of trouble."

"I'm sure it will come in soon," Origen said.

"I'm sure it will," Bernardine answered.

"I had a wonderful day," Rose said. "First I, uh, checked on the dried flowers; they're coming along very nicely, you know. I love dried flowers, especially the darker ones, though the bright colors are nice as well. Then…let me see…oh yes, I did some washing and ironing. I love the smell of detergent, by the way (don't you?), especially the new kind that we just got (what is its name?), you know…the one that smells of citrus. I don't remember who bought that, but I'd certainly like to thank them again.

"After the ironing I straightened my room (I always change the sheets on Wednesdays)…then I read a little…not in my room, but down in the refectory. Or did I go back to my room? No, I stayed in the refectory. Yes, that's right. I made myself a cup of tea, found a sunny window, and read a biography of the Little Flower. Did I tell you all about it? I thought I did. Well, it's quite good, though there is all this business about France that you don't really need to know. Anyway, I read that book and then, before I knew it, it was time for lunch. Wait, no, I went to chapel for a minute or two, and then to lunch. It's so nice to be retired, except, of course, for the fact that it's a little quiet during the day when I'm more or less by myself, but I do have my thoughts and my prayers. It's just that I so look forward to seeing all of you like this and sharing the parts of my life with you."

Rose looked around. Terence was poking at the fire again and Bernardine's arm had fallen off the side of her rocker; her eyes were also closed and her mouth open. "I'm sorry," Rose said. "I shouldn't run on like that. I'm sure one of you had a much more interesting day than I."

"I know that I did," Roberta said.

"Tell us about it," Virgilia answered.

"It started very normally. We did our little collection for the missions and then talked about the rosary. The collection went very well; I find that distributing holy cards to those who are most generous helps a great deal. One little girl brought me fifty cents."

"Probably her lunch money," Terence said. "She didn't want to be embarrassed in front of her classmates."

"No, I asked her," Roberta said, "and she told me that it was money she had saved. I thought that was very sweet. I gave her a picture of St. Francis.

"Then we did our reading and our social studies, and some art. Did I tell you that I received those reproductions from the National Gallery? I asked the pupils to identify the works of the old masters and then we talked awhile about religious art. By then it was time for lunch. That's when things began to get interesting."

"What was so interesting about lunch?" Bernardine asked, her eyes now open and her curiosity piqued.

"It wasn't the lunch that was interesting; it was what happened afterwards."

"And what was that?" Carlotta asked, joining them and sitting on the stone ledge next to the fireplace.

"Well," Roberta said, "there is this boy. His name is Charles. Charles Albritton. He's very big for his age and very difficult to control. Today he spent most of the time on the playground tormenting his classmates. Then he went behind the bingo hall and found this pile of ice that the workmen had left. He found a plastic bag, filled it with the ice shavings, and ran around the playground, putting pieces of ice down the other pupils' backs, especially the girls'."

Terence smiled.

"It's not amusing," Roberta said. "It was very cold and windy and the ice was very bothersome."

"So what did you do?" Carlotta asked.

"Well…first I made him stand by himself behind the school, right near the northwest corner where he could feel the wind and think about what he'd done. He didn't like that very much; he was moving from foot to foot, muttering under his breath.

"Then we came inside and I marched him to the front of the room and asked him what he had done and why.

"I had to drag it out of him, but he finally admitted that he had put pieces of ice down the girls' backs. I asked him why he had done it and he said that he thought that it would be funny.

"'Funny to who?' I asked. 'Certainly not to the people you were tormenting.'

"Then we talked about health and hygiene and about the privacy of the body and how 'he had endangered the former and invaded the latter.'"

"What did you do then?" Terence asked.

"I told him to hold out his hands. I let him stand that way for awhile while I walked slowly to my desk. I opened the top drawer and removed my ruler, the one with the leather thong around the end.

"He was growing progressively more nervous; I could see it in his eyes. I wanted to strike quickly, while his hands were still cold, but I also wanted to see his fear and apprehension.

"I slipped the thong over my fingers and onto my wrist—all very slowly and deliberately, of course. Then I tapped the flat side of the ruler against my hand, as if I were testing it.

"By the time I stood in front of him I could see the tears welling in his eyes. 'Think about this the next time you consider bothering your classmates,' I said. Then I struck him.

"I should tell you that he is one of those annoying sorts who have never been properly disciplined. He probably runs loose at home and expects to be able to do that in school as well.

"Anyway, I told him to hold his hands still. They were shaking, you see. I grabbed them and held them for a moment, in part, of course, to see if they were still cold, which they were.

"Then I struck his open right palm with the end of the ruler. Then the left. Then the right and then the left, a second time. 'Do you intend to continue to torment your classmates?' I asked.

"'No, 'Ster,' he said. I informed him that I was to be addressed as Sister, not 'Ster.'

"By now he was shaking. I looked at the class and their mouths were open. Finally I had their full attention. 'Sit down!' I said to him and he walked quietly to his seat.

"He put his head in his hands, covering his tears and trying to regain his composure. I can't tell you how good that felt. Every day I see these children doing just as they please, running about, touching and poking one another, never giving any thought to what trouble they might be causing or pain they might be inflicting. For just a few moments I felt as if I had made an impression."

"I'm sure you made an impression on his hands," Terence said. "Are you sure you didn't break one of his fingers?"

"Don't be ridiculous," Roberta said, taking a deep sip of her toddy.

For a second there was a sense of collective embarrassment, though some obviously wished to hear more of Roberta's story.

"I'll just make some more toddies," Carlotta said, rising and walking toward the kitchen. She went through the swinging door, put down the drench jar, and left the kitchen by the rear door, walking quickly down the hallway. When she knocked at the door a voice answered promptly. "Yes, what is it?"

"Forgive me for bothering you, Mother," Carlotta said. "There's something I believe you should know."

Mother put down her pencil, closed her ledger, and set it aside. "Why don't we have a little tea, Carlotta?" she said.

"Certainly, Mother," Carlotta responded, hurrying out of the room and back down the hall. She returned a few minutes later.

"It's so thoughtful the way you keep a kettle on the stove, Carlotta. May I pour?" Mother looked at Carlotta standing before her and then at the small table next to the sofa and wing chair, but finally decided to stay behind her desk. Eventually she pointed to the wing chair and Carlotta turned it toward the desk. When Mother gestured a second time Carlotta sat down, but stayed poised at the front of the cushion. Mother reached halfheartedly toward the handle of the pot.

"I'll do it, Mother," Carlotta said, as Mother leaned back in her maroon leather chair.

"Just a little sugar, dear, and less of the cream than usual," Mother said. "I still have much to do."

"Here, Mother," Carlotta said, slipping a napkin on her desk next to the ledger and putting the cup and saucer on it. Mother lifted the small spoon from the side of the saucer and stirred the tea deliberately. "This is so good of you," she said. "Are you comfortable?"

Carlotta sat up in her chair, took the cup away from her lip and promptly responded, "Yes, Mother."

"Good. Now what is it you wanted to tell me, dear?"

"It concerns Roberta, Mother."

"Yes?"

"Roberta has the sixth grade, you know."

"Yes, I know that, dear."

"Well…there was an incident today."

"An incident?"

"Yes, Mother."

"What kind of an incident?"

"An incident with one of her pupils."

"And what is the pupil's name?"

"Charles Albritton, Mother."

"Really? And what was the nature of this incident?"

"Well, Mother, you know that the boy is very big for his age…"

"Yes…"

"And very, very exuberant."

"High spirited."

"Yes, Mother, very high spirited."

"And…?"

"Well, Charles found some ice that was left behind the bingo hall and proceeded to put it down the backs of other pupils."

"The girls?"

"Yes, Mother."

"And…?"

"And Sister Roberta disciplined him for it."

"Was the discipline harsh?"

"That's hard for me to say, Mother…"

"What did she do?"

"She struck his hands with her ruler. Several times."

"When they were still cold?"

"Yes, Mother."

"And how did the boy take it?"

"I believe he was very upset, Mother."

"And how did you come to learn this?"

"Roberta told us. We were sitting around the fire, enjoying some refreshments and talking about our day. She told us about her incident with Charles."

"And did she seem to enjoy it—this incident?"

"Yes, Mother. She thought that he was in need of discipline and she was happy that she could provide it. It also helped fix the attention of the class. That could contribute to better learning."

'Yes, it certainly could," Mother said. "Would you mind refilling my cup, dear?"

"No, not at all, Mother."

"Take some for yourself."

"No, I'm fine," Carlotta said.

"Would you do me a favor?" Mother asked, picking up her pencil and a small slip of paper.

"Yes, Mother?"

"Put this note on Roberta's pillow." She wrote something quickly and folded the paper in half. "You needn't do it right away. I'm sure you'd like to retain some anonymity here."

"Yes, Mother."

"And you needn't fear; I won't mention that we had this discussion."

"Thank you, Mother. Should I leave the pot?"

"No. Take everything with you, dear."

Carlotta bowed slightly, picked up the tray, and backed out of the room.

An hour and a half later there was a knock at the door. "Who is it?" Mother asked.

"Roberta," the muffled voice replied.

"Come in, Roberta," Mother said.

Roberta stood in front of Mother's desk. "You wanted to see me, Mother?"

"As a matter of fact I did," Mother responded, letting Roberta continue to stand. The chair which normally sat on the opposite side of Mother's desk had been placed in a distant corner of the room.

"I received a call a little while ago from one of your pupils' parents."

"You did, Mother?"

"Yes, I did. I gather that you had an incident in your class today."

"An incident, Mother?"

"Are you being coy with me, Roberta?"

"No, Mother. Do you mean the disciplining of the Albritton boy?"

"Did anything else happen of comparable importance?"

"No, Mother."

"Then that's what I mean."

"His parents called you?"

"I didn't say it was his parents, Roberta. I said it was the parents of one of your pupils. From what I was told I gather that the other children were upset by your actions."

"I wouldn't say they were upset. I would say that they were… attentive."

"Attentive, you say?"

"Yes, they paid close attention to what was occurring."

"Tell me, Roberta. Is it common for you to return from the classroom and begin vomiting uncontrollably?"

"No, Mother. Of course not."

"And is it common for you to be unable to eat or to sleep?"

"No, Mother. Why do you ask?"

"Did you enjoy your toddy this evening?"

"Yes, Mother."

"Then I would suggest to you that your response to what happened was different from the response of at least one of your pupils."

"I see."

"I'm not yet persuaded that you do. How well do you know the Albrittons?"

"I haven't met them yet, Mother. It's still early in the school year."

"It's the end of November, Roberta. Classes began on August 28th."

"Yes, Mother."

"Do you read the local newspaper, Roberta?"

"Of course, Mother."

"Do you read all of it?"

"No, not all of it. Just the essential parts."

"Essential, did you say?"

"Yes, Mother."

"Would you consider the Business section essential?"

"Not to me, Mother."

"Then there are some things that have escaped your attention. Tell me, did you strike the Albritton boy in a way that could have done permanent damage?"

"Certainly not, Mother. I disciplined him in an appropriate manner."

"Let me tell you something about Charles Albritton's family," Mother said, slipping on her rimless glasses and fixing Roberta in a focused gaze. "Charles's father, Louis Albritton, owns a printing company. The firm was established by Louis' father, Louis Sr. The company has been in existence for forty-seven years. It is the largest printing company in the city. Indeed, it is the largest printing company in the state, and, for that matter, the largest in the tri-state region.

"Last year, Centennial Printing did six hundred and seventy-five million dollars worth of printing. Do you read the *Telegraph Register*, Roberta?"

"Yes, Mother."

"It's printed by Centennial Printing. Do you use the hymnals in the parish church?"

"Yes, of course, Mother."

"The hymnals are printed by Centennial Printing. They have been so printed for the last twenty-five years. The Holy See purchases approximately seven million copies of those hymnals every time they are reedited and reissued." Mother let that sink in. "While you're here let me show you something." Mother picked up an envelope, the side of which had been slipped under the blotter holder on her desk. "I don't believe you've seen this," she said, handing it to Roberta.

Roberta began to open the envelope flap but the end had been glued. She slit it open with her fingertip. She opened it and took out the card that was contained inside.

"What you have in your hand is Monsignor Sheridan's Christmas card. It's very handsome, don't you think? Have a look at the back."

Roberta turned the card over and saw the small gold lettering indicating that the card had been produced by Centennial Printing.

"Do you know why the Monsignor contracts with Centennial for his card?"

Roberta hesitated. "It's a very nice card…"

"Yes, but there are many very nice cards. The Monsignor gives the contract to Louis Albritton because Mr. Albritton has made a pledge to pay the cost of repairing the roof of our parish church. Do you have any idea of the extent of that cost?"

"No, Mother," Roberta said. "I don't."

"It's a slate roof and a rather large one. The Monsignor was not aware that considerable damage had also been sustained by the underlying rafters when some of the flashing deteriorated. Large parts of the roof will now need to be completely replaced. The best bid that the Monsignor has received is one of three hundred and seventeen thousand dollars. That figure rises 5% every six months that the project is deferred. Mr. Albritton's gift would thus prove very helpful. It would be very helpful to the Monsignor, very helpful to the parish, and very helpful to all of those such as ourselves who depend upon the charity of the parishioners, particularly the charity of the more well-to-do parishioners. Unfortunately there is no gift as yet, merely a pledge, and the pledge is no more than that. It could be revoked at any time and for any reason."

"Mother, I…" Roberta said.

"You what?" Mother said.

"Nothing."

"Nothing? I don't believe that quite covers the case. You not only humiliated Mr. Albritton's son in front of his classmates; you struck him brutally."

"I wasn't brutal, Mother. Truly, I wasn't…"

"Do you wish to speak of brutality, Roberta? I'd be quite happy to if that's your wish."

Roberta stood silent.

"Perhaps I can summarize your thinking. Brutes are thick and stupid, like some animals. We deal with them in kind, in ways that they will understand. We chain them and strike them. Sometimes we use steel devices. Sometimes we use threats. We might even use promises. Like cubs, the poor things must somehow be licked into shape. The responsibility falls to us to do it and it helps ever so much that we can offer the promises of heavenly bliss or hellish fire. Brutes understand comfort after all and they certainly understand pain. We both promise and inflict; those are our twin roles and we embrace them happily because our ends are so pure and so dear.

"Don't you agree?"

Roberta remained silent. She was moving from foot to foot now, knotting her fingers together, though trying to conceal the fact from Mother.

"We have been the protectors of a church of immigrants. As such we have had certain responsibilities. The men have shirked them, of course, as they always will. Better to play daddy and eat thick beefsteaks in the main house.

"We enforce and they then reap the fruits. Very convenient for them. We understand that. I understand that, Roberta. But what if we overstep? What if we strike once too often or once too hard? What if we strike a patron, as you have, Roberta?"

"I…I," Roberta stammered.

"You what?" Mother said.

"Nothing."

"Stop making those ridiculous denials. Speak your mind!"

Roberta took a deep breath and then began. "I could apologize…I could explain that I had been too severe. It was out of love and concern. Charles is a good boy, a well-meaning boy. I so wish him to do well. The means were wrong but the intention was pure."

"You would say that?" Mother said.

"Yes, I…I would."

"To his father?"

"Yes."

"And to the boy?"

"Yes, if you think it would help, Mother."

"You really are a perfect fool, aren't you?"

"Mother…?"

"You don't see it, do you?"

"See what, Mother?"

"Any of it."

"I don't know what you mean, Mother."

"Let me make it simple enough for you to comprehend, Roberta. Pay attention. And stop shifting from foot to foot. Put your hands at your sides."

"Yes, Mother."

"Now, think about this. If you once admit that you have been wrong there is no going back. If you once admit that the discipline you administered was unnecessary or extreme, you are a changed person in their eyes. If you once admit that you abused your authority your authority ceases to exist. Don't you see it, you fool? The whole house of cards tumbles to the ground and you're suddenly just…like…them."

"Mother…?"

"What?"

"What would you have me do?" Roberta asked.

"Let me attempt to show you. Go to the window and put the palms of your hands against the panes." Roberta stood there, not comprehending.

"Don't stand there gaping. Do it."

Roberta walked across the room and held her hands against the windows, looking back for further directions. Mother had pushed her glasses closer to her eyes and was studying some papers on her desk.

"Mother…?" Roberta asked.

"Silence," she responded. "Just stand there until I tell you to move."

A full ten minutes later Mother opened her side desk drawer. "Come here," she said. As Roberta approached, Mother reached into the back of the drawer and took out a ruler. "Stand in front of the desk," she said.

Roberta stood there, her hands trembling. "Hold out the palms of your hands," Mother said. Roberta extended her hands; they were shaking.

Mother approached her and touched the center of her right hand with the index finger of her own left hand. "Nice and cold now," she said.

She stood back, gripped the ruler firmly in her right hand, raised it slowly in the air and brought it down, swiftly and violently, across the palm of Roberta's left hand. Roberta's lower lip quivered in fear and pain.

"Hold them still!" Mother said. She stepped back and then brought the ruler down across Roberta's right hand. This time she snapped her wrist to increase the force of the blow. By now Roberta was crying audibly.

"Put your palms down on my desk," Mother said. As Roberta did so Mother ran the fingernail of her left index finger along the metal straightedge that protruded across the top of the ruler. She turned the ruler over in her hand and held it in the air above the rear knuckles of Roberta's hands. She raised the ruler in the air, looked into Roberta's eyes, and then suddenly brought it down very slowly, resting the straightedge across her knuckles. Roberta exhaled and relaxed for a moment. Suddenly Mother increased the pressure of the straitedge across the knuckles and then pulled it away savagely, raking the sharp metal across the backs of Roberta's hands.

Roberta gasped and let out a sharp, prolonged cry of pain. "Silence!" Mother screamed. "It's too thick to cut deeply, you fool." Roberta continued to shake, the spasms of pain and fear increasing with each rapid breath.

"Stand still!" Mother said, seizing her by the shoulders. Roberta stared at her through tear-soaked eyes. Her nose and cheeks were red and wet.

Mother reached into a hidden pocket in the folds of her habit and removed a small lace handkerchief. "Here, child," she said, handing it to Roberta. "You may keep that. Now, come here." Mother put her arms around her and held her until she stopped shaking, patting the base of her neck and the center of her back as if she were a frightened child awakened by an electrical storm.

Finally she stepped back and took Roberta's hands in her own, lifting them to her face and pressing her lips against the angry red line that ran across her knuckles. "Everyone makes mistakes, child. Even the holy father. The important thing is that we learn from them and that we never forget that we are loved by God and all of His servants within the Church. Do you understand, child?"

"Y-yes, Mother," Roberta said, stepping into her kindly embrace a second time.

"The pains of this life are nothing in comparison to the pains of the next if we fail to do God's work. Now think about what you have done, remember that you will always be a child of God, and tomorrow we will proceed as if this never happened."

"Yes, Mother. Thank you, Mother," Roberta said.

"Well," Mother said, "Do you see now? Do you understand what to do?"

"Yes, Mother, I think so," Roberta said. Before Mother could respond Roberta bowed and walked quietly out of the room, closing the door behind her and pulling it slowly against the jamb to avoid any unnecessary noise.

Mother returned to her desk, opened the top side drawer, tossed in the ruler, shook her head, and reached for her ledger. A few minutes later there was a knock at the door.

"Yes?" Mother said.

The door opened and Carlotta entered, carrying a tea tray with a steaming pot, cup and saucer, and a plate of fresh cakes.

"Just leave them on the table," Mother said.

VI

___

SISTERS

It's funny how different the place is now. You throw up a building or reroute a highway and suddenly you've got a different kind of clientele. The change isn't always for the better.

I usually come on around 4:00, a few minutes before the first wave of regulars drifts in. Three or four want to eat. They missed lunch or want to get an early start on dinner. A few nibble on the free leftovers from lunch that we repackage and put out on an Army-surplus steam tray. When you get right down to it, though, we don't really do much of an evening food business. There's an old grill, a microwave, and a deep fryer but the menu is pretty simple and I can't honestly say that I'd recommend any of it. Most of our customers have always pretty much just come in to drink and the majority have come in to drink for most of the evening. It was never really the kind of place where people popped in for cocktails and expected them to come with stir sticks, truly fresh fruit and monogrammed napkins.

The change began about four years ago. When the economy picked up and they started developing the far south and southwest parts of town and the row of strip malls and restaurant chains along the interstate, we started to see a more or less steady stream of workers from downstate. There's not enough skilled labor in the area to meet the demand, so the big contractors had to go to the south counties to find the men to bring up here. These days they probably also hired a woman or two but we don't see them very often in here.

They generally come in for a few months, complete their projects, and then go back home to their families. Some come back for a second or third job, but most don't. When they're here we become whatever family they have. Since they start working early they're finished by the late afternoon. At six o'clock the parking lot's already pretty well filled, as is the bar and the set of tables we recently set up near the telephone by the ladies' room.

Most of the calls are for drafts and bar whiskey. We carry Modelo, Stella and Michelob for the big spenders. Most will drink a few Miller Lites and then say, "Heat the next one up." That means they want a jigger of bourbon between drafts. The stuff isn't too bad. Not that I'd drink it myself, but I don't feel too guilty about serving it. These are basically nice people, at least while they're sober. Sometimes I have to ask the bartender to step in, but most of the time I don't. Our patrons are not looking for trouble and the great majority are not looking for women. They're just coming in to gear down and end their day around people they know.

The three motels down the highway that were barely scraping by are all filled now. They like the long-term business and they'd rather have skilled workmen just coming in to sleep than underage kids on a sweaty date or tourist families that keep calling for more towels and wash cloths and toilet paper.

My uncle used to run one of them--the Monte Vista--and he told dinner-table stories that could make you lose your appetite for dessert. That's all changed with the contractors coming in. Somebody said the motels are now really short-term apartments and I guess that's a fair description.

The men don't ask for much and the rooms are clean and cheap, so everybody's happy. I know most of them by name and most of them know me and the other waitresses. There's no need for nametags. The place is called Hal's, though the owner's name is actually Jerry. He's OK.

He lets us dress comfortably. We don't have to whore for tips with tight pants or short skirts. Since I'm taking classes over at the community college I can come straight to work without changing clothes. It's easier all around. All Jerry asks is that we be on time, keep the drinks coming, and try to be cheerful. That's fair enough.

I'd rather work the bar than the tables. There's more business there and you get a chance to talk to the men. I don't understand what they're talking about most of the time, but I like to hear their voices. They keep talking about things that are in or out of plumb, about the best ways to snap a chalk line, about how all rooms are basically out of square, how you shouldn't chintz on the pea gravel, and how the energy codes are making it harder and harder to put up buildings that can breathe. Every now and then one of them will get injured on the job. They like to show their wounds and scars to one another, since their wives aren't here to look at them and commiserate.

They all seem to have started young and then got old fast. Most of the time they're working in the elements and they're pushing their bodies a little farther than they're meant to be pushed. When they were young they'd be tan and lean but as they got older the lines in their faces started to settle in and their fingers got so that they would never really ever be clean again. You don't smell their bodies so much as you smell the grease and oil from their tools and machines.

I like them though. You know they'd take care of you if you needed them to. They're the kind that hold the world together but don't get proper credit for it. And they don't expect it. They're happy just to have the work and a fair wage. There's an honesty in that which I respect.

The nine o'clock crowd is altogether different. They're new in town too but they're all from out of state. Techie types, but not so much cybergeeks themselves. These are the ones who make money off of the cybergeeks. These are the people who came in from the big dotcoms to swallow up the locals. They hid it pretty well at first, back when they were basically just picking off the low-hanging fruit. After they plucked it they sat back for awhile, then offered their own products with just enough new bells and whistles to justify the inflated prices. They all dress in soft, tailored suits, but you don't see many ties. The occasional dark on dark they call a 'full Reeg' and they make fun of the wearer, smiling behind their call-brand cocktails. The other day Jerry had to put in an order for a case of Jägermeister and some other stuff. Like he always says, if we don't sell it somebody else will.

When the construction types have had too much to drink they begin to just slip away. Their eyelids get heavy. They blink a little more. They slump down over their crossed arms. Sometimes they slide off their stools, push away from the bar, and start lurching toward their pickups. When I see it coming I try to get some coffee into them first. The thick stuff—no charge.

When the younger set have had too much, things start to turn nasty. Sometimes it's a word or two with a sharp edge. Sometimes it's an off-color joke or a comment about somebody—usually something physical. Sometimes it goes beyond that and nasty turns into ugly.

It happened last week. We didn't know at first what was really going on. Like I said, they tend to hide things at first and go after you later. They can seem nice if you don't know them, but they're basically users. They think it's all theirs by right and if you don't automatically give it to them they find ways to take it.

Like I said, we had a problem last week. One of the waitresses, a girl named Jeannie, went out with one of them. I warned her not to, but she's young and thought nothing could ever go wrong. She doesn't think that anymore. She's a college kid working part-time. This time she had to learn things the hard way.

The guy's name was Spence—his first name, not his last. He's around here a lot. He's loud and full of himself. Every other sentence is a brag about something he's done or some chunk of money he's earned. For a week or so he softened her up with good tips, then asked her if she'd like to go out to dinner with him. She did and everything seemed to go all right. Then he asked if she wanted to go to a party at a friend's house. That seemed tame enough, so she went.

They got there about 10:30. Jeannie doesn't remember much after that. She figures he put something in one of her drinks because she said she started to feel sleepy and relaxed. I had some back problems a year and a half ago and the doctor prescribed Valium to relax my muscles. Jeannie's description of how she felt sounded as if she had taken a whole handful of them.

She later awoke in a guest room bed. It was just before dawn and there was a note from this Spence guy on the nightstand. She had a lot of pain below the waist and there were some bruises on her shoulders and upper arms. It was pretty clear that she had been raped but she didn't know how many were involved. The note just made some comment about what a great time everybody'd had.

I told her to get tested for disease right away (and she did), but she's still waiting for the full results. She didn't get tested for drugs until a couple days later though and by then it was too late. She'd been dizzy and her vision was a little blurred, so they figure that somebody had probably given her roofies. You read about this kind of thing all the time. You see the statistics and the little drawings in USAToday, you hear about it on the evening news, but like they say, it's never real to you until it happens to somebody you know. When you see them shake and keep looking over their shoulder, when you smell their fear and see their tears, when they start telling you things they've never said to you before—that's when you start to get some idea of what they must have gone through.

It'll be awhile before she's anything like normal again, but Jeannie and I talked about it and I told her there might be something we could do in the meantime. I've got a regular named Terry. Terry Hostert. She was an engineer or something once, but decided she wanted to work with her hands. Now she's a finish carpenter. She came up from Simpson County about three or four months ago and is known for doing quality work; Jerry even had her do some things around the bar. A nice person.

I brought her into this and we talked. She had some good ideas. We decided that we shouldn't just let it go and that there was something that we could try that might get Spence's attention.

Last night I started to put things in motion. Spence came in with a couple of his friends around 10:15--a woman named Stacey and a guy named Brad. None of them ever have regular names. Brad's the puppy dog, licking Spence's hand and listening to his stories. Stacey's the big-hair, high-heels type, always wearing something tight, always expressing herself by jutting out her boobs, and usually trading quick feels for free drinks.

Brad always has whatever Spence is having; Stacey always makes us recite the list of white wines we sell by the glass. Then she frowns and orders lemon Stoli. A couple years ago I hadn't even heard of it. They were on their third round when Stacey slid off her stool and made her way to the toilet. She always makes a little sound when she does it, as if she's getting her jollies in the process. She brushed Spence's left arm with the tip of her left boob as she turned. Maybe she wanted him to have something to remember her by while she was in the toilet. Like those women who spray their perfume on their boyfriends' coats when they're out of the room—so the memory will stay with them. I gave her a minute or two to get settled and then I walked over to Spence and Brad.

"Hey, you two aren't staring into each other's left eye, are you?" I asked.

"What do you mean?" Spence answered.

"That's the window into the soul," I said. "For a second there, I was afraid that I might have to worry about you two."

"Why the left eye?" Brad asked.

"I don't know; I heard it on HBO the other night," I answered.

"Tantric sex," Spence said, smiling at me like he was ready to start undressing me and nodding at Brad as if he was ten years old and should sit at the feet of the master and start listening up.

"I wouldn't know about that," I said. "I was just channel hopping."

"The couple was sitting on the side of the hill with no clothes on," Spence said. "You mean you didn't stop for a second to see what was going on?"

"Certainly not," I said. "After I got over my shock I turned on the Antiques Road Show."

"Yeah, right," Spence said. "You didn't wait long enough to hear about the tantric sex orgasms—the kind you feel in every cell of your body?"

"No, and I'm not sure that's possible."

"Stare into my left eye for a second and tell me what you see," Spence said.

"I just did," I answered, "and I think I saw a request for another round of drinks."

"Sounds good," Spence answered. "What's your name again?"

"Deb," I said. "I'll be right back with those drinks."

As I walked toward the bar I could hear whispers and giggles behind me. This was going to be easy.

I returned with the drinks six minutes later. By then Stacey was back. She had run a comb through her hair and freshened her lipstick. It looked as if she had pulled her sweater down into her skirt to get a little more lift and separation. When the boys didn't take immediate notice of the fact she seemed disappointed. As I put the drinks on the table she looked at me as if I was a house servant. I stared through her, putting her glass a few inches in front of her and sliding Spence's into his hand. Brad was focused on my chest and didn't notice, but Spence smiled.

The next night the three of them came in a little later. They had had a late dinner and wanted nightcaps. They were sitting at one of Katie's tables, but as soon as Spence noticed me I whispered something to her. As she walked toward the other side of the room I approached them.

"Late tonight, huh? What can I get you?"

"Hi, Deb," Spence said. I had taken off my apron a few minutes earlier and was wearing a snug blouse and tight jeans. Brad seemed to approve. Stacey didn't. She was twisting her neck, looking in another direction.

"Kahlua and cognac," she said. It was more of an order than a request.

"Gentlemen?" I said, with a slightly softer voice.

"Irish coffee," Spence said, his tone blending with mine.

"The same for me," Brad said.

"I'll make fresh," I said, as Stacey got up and walked toward the ladies' room. I could feel their eyes on me as I walked back to the bar.

The next night Spence came in earlier. Only Brad was with him.

"Where's your friend?" I asked.

"Working late," Spence said.

"That's a pity," I said, in my most understanding voice.

"We'll try to soldier on," Spence said. "You could always take a little break and join us."

"Terry couldn't come in tonight," I said. "I've got to cover her tables. Maybe later if things slow down."

I knew it would be slow, but I let them wait awhile, walking past them whenever I got the chance. After the contractors went home and things were under control I walked over to their table.

"Does that offer still hold?" I asked, "because if it does, I'm thirsty."

"Have a seat," Spence said, sliding one between their two chairs but leaving very little room.

"This is cozy," I said, settling in between them. Ruth came over and took our orders. "What are you drinking?" I said to Spence.

"Macallan; make it a double," he said.

"Sounds good to me," I said, "just a single, on the rocks, Ruthie."

We talked and had a few more drinks. Mostly boring stuff about Spence's sales and how he was going to personally turn IBM's bottom line red. Then some crap about his wardrobe and how hard it is to get Italian shirts and British socks in this town. Brad was lapping it up, making goo-goo eyes from the Amen corner. I did my best to act interested, asking questions and throwing in light compliments.

After an hour or so, Spence asked what I was doing Saturday night. I leaned into him and opened my eyes a little wider. He suggested an early dinner and then perhaps a show. Maybe even a party later. In the meantime he'd try to see what was shaking and get back to me. "I think you'd like *Pastille*," he said.

"I've heard it's very nice," I answered.

"Let's do it around seven," he said.

"You mean go out to dinner?" I said.

"Of course, what did you think I meant?" he answered.

I just smiled. "Seven," I said. "You can meet me here."

"Done," he said.

Pastille is one of those pricey places that always has entrées with one too many ingredients. It's all chrome and pastels with black accents and uncomfortable chairs. The waiter's name was Jay; Spence read the wine list while he dutifully recited the specials. I ordered something with mashed potatoes to line my stomach. Spence asked for something that wasn't on the menu, assuring the waiter that the chef would make it for him.

"Do you like penne with aurora sauce?" he asked.

"I'll try some of yours," I answered.

When the wine came Spence checked the year on the bottle and told the waiter he wanted the 2018, not the 2019.

'That's all we have," Jay said.

"How about a Querciabella?" Spence asked.

"I don't think so; I've never heard of that," Jay answered.

"What have you heard of?" Spence responded.

"Would you like me to ask the chef what he would recommend?" Jay answered.

"No, just bring us a bottle of the Silverado," Spence said.

"Chardonnay or Cabernet?" Jay answered.

"Cabernet," Spence said, as if he was the last man on earth with a functioning brain.

"It's very good," I said.

"The 2017 was better, but this isn't too bad."

"So what have you been up to?" I asked. Spence smiled. Finally a subject that pleased him. He talked for at least twenty minutes nonstop, pausing only to sip his wine. From time to time he gestured with his fork, stabbing in the air to make a point. I dug my fingernails into the palms of my hands, forcing myself to stay alert and appear interested.

I passed on dessert and watched Spence drink his double espresso. I also passed on the cognac which followed it. Instead of looking at the table I focused on Spence's eyes. At first it made him nervous but eventually he took it as a good sign and upped the flirtation ante with a comment on my dress and then one on my lipstick. "Still up for a party?" he asked.

"I thought we were going to a show."

"Nothing worth seeing," he said.

"OK," I said. "I'm up for anything."

That brought a smile.

"You'll like these people," he said. "Very hip. Not like the white socks group that you see around the bar."

"I can do hip," I said, letting the word hang there in the air.

"I thought so," he answered, his eyes moving down to my mouth and then the top of my dress.

The party, as he called it, was in a condo on the west side of town. He said it was close to his friends' work. It sat on the edge of an industrial park with five low-slung brick boxes with interspersed fountains. There was some limestone facing along the bottom of each building and then a lot of glass and remote-control blinds. His friends' place was on the top floor. When the door opened right after his knock there was the heavy smell of cigar smoke and the sound of a baritone sax seeping around the frame.

"So who lives here," I asked, "a jazz critic?"

He broke into a wide smile. "Close," he said.

After introducing me to three other men and a lone woman, he asked me what I wanted to drink. "Let me think about it," I said, and excused myself.

The powder room was down the hall, across from a bedroom. I combed my hair, touched up my lipstick, and checked out the rest of me. When I returned, I slipped into the kitchen and made my own drink. It was mostly tonic water, but I drizzled some gin down the side of the glass and dabbed some on the edge of my upper lip so that he would catch the scent and think I was ready for something serious.

"I could have gotten you that," he said, when I returned.

"I know you could have," I responded, "but my legs still work so I figured I'd use them."

The host was a guy named Rick. His live-in's name was Bree, pronounced like the cheese. The other two men were named Blake and Brooks. "The three B's," Spence said. They looked like movie extras with patches of hair in unexpected parts of their faces. Blake was bald and had a turtleneck. Brooks had a silk shirt, open to the second button. Rick and Bree each had on red tee shirts. Rick kept patting her ass and leaning toward her as if he was trying to smell her neck.

I could have used a stiffer drink; I didn't like the feel of this at all. Instead I nursed the glass of tonic water for an hour. Spence asked three times if he could freshen it for me. Instead I sat closer to him on the couch, crossed my legs, let my dress slide up an inch or so at a time and brushed my ankle against his calf. It didn't take much to hold his attention.

When he asked a fourth time I said, "Sure, I'll have another." I thought about telling him to make it strong but I knew he wouldn't need any encouragement. He was in the kitchen longer than he needed to be and when he returned and handed me the glass I could see tiny particles clinging to the ice cubes at the surface. "Enjoy," he said.

"I'm sure I will," I answered, bringing the glass to my lips and moistening them, but not taking in more than a drop or two. Rick and Bree were dancing and I asked Spence when he and I were going to join them. That seemed to surprise him, but he said, "Why not now?" and led me across the living room to a section of exposed hardwood floor. He started out with his right hand on the small of my back and started to work his way south. Before he could settle into that position I leaned in closer and looked into his eyes. He didn't know whether I was going to complain or purr and I let him wonder for a second before I straightened up, looked at my watch, and told him I had to make a call.

I went back to the couch, opened my purse, took out my phone, picked up my drink, and turned to walk toward the back of the apartment. "This shouldn't take too long," I said.

Thinking that this group was not above listening by the door I called my sister on the coast and asked her how her daughter was doing after having her appendix out. "I know I promised I'd call sooner," I said, "but I've been tied up."

If they were listening to what I said to Carol they might have gotten the impression that I was a little careless and irresponsible. They would have liked that. Eventually I hung up, poured two-thirds of my drink into the dirt of a Norfolk pine plant in a blue crock, and returned to the living room.

"Everything OK?" Spence asked.

"Oh sure," I said. "My niece just had her appendix out and I promised to call earlier today, but forgot."

Blake was talking about the new incarnation of Taxicab Confessions on HBO and was telling Spence and Brooks about a guy from Nebraska and his experience in a Las Vegas massage parlor. He didn't spare the details in my presence. Bree and Rick were in the far corner of the living room, rubbing up against one another and kissing with their mouths open and their tongues active. I wondered if this was for my benefit or part of their usual routine.

After Blake finished his story and answered followup questions from Brooks I let my eyelids fall and began to yawn. "God, I suddenly feel so relaxed," I said. "I'm afraid I'm gonna fall asleep." Then I reached over and put my hand on Spence's thigh. "How about some coffee? I'm afraid I might conk out and miss something."

"Coffee?" he said. "Sure."

While he went out to the kitchen I picked up my purse and went into the toilet. I took some Vivarin to go with the dose I had had earlier, checked my hair and lipstick, and returned to the living room.

"I'm afraid this is Instant," he said. "Is that OK?"

"Sure," I said. Probably Decaf, I thought. They wouldn't want me any more alert than I was then. When he handed me the cup and saucer I brought the cup to my lips, and noticed some more flecks floating on the surface. What the hell is he trying to do, I wondered, put me out forever?

"That's good," I said. "Thanks, but it's a little hot yet." I put the cup and saucer down on the table and went back to resting my hand on his leg, as if that's what I really wanted to do. He didn't move away. After a few seconds he put his right hand on top of mine and slid it slightly higher. I flashed him the big eyes.

Ten minutes and three of Blake's stories later, I let my head fall against his shoulder. "Are you sleepy?" he asked. "You want to lay down for awhile?"

"That sounds good," I said. "Why don't we go to your place?"

"Tell you what," he said, "I need to talk to Rick about something, if

I can pry him away from Bree for a few minutes. You go in and lay down and I'll come get you in a couple minutes."

"OK," I said, "but don't be too long."

"Don't worry about that," he said.

I barely heard it when they came in. There was only a slight scuffing sound as the hollow door moved across the surface of the wall-to-wall carpet. I could hear the sound of several feet. I tightened up, digging myself into the folds of the bedspread, and suddenly the footsteps stopped. Then the side of the bed went down as Spence got in beside me. I could feel his leg against mine; it was bare.

I moved again and he put his arm around me, slowly rubbing my back and the side of my neck. Then he moved in closer and started to unbutton my dress. I blinked my eyes and he stopped. When I closed them again he slipped his hand between my legs, moving his fingers higher.

While it's not a skill that I've ever had to use very often, I can swallow my tongue to the point that it kicks in my gag reflex. To that I added some twitches which eventually turned into what he might have thought were convulsions. By now he had pulled his hand back as if it were on fire. While he watched me lay there, shaking, I swallowed my tongue just enough to make me vomit. I don't know whose feet caught the first wave, but Spence was soaked by it and so was the bed and the surrounding floor. After the first release the reality set in as the smell filled the room.

Not a romantic moment, and the fact that I was still shaking raised fears that I might be seriously ill and they might be in very, very deep shit. Spence squelched any talk of the emergency room and instead called for a wet washcloth, which he used to cool my head and clean my face. I coughed and sputtered in his general direction, covering him with sour breath and retching sounds.

I let him hold the washcloth against my forehead for another minute or two and then slowly spoke. I asked for help in getting to the bathroom, closed the door behind me, started in again with the sound effects, and let them stand outside, squirming.

Eventually I let Spence take me back to Hal's, told him I'd be all right and that I'd see him later. He didn't try to kiss me goodnight. I got into my car, watched his taillights get smaller and dimmer, and then checked my watch. Thirty minutes later I was home, scrubbed, and in bed.

I didn't see Spence again for several weeks. He came in with a guy in an Italian suit who he said was his lawyer. "You're going to jail," he said to me.

"What are you talking about?" I answered.

"The night of our date somebody broke into my apartment. They crashed my hard drive just before they transferred the money in my mutual fund account to a goddam bank in another state."

"Who in the hell do you think you are?" I said. "You come in here making accusations like that…how would anybody be able to transfer your money without your password? And why do you think it was me?"

"Listen…" he said.

"No, you listen, you yuppie prick," I answered. "I called my doctor right after you dropped me off that night. He sent me to the emergency room. They identified the shit you put in my drink. And there was a hell of a lot of it. I told one of my friends about it and after we talked for awhile she told me that she had passed out on a date with you and that you and your friends had raped her. I took her to the doctor's and she still had a trace of the drug in her system. They tested her hair follicles. You probably didn't know they could do that, did you? How many other people did you drug and rape? It shouldn't be too hard to find out, now that two of us are ready to testify. You'll do twenty years, you son-of-a-bitch, maybe more. Now get the hell out of here and take your lawyer with you."

"You'll be hearing from me, you bitch!" he said, jerking his head and shaking his fist, but of course I never did. Somehow it's always easier with the ones who think they know everything. Terry Hostert said that his password was NumeroUno. It took Terry's search software about three seconds to find it. The stuff about the roofies still being detectable was in part a bluff, but he didn't want to test it in court, especially with two of us ready to testify. Actually Jeannie wasn't ready to testify; she'd already moved to Colorado with the $287,000 stake from Spence that Terry had bounced from account to account so many times that it could have been a super ball slapping against a prison cell wall.

Technically we were flirting with a grand larceny charge, but compared with the prospect of twenty years in a seventy square-foot concrete room, a dogbreath cellmate and endless bologna sandwiches, little Spencer thought he had gotten off pretty well. Personally, I never gave it a second thought. Somebody's got to stand up to these pricks. They come in here and act like we should fall at their feet. They see some dirt on our jeans and they think since they know how to order wine they can take whatever they want. We're hicks, here to service them whenever they feel like it. They think we should be grateful. It's their world and they feel generous if they let us share it from time to time. That's the way things are. At least that's what they believe. It's always fun to see them piss down their pantslegs when they find out it doesn't always work out that way. The drop of their eyes and the quivering in their stomachs is a pleasant add-on. They thought they owned the town and could turn all of us into their slaves and servants. Then they find out that the small-town hicks have always dealt with far worse and can crush them with the heels of their shoes. When I told little Spencie to get the hell out of town he noticed that a couple of the construction guys had overheard our conversation and he realized that whatever he might have won in court would have been more than balanced out with what he and his lawyer friend might lose on a long night in a dark alley with enough small animal sounds to muffle human screams. People like us, people who work for a living…we tend to stick together.

VII

QUEEN CITY P. I.

You'd think by now that everybody would have figured out the kind of work we really do. Flash: we don't catch murderers and we don't save cities. We never wear trench coats or brimmed hats. I own two ties. One's too stained to clean and the other's too wrinkled to wear. And you can't iron them because if you try, the material on the other side forms lines on the front when you press down and the lines stay there forever. Mostly what we do is sit in cars with soggy-edged coffee cups and screaming bladders, working for lawyers representing husbands or wives with cupcakes or poolboys on the side, except there aren't that many pools around here, so the boys are usually plumbers or electricians or landscapers. Those of us with a little more luck work for flush companies on workmen's comp cases, chasing down bullshit artists on long term disability whose asses should be at work instead of at home on the family porch swing. The whiplash and lower back crowd. Think about it: all you have to do is get a picture of them lifting a cinder block or a giant bag of Wal-Mart dog food and you're home. Better than taking pictures through a bedroom window in a world full of handguns and lawn sprinklers.

I saw this show on television once; it was about a foundry. Everybody was squatting and straining and sweating. They interviewed the foreman. He said that it might seem odd, but that men naturally like to work, even if they have to do work like this. Not my guys. They don't want any part of it, least of all the hard part. Sure, they have to take a big hit in pay, but 60% for doing nothing is still the best job in town, especially when it leaves time for other things.

It may mean that they have to work paperless, but most of these guys aren't worried about the challenges of responsible citizenship. They weren't hanging out in the executive men's room to begin with and they don't mind a little cash-only work to supplement the 60% they're ripping off, particularly if the work isn't too difficult.

When they're in the mood, some of them drive gypsy cabs. Some of them wait in line for yuppies to get their cars registered or their license plates renewed, at least they did when we had yuppies, before the Over-the-Rhine developments went south and business went to shit. They can do odd jobs for old ladies or sit behind a counter on a slow day when the owner's out. There's plenty of ways to make money without leaving any record of it, especially if you're not doing or expecting very much. I knew one guy who became a professional beggar. He was spending all his time riding a folding chair anyway, so all he had to do was find a better location, get a styrofoam cup, and stick out his hand. Another cruised neighborhoods for a group of burglars, checking driveways for newspaper piles or looking for vacant curbs on garbage days.

No one case represents a lot of money to a big company; some of these guys were worth next to nothing when they did show up for work. The trouble is there's so damned many of them now that when you add all those 60 percenters together things start to get annoying. The good thing is that I don't have to catch all of them. Just catching one or two usually gets the attention of the rest, especially if the ones I catch have to do a little time in addition to returning what they've ripped off. Paying back means they're not just working, they're working for nothing and that hurts like a sonofabitch.

My only regret is that the postal inspectors keep all the post office work for themselves. If my agency could get a piece of that market we could redline everything else. I actually got into the business because of a parcel post driver who was related to my wife's sister's boyfriend. He went out on a long-term after pulling a back muscle, lifting a box on a Mt. Adams delivery. I had a little sympathy at first. I can never figure out how they get a whole set of snack tables in an 18" x 12" x 6" box. By the time you've got it off the ground you realize it's denser than concrete. Anyway, the muscle pull was legit, but the guy got used to his Ben-Gay and barcalounger and settled in for an extra month or two. The months became a year, then two, and eventually the inspectors got some pictures of him handling bales of peat moss and bags of charcoal briquets and suddenly he was back on the truck surrounded by brown boxes.

Not bad, I figured, and a hell of a lot better than chasing dealers down dirty alleys and over high walls topped with rusty concertina wire or getting caught in the middle of a domestic when the husband was handling a knife and the wife was countering with an electric drill. I left the department after twenty, joined Cincinnati Security Systems, got an inconspicuous Taurus and a digital camera and started tracking long-termers. The guy I was working was named Leo Cooper. It's a long story, but Leo's a former bricklayer who worked for a company that has a permanent crew at P&G. They're always adding new product lines and new labs and that means new construction. The company (Milford Brick and Tile) negotiated a deal with P&G by which the crew stationed there would get P&G benefits, so while old Leo was technically working for Milford it's P&G that's getting ripped off and since CSS's contract with P&G is a sweet one I've been told to give this my very best work, which I'm doing.

Leo lives in Price Hill, just on the Delhi border, but today he's in a bar at Eighth and State. This is the part of town that has bars with signs that say "Whiskey" and restaurants with blinking neon signs that say "Eat." I don't even like to drive through these streets and I'm wondering if Leo has made me and is drawing me here to have some fun at my expense. You don't know unless you keep playing, so after I park the

Taurus and check three times to make sure it's locked, I follow Leo into a bar and order a beer.

The bartender's name is Smitty and the only thing he has on tap is the local swill, so I have a glass and rub my head a lot as if I'm tired and thirsty and needed this one bad, even with all the thumbprints on the glass and the brown hint of old lipstick which is still visible around the rim. I turn the glass as inconspicuously as I can and take a deep sip. Leo's in the corner next to the telephone, nursing a shot of something clear, probably vodka, and when the phone rings he reaches up immediately and answers it. After a word or two with the caller he hangs up and takes another sip. I'm trying not to be too obvious about watching him, so I tell Smitty that his beer tastes good and try to look through him as if I'm lost in the moment. After I blink and look back in the mirror for Leo's reflection he's gone. Out the back door. Sonofabitch.

I can't follow right away so I wait a few seconds, finish the beer, leave three dollars, and walk back out into the sunlight. I get in the Taurus and drive up and down the adjoining streets, but it's clear that I've lost him and I'm going to have to start all over again.

The next day Leo stays home all day, so that's a bust even if I am getting paid for it, but the morning after--a Thursday--he comes out of his house on Delridge Drive and walks south, toward the bus stop. He looks serious and determined, like he's going to work. I'm in the parking lot of the playground at the end of the street, checking him out with some field glasses and trying not to give it all away by catching the lenses in the sunlight. The bus arrives in three and a half minutes and after a layover at Foley and Pedretti he's on his way to Eighth and State again. This time I don't follow him into the bar; I sit in the Taurus at the edge of the alley behind it, watching the back door.

At least old Leo is consistent; he's in the bar for about six or seven minutes and then he's back on the street. He walks down the alleyway, looks in both directions, and comes back onto West Eighth Street. He walks east and just before the viaduct he walks into a commercial building and closes the door behind him. The first floor used to have a jewelry store on the east and a barber shop on the west (my Uncle Lou went there all his life), but both have been closed for years. The second-floor windows are still intact and they haven't been replaced by plywood, so I park on a one-way street that intersects West Eighth and reach for my field glasses.

I can't see anything but smudges on the glass and some drapes that look like they might have been installed a few months before the Ohio River started to flow. I'm nursing my coffee now and wishing like hell I had stopped for some donuts or danish at the Bizy Bee. Maybe some of those upside-down cupcakes with the thick chocolate drizzled over them or the rolls with the raspberry jelly that they make in pans and break off a few at a time.

I'm not worrying too much about the coffee, since I'm thinking that no one could stand to be in a building at Eighth and State for longer than a half hour and my bladder could easily hold out that long, but it turns out that I'm wrong. After an hour I have to cover up with the day-old newspaper on the seat beside me and begin to relieve myself in the coffee cup. It's an old trick, known to all professional detectives, and it's always guaranteed to bring out the perp a minute too soon. The moment I settle in and start to ease myself, the door opens and out comes someone of Leo's height and weight who doesn't look like Leo. At least not right away.

He's wearing an outfit that's just this side of a full Cleveland: light slacks and a plaid sport coat in a large pattern, a lime-green shirt and horse blanket tie, suede shoes with thick rubber soles, Buddy Holly glasses, and the obligatory toothpick between the lips. The eyebrows seem thicker and the sideburns darker, but the walk is exaggerated and unnatural and my bullshit alarm is starting to sound.

No one else has gone in or out in the last hour and this is a guy who would have been hard to forget even if I'd seen him in one of those New York movies, walking in slow-mo down the street with ten or fifteen thousand other people. Besides, he's carrying an old brief case that's big enough to hold a pair of shoes, pants, and a shirt if he wants to make another change. And why would he need a brief case if he's doing business at Eighth and State, where there's no business but the drug business? After he closes the door behind him he walks west, back toward the bus stop. I take a risk and drive ahead, positioning myself for a second look with the field glasses. I don't get a good look but I get one that's good enough to take a chance on, so when the bus comes I follow it into town.

Suddenly this all gets very interesting, since the guy I've been following gets off the bus at Government Square and then walks down to 4th Street before turning around and walking north on Main. He doesn't go in any stores; he doesn't stop to buy cigarettes or a drink. Nothing. And while it's hard for me to keep an eye on him all the time I never see him look at his watch. So I figure he's not so much killing time as he is shaking anybody who might be following him.

He goes down Main to Court Street and hangs a left. I figure it's time for me to start following on foot, especially since there's an open meter on Court Street and I don't have to futz around with one of the local lots. My bladder's calling out again but this time I tell it I'm just not listening.

He's standing in the store front of what used to be an old candy company. He sets down the brief case, adjusts his Buddy Holly glasses, and takes a look at his watch. Then he scratches above his right ear and I'm thinking—new rug, maybe some bad glue that's starting to dry and tickle.

I remember the old candy store; they had the wholesale and retail business under the same roof. It was called Bissle's or something close to that. Bissle's Candy Factory. There was a huge marble table in the front room, with a large chunk broken off of the right-rear corner. They used it for multiple purposes, but especially for cutting the vanilla and chocolate fudge. My favorites were their coconut creams: coconut opera cream on the inside, dark chocolate on the outside, and a little nest of fresh coconut on the top. Whenever I got the chance I'd have five or six of them instead of lunch. It'd make me sick sometimes but I'd go right back the next time and do it all over again. The caramels were something special too. They had the red and the licorice kind, not just the brown.

Leo wasn't having any candy. And I was now sure it was Leo, even in those clothes and with that makeup and hair. He was talking on a cell phone and fishing through his pockets for a cigarette. When he couldn't find one he opened up the bag at his feet and checked there. Nothing.

He finished his call and walked quickly to the Court House, climbed the steps and stopped at the cigar stand in the south corner of the first floor. It was operated by a blind man with the largest German Shepherd I'd ever seen. The dog had blackish hair and was curled up on the floor behind the man's stool. Leo gave the proprietor a ten-dollar bill and the man asked another customer to verify that it was indeed a ten. Then he gave Leo a pack of cigarettes with his change. Leo lit up before he was out the door. He walked east on 9th Street, looked over his shoulder, and then worked his way south to the old Times Star Building, a remnant from the days when we had both a morning and evening paper. The building is what they call art deco. It's got towers and statues and gargoyly things. Very nice when it was in its prime.

There weren't many people on the street and I had to be careful to keep my distance. When he turned left into the building I had to hurry to catch the floor number on the elevator. The elevators have those old semicircular brass things that look like half of a clock, but with one hand. Most of the building contains county offices and juvenile court, but the county rents out a couple of floors for private businesses. His elevator stopped at the fourth floor. I checked the building directory. There were three suites on the fourth floor—a lawyer's office, an insurance company I'd never heard of, and something called Carson Enterprises, which could have been anything. I walked over to the bank of elevators, hit the UP button, waited for a light to blink and a door to open, and then hit the number 4. Taking another chance.

The fourth floor hallway was dark. The tile floor had no carpet but the plaster had been patched over the years. Each of the office suites had opaque glass with green lettering in a gold border. Reflected, natural light illuminated the windows. The hall was quiet and there were no natural nooks or crannies where I could stand. Now that I had gone that far I couldn't afford to be made, so I hit the elevator button and waited. Suddenly one of the suite doors opened.

It was the door for Carson Enterprises. I didn't turn or look up. When the elevator door opened I stepped into the car and held the door, appearing to be polite but avoiding direct eye contact. I didn't need it; I recognized the guy immediately.

It wasn't Leo Cooper. It was Tito Boyer, a street hood from Covington with career aspirations. His path never really crosses with mine; I just see his face in the paper sometimes. When Mr. Morality, Charlie Keating, drove the dirty bookstores out of Cincinnati and across the river Tito's Uncle Ray was sitting in Covington licking his lips. With some backing from the Cleveland syndicate he put up some fresh neon, added some phone sex services and massage parlors, and eventually cut into Newport's market share so deep that he was able to force everybody else out without spilling any serious blood. Ray died and his younger brother Lou took over the smut empire. Now Tito's the heir apparent, except he's got a bad temper, a taste for dope, and other baggage that keeps putting him in the local headlines.

Tito got on the elevator and stood near the door exposing his back to me. It just goes to show how dumb he is. Probably figures he can kick or bite his way out of anything. He was wearing a silk suit with a dark shirt and matching tie. His shoes looked like real alligator. No pinkie ring, but he had a gold bracelet that he kept futzing with as the elevator descended. When he got off and walked through the main building doors a car pulled up, as if on cue. He must have called the driver from upstairs. What was a scumbag like him doing on the same floor of the Times Star Building with a small-time lowlife like Leo Cooper?

I thought about going back upstairs when suddenly an elevator door opened and Leo walked right past me in the building's lobby. He hit the sidewalk, turned left, and I followed. He turned right on 8th Street, passed the site of Andy Schain's old Studebaker dealership (Jesus, am I dating myself) and then headed up to Main, walked around what used to be Bert Smith's Acres of Books, and returned to Government Square, where he caught the bus for 8th and State and headed off into the sunset.

He must have been going there to change into his other clothes. For some reason or other he didn't want to be seen in the electric plaid back on Delridge Drive. I couldn't follow him anyway, since I had to go back to Court Street to pick up my car.

I stood there in the street for a second, thinking about the old city, thought about how they'd actually moved the fountain on Fountain Square, and stared in the general direction of the spot where the Albee Theatre used to stand. An old vaudeville palace, you could still see the stage slots for the cards announcing the acts. The marble bathrooms sat at the base of sweeping staircases—facilities nicer than any house most of us ever lived in. Great velvet curtains and broad balconies, smartly-uniformed ushers--all gone now. And in its place industrial cineplexes in weedy parking lots and Lou Boyer peep shows with wadded kleenex under the wooden bench seats and the constant smell of roach spray.

It's hell to grow old and remember the way things used to be and see how they are now. That's why I stopped off at the Crow's Nest on my way to check out Leo. Even after three Buds and a couple visits from Old Grand Dad I could see that he was safely tucked away for the night. When he stood up and stretched in front of the living room window I could see his tank top undershirt and plaid boxers. I figured him for some kind of method actor whose underwear had to match whatever he was wearing outside—just to keep him in the mood and help him feel the part.

The next day it was the same routine. First to 8th and State and then into the old building to change his clothes, only this time he came out dressed like Leisure Suit Larry. He was wearing this aqua outfit (the old Studebaker color would have been 'Tahoe Blue') with white shoes, a ruffly shirt open at the neck, and a gold necklace. He had on a brown rug that looked like quality but having got used to his regular look it seemed like a half inch too high on the top and a little loose around the ears.

When he got to town he headed for 4th Street, checked out some shops, dropped into a bar for a drink or two, came back out, looked at his watch, and walked briskly to the Times Star Building. I followed him in my car until I saw an open space on Main. I parked quickly, noticed that the rear end of my car was sticking out too far, but let it go and hurried to catch up with him. Same old same old at the Times Star Building; he got onto the elevator alone and just like clockwork the car stopped on 4. I waited five minutes and followed. Exactly seventeen minutes later the door for Carson Enterprises opened and a woman walked out--a tall brunette with deep green eyes. She was wearing something short and tight and an expression that spelled relief.

I had already pushed the button for the elevator. When it came I held the door for her and she smiled. There was more sincerity in her face than I'd seen in a week and we rode silently to the lobby. Leo followed eight minutes later, hit the sidewalk, hung a left, and walked straight to Government Square.

For the next several days he stayed at home, putzing in the yard for a few minutes one day, hitting the Delhi Pike Kroger's the next. I could see the smoke from his backyard grill late in the afternoon and heard the sound of his power mower in the early evening. He was one of those people who cut his grass in sections, doing the backyard one day and leaving the front for later, even if the two don't match. Not a Cincinnati guy at all.

Monday morning he slept in, then cut his front yard, diddled in the garage for awhile, and finally sat down in a plastic folding chair at the top of his driveway, nursing a Schoenling Little Kings. Then he drank a second. I didn't know he had that much courage.

Tuesday he went back to work. I beat the bus to 8th and State—not a wise move, since he could have been going some other place, but by now I had a favorite parking place and I wanted to be sure I either got it or something close. Four minutes later he got off the bus. I was just biting into a wedge of coconut coffee cake I had picked up at Bizy's. It's still the best, especially when they don't scrimp on the drizzled sugar. Their coffee's not as good as White Castle's, but the nearest Castle is way the hell over on Boudinot and I didn't have time for a side trip.

I was half way through the coffee cake when the door opened and Leo walked out onto the sidewalk. This time he was dressed for business: a dark wool suit with faint chalk stripes, starched white shirt, blue silk tie, gray socks and black leather wingtips. The only thing that didn't fit was the hair. Teased into a fright wig, it was too young for him. With the heavy glasses he was all Hart, Schaffner, and Harpo Marx.

The route was different but the destination was the same. This time he headed west/northwest from the Square, walking by the Lazarus Building, which for me at least is still Shillito's, then turned right and after a block jogged left, past the sites of the old Cinerama Theatre and the Gayety Burlesque House. I've always kind of liked the fact that the Library now sits on the east side of the Gayety site. Different people learn in different ways and we should respect those differences. At least that's what they say at the School Board meetings.

He was at the Times Star Building by 11:10 and out at 11:47, having been preceded by another suit, this one carrying an umbrella, which I hoped he wouldn't need, since I didn't have one. The guy was about fifty, plump and prosperous, with a good haircut and dye job. I had no trouble imagining him at the Sunday buffet at the Losantiville Country Club. He didn't say anything to me on the elevator, but he looked me up and down and didn't seem pleased by what he saw.

Since no one at Carson Enterprises was going to invite me to the next meeting with the newest version of Leo I figured I had to go in and check things out for myself. Fortunately it's not as hard as it sounds. And no, you never go in at night. The watchman won't know you if he catches you and you could end up getting shot. Instead, you go in at five o'clock when everybody's anxious to go home and you go in with a plausible excuse for being there. I also figured that two could play the Leo game and it was my turn.

I moved my car, had some lunch, drank three cups of coffee and saw a French movie at the art house near Shillito's (it had something to do with three girls who couldn't make up their minds whether they wanted to be boys or commit suicide). By then it was nearly four o'clock. I went back to my car, finished off the remains of the coconut coffee cake, got a bag out of the trunk, and walked over to the library. The third floor Men's room has a handicapped stall which is bigger than most dressing rooms. I took off my street clothes and put on my uniform. Then I drove to the Times Star Building, put the OFFICIAL BUSINESS card on my dash, and walked up to the lobby.

I love the internet. You can get pictures, print them off on this paper you get at Office Depot, and then iron them onto a white shirt. An instant uniform. Mine was the most trusted name in pest control in the Queen City. It read:

SINCE 1934
ScherZinger
STOPS Z BUGS

I had a little matching white hat, which is always a nice touch and I added a gallon-size plastic tank with a plunger and hose that I got at Wal-Mart to spray Roundup. I printed the Scherzinger logo on some label paper and glued one on the side. I looked so damn official I nearly fooled myself. The tank was half-filled with water and some cheap perfume. I always like to spray a little on the outside of the tank before I go in, so people are thinking, "Oh yeah, it's that shit that's supposed to smell like something other than bug spray, but we know what it really is." I clipped a chain full of old keys to the belt loop above my right pocket and I was ready for business.

I got to Carson Enterprises at exactly 4:58 but the door was locked. The glass was dark, as was the door of the Lawyer's office. When I tried to turn the knob it wouldn't budge. Strike two. I could always pick the lock but I prefer the path of least resistance and I don't like to be seen bent over in a hallway doing something illegal. The insurance company was called Hearthstone. I tried the knob and it turned. I entered and found a woman gathering up her shopping bags and reaching for her purse.

"We're closing," she said, without looking up. Then she turned, looked at me, and said, "Sorry, I thought you were a customer."

"Right," I answered. "I don't like to spray when people are still here."

"We appreciate that," she said. "Would you make sure that the door locks behind you?"

"I certainly will, ma'am. You have a nice evening."

She moved some things around on her desk, even though everything looked straight, smiled, picked up her various bags, and said, "Good night."

It only took me a few seconds to find the connecting door. These places always have them so that the space can be reconfigured for different renters. The lock was an old Yale job that only took four or five minutes to get past. I picked up my bug spray tank and walked into the offices of Carson Enterprises.

Carson consisted of a single room and it couldn't have been conducting too many enterprises because there was no computer, no fax machine, no phone, and no furniture, just a bare room, a stained rug, and a single window that looked like it was last cleaned the day the Times Star announced the crest of the 1937 flood.

This was a breezeway, not an office. I walked over to the connecting door to the law offices of Stanley and Stanley and listened. There was no sound. I tried the knob, but it was locked. It took me nearly ten minutes to pick the lock and when I did I opened the door slowly. Then I got another surprise.

The office of Stanley and Stanley only had room for one Stanley and that Stanley would have difficulty practicing law. The suite consisted of a small anteroom with nothing beyond a bare desk and a tiny office with a desk, chair, and three client chairs. There were no computers, no fax machine, no telephones and no law books. The office contained a small file cabinet with a large lock. On top of the cabinet was a set of aged phone directories. There was a phone jack on the wall next to the desk. Whoever was using the office, and somebody obviously was, was working with cell phones and a laptop computer (if that). How did they attract clients? If they weren't working in secret their approach to advertising gave new meaning to the word 'narrowcasting.' They made the drug dealers on Vine Street look like Anheuser Busch or Unilever.

As I thought about these things I heard a key in the lock of the door in the anteroom. Trying desperately for a quick counter move, I hurried to meet the person as he entered. Before he could speak, I said, "Just laying down a coat of spray. If you want me to come back later I'll be happy to."

He was tall and broad and his eyes were staring holes in my forehead. He didn't speak at first. Finally he said, "We didn't call an exterminator."

"The building management handles the contract," I said. "If we don't spray everywhere the bugs will all concentrate in the areas we skip. This is the only way we can do an effective treatment."

"Come back some other time," he said. "No rush."

"Will do," I said, tapping the bill of my cap and walking toward the connecting door to Carson Enterprises.

"You don't need to do them either," he said.

"OK," I said, asking him to excuse me, as I walked past him into the hallway. When I got there I pumped the plunger on the tank and aimed the stream of perfumed water at the top of the floor molding and along the edge of the quarter round trim. I was taking a risk, giving him enough time to check with the building super, but I figured I had to complete the performance if I was going to con him successfully. I sprayed the area around the door a second time, so he could pick up the scent, which resembled a urinal cake soaked in kerosene.

So just who in the hell was he? He looked like an educated bouncer, shrewd in the eyes but thick in the neck and shoulders. If he had doubts about me he wasn't giving much away, since that would only feed my own suspicions. Besides, he could always say that he was just moving in. What could I say when the building management announced that their pest control contract was with another company?

I sprayed for about three minutes and then hit the elevator button. The door opened suddenly and out walked a woman with Tammy Faye eyes and the kind of sequined jean suit you see in Palm Springs remnant stores. Her hair was high and frosted and most of the rest of her seemed to be held in with industrial-strength elastic.

"Evening," I said, looking down. I followed it with a sucking nasal sound designed to suggest that I had spent too many years with too much bug spray. She didn't respond. She just looked at the heel of her right shoe as if she might have unintentionally stepped in something.

I got off at the second floor, went down the rear stairs, and exited through the loading dock door. Fifteen minutes later I was in a men's room at a River Road service station, changing my clothes. Twenty five minutes later I was at the Crow's Nest, using my fingertip to connect the moisture dots on my beer glass, and trying to figure out what Leo Cooper might have been up to.

It took me three beers, a bag of bacon rinds, and then two more beers before it finally hit me. I must have made some sound, since the bartender, a guy named Carl, came over and asked me what I wanted. "Nothing," I said. "I was just trying to figure something out."

"Here," Carl said, handing me a fresh draft. "We don't want too much thinking in here; it's bad for business."

The problem now was avoiding payback. Leo would take a lot of people down with him, people who wouldn't appreciate that fact and would come looking for the person who dropped the dime. The quarter now. Actually two of them. They don't come right away; they know you'll be waiting. They let a month or two pass, maybe even a year. Then you get introduced to the baseball bats, or worse. And you can't count on the cops to guard you. Maybe if you were some kind of babe who didn't like to pull the blinds, or some rich, Indian Hill type who would give them something on the side…but the cops don't want to sit in a stuffy car across the street from a place like mine every night.

And like I said earlier, this is not the kind of job that involves a lot of heroics, so why take the risks that go with that? Besides, I had a friend who could help. He was still in the force, a short-timer with his eye on the calendar. We used to fish together at a pay lake in Springdale. It had the worse smelling outhouse I've ever been in in my life. We never caught anything but bluegills, but we drank a lot of beer. His name was Ralph Hahnhorst. I gave him a call, told him my theory, he went to his captain, told him he had gotten an anonymous tip, and the wheels started to grind.

They picked up Leo outside of what is still called old Judge Leis's courtroom, confronted him, and took him down. The various fingerprint matches were enough to loosen his tongue. His hands were red; his only choice was to go into mitigation mode. He drew ten to fifteen. Judges don't like perjurers, especially those who do it for money. Leo had developed a whole repertoire. He'd go to the lawyer's office in the Times Star Building and meet with the shyster; the clients would come in, check him out, go over the story he was supposed to tell, and the next time they all met it was in court. He was always dressed for the part at hand and had enough makeup and changes of wardrobe to keep the bailiffs guessing. He did upscale, downscale and first-time-in-a-tie.

I had to hand it to him for staying in character the way he did. When they started checking around they found that he had duped at least sixteen separate juries. They never found any money though, so that would be waiting for him when he got out. That wasn't important to me. Guests of the state like Leo couldn't draw disability checks from P&G, so my part was finished. There were enough headlines to make cheaters like him stop and think a little, so that part worked out OK too.

When the cops hit his dressing room on 8th Street they found all manner of things, including some corsets and a padded jock that made him look like a disco dancer with an industrial package. The local media lapped it up. One of the shock jocks made a joke about "Make Believe Ballroom Time," a former radio show in town that the old folks still remembered. The whole thing got a lot of play. Personally, I just drew my monthly check and went on to the next case, a wayward husband from Terrace Park who had a little friend across the river, in Florence. It wouldn't be a tough job or a big settlement; the wife—my boss's second cousin--stressed the principle of the thing. Whatever. No matter how it goes down or what the agency receives, I still draw the same check. It's not like a job in a John Ford western where you ride in with the cavalry and save the women and the men in white hats to a Max Steiner score, but then you never really get serious saddle sores or have to take an arrow in the ass and you gotta understand that when you get to be my age that is one ginormous fringe benefit that definitely has its attractions.

VIII

LOST WEEKEND

I didn't really want to do it, but Roger insisted. He told me that it was impossible to back out once he had agreed to it and besides, it would be fun. And why did you agree to it without consulting with me first, I asked, and he said that I had been busy and that they had asked for a prompt response. And why was I making such a thing of it, when most people would jump at such an opportunity.

"I don't like the feel of it," I said.

"The feel of it? What are you talking about?"

"We barely know them," I said. "In fact, I don't know them at all, and I don't feel comfortable spending a weekend at their home."

"And why not? There wasn't anything else planned. Are you afraid of something?"

"Why do you say that?" I asked.

"Why shouldn't I?" he answered. "There must be something worrying you or you wouldn't be acting like this. Most people would leap at a chance like this…no, I know…don't bother saying it…you're not 'most people'."

"Most of my friends wouldn't do it," I said. "In the first place I don't even know the people. Second, the place is remote and I'm not interested in starring in some sort of Blair Witch Project III."

"It's not remote," Roger answered. "It's twenty-five minutes from downtown Sonoma."

"On the side of a mountain, off of a gravel road…"

"A few feet from a road that gets regular traffic."

"This isn't my idea of regular traffic," I said, as we slowed to 10 miles an hour, negotiating a series of sharp turns. "The only other vehicle we've seen so far was that pickup rusting in the ravine behind that shack."

"Oh really?" Roger answered, as a small foreign car passed by us in the opposite lane.

"Did you look at the driver?" I asked.

"What about him?"

"He looked like something out of a lineup."

"Don't be ridiculous. This is an agricultural community. The vineyards get dusty. So do the people who work in them."

"He looked like somebody who would spend his weekends dismembering bodies. He looked strange and malnourished, like that boy with the banjo in *Deliverance*."

When I checked the lock on my door Roger said something under his breath.

"I met them at a tasting in the city," Roger said. "A very exclusive tasting. The publisher of the *Wine Spectator* was there. Marvin Shanken."

"A shank is another name for a homemade knife," I said.

"First thing Monday morning I'm putting you in therapy," Roger answered. "He was very, very nice."

"The Shankman?"

"No. Dennis. So is his wife, Deirdre."

"I don't like people whose names alliterate," I said. "I know that sounds silly, but I just don't. It's as if I'm suddenly stuck in a bad play. They know their lines. Everything's all planned. David and Deborah.

Daniel and Daphne. Dylan and Diana. Dennis and Deirdre. It's a bad English play…and it ends in a nasty way."

"What are you talking about?"

"I'm talking about being brought into some quaint and tidy little setting and finding out the couple who live there—the ones with alliterating names--have been waiting for someone to do unspeakable things to."

"Well it probably won't be quaint or tidy. It will be sprawling and grand and the only unspeakable thing you could look forward to would be some sort of sauvignon blanc from the central coast with a grassy, herbaceous taste somewhere between asparagus and fermented hay. Except that that won't happen, because Dennis wouldn't let it happen. His taste runs to Margaux and Medoc-style claret blends and Deirdre likes chardonnays with the complexity of a good Puligny-Montrachet but the kind of forward fruit you only find in California."

"Forward fruit? You mean like your cousin Leon who was thrown off the West Hollywood Board of Supervisors?"

"How politically incorrect of you, Laura," he said. "You seem to be loosening up. Lean over and give me a kiss."

"Not on this road," I said. "If I successfully escape Daffy and Daisy I don't want to die from driving off of this mountain."

"You won't, sweetie, don't worry. That's why we're staying for the weekend, so we can sober up and get back down to the valley safely."

"All right," I said, doing my best to be accommodating. The sun was warm and lovely, after all, and the scent of eucalyptus increased with every turn. "Is that Spanish moss?"

"On the live oaks? I don't know. It looks like it, but I thought the Spanish moss was only in the swamps."

"It must get very damp up here in the winter. And cold. Did you see the sign about the tire chains?"

"Yes, but fortunately it's only October."

"That moss, or whatever it is, looks ominous. I don't like things hanging from trees."

"Laura, you fell asleep watching the Blair Witch Project. Why does it bother you now?"

"Because it's real."

"Well, so is the wine Dennis has been promising and I can't wait to taste it."

"I'd stay sober if I were you."

"Now why do you say that?"

"Because you never know what might happen. I want you to be alert."

"All right. What have you been reading? P. D. James? Ruth Rendell? We've got to move past this nonsense. I want you to have fun. Kick back. Enjoy the sunshine. Enjoy the view. Enjoy the wine. Enjoy the pool. You're about to have three days and two nights in paradise."

"Just stay alert," I said, as Roger hit a curve too quickly and had to wrestle the steering back into equilibrium. Actually I hadn't been reading P. D. James. Or Ruth Rendell or any of the mystery sisterhood. I had been reading about the California wine industry so that I could humor Roger and try to understand what the fuss was all about. I was trying to enjoy the sun and the views and the wine, but somehow it wasn't working out.

For starters I found out about the Hungarian soldier, Agoston Harazsthy, who most consider the father of the California wine industry. Not Father Junipero Serra, who planted the first vineyard and not Jean-Louis Vignes who planted the first vines of vitis vinifera (the real, European McCoy), but Count Harazsthy, who founded what is now the Buena Vista winery in Sonoma in the mid nineteenth century.

Except that he didn't start there. He started in Wisconsin. Now what kind of an expert was the Count (I didn't like that 'Count' business at all, with visions of Dracula and other such) if he tried to grow grapes in Wisconsin? That wasn't the worst of it. The worst of it was that his wife became depressed by the winters in the upper midwest and walked into the Wisconsin River until her hat floated. Then and only then did the Count pick up and move to California, so the real kickoff to the fathering of the wine industry in the golden state was the violent death of the Countess. So…was he happy he left? Did he toast her memory, thinking about that hat floating down the river? Was there something going on here that we should know about?

As we approached Dilbert and Dina's home we could see a spray of bougainvillea across the yellow walls on each side of the gate. The gate itself was heavy, black iron and it was open. That was very welcoming, I thought. On the other hand, what good is an iron gate if you leave it open? As we drove through the entry the gates closed behind us. There must have been some triggering device, but I couldn't see one. The roadway was white gravel and there was no pattern in it that suggested a signalling device. I looked for a closed-circuit TV camera on the wall, but couldn't find one.

"What are you twisting around for?" Roger asked.

"I'm trying to find a camera or light beam or something that could signal the gate to close behind us."

"Did you look up in the trees?"

"Yes, but I didn't see anything."

"Maybe there's something in the road that sets it off," Roger said.

"Perhaps," I answered.

The roadway approached the house from the south. A side-load, four-car garage came into view. We drove past it as the roadway became cement with interspersed rows of pink tile. It curved around the front of the house, past a fountain and parterres of roses and birds of paradise. The fountain looked Italian. It wasn't the sort of thing that could be purchased off the shelf. There were satyrs and naiads striking erotic poses amid the spray. Roger said they looked as if they could use a cold shower and I smiled politely.

Roger parked the car just beyond the front doors, leaving room for anyone else who might be invited to park behind us. The double doors were at least eight feet in height, probably Italian oak. It was hard to tell with the weathering. The carvings had lost some of their curves and angles with the passage of time. They appeared to be parts of a set of framed tableaux illustrating the garden of Eden and the expulsion therefrom of its nude occupants. "Somebody's got sex on the brain," Roger said. "Yes, dear," I answered.

The door knocker was black iron. Roger struck it against the backplate three times, each time louder than before. When he turned the knob it opened. He called out, "Dennis…Dee Dee…"

"I thought her name was Deirdre," I said.

"She goes by Dee Dee," Roger answered.

I held my expression and my thoughts.

He called out a second and then a third time. There was no answer. "Perhaps they're in the back," he said. "We could walk around, but I don't think they'll mind if we go through the house."

"You know them," I said. "I'll follow you."

The front doors opened onto a breezeway. To the right was the garage area, so we turned left and walked toward the center of the house. I would have thought that the Italianate style would have called for greater symmetry, but I said nothing and followed Roger. Perhaps there was an orangery at the other end of the house which balanced off the garage. Not that you'd need one in California, but the form—if not the function—could have satisfied a picky architect. Unless of course it cooled off enough during the winter months to actually be necessary. Not that it mattered. I realized suddenly that I was filling my mind with this business to distract myself from the fact that we were walking around, uninvited, in a remote house with a long driveway with a large iron gate that had closed behind us.

"Look," Roger said, "paradise."

The hallway had led us to a large dining area with metal candelabras holding real candles. The table and sideboard were antiques, probably

Italian, and probably worth a small fortune. The table was covered with glasses of various shapes and sizes, all symmetrically arranged in rows. Beneath them were long sheets of bright white paper.

"Riedel," Roger said.

"I beg your pardon?"

"Riedel crystal," he said. "Top of the line for tasting."

"I see. And the white paper?"

"To check the color of the wine. You tip the glass and hold the wine over the white surface."

"Very handy," I said.

"Oh my," he answered, as he inspected the bottles at the center of the table.

Roger described each of the eight wines in exhaustive detail, checking each of the bottles to make sure that they remained, more or less, at cellar temperature. This was a problem, as one of the skylights was letting in enough sun to counter the effects of the air conditioner, Roger fearing that the wines would soon reach room temperature.

There were three whites and five reds. The whites included a Chassagne-Montrachet, Puligny-Montrachet, and Dehlinger unfiltered Chardonnay made with French yeast. "Ah ha," Roger said. "At first I thought it was Burgundy versus the Russian River Valley, but I can see that Dennis has simply brought out his personal favorites. Look at these reds." They included a Heitz/Martha's Vineyard, Penfolds Hermitage, '90 Latour, '66 Romanee Conti Grands Echezeaux, and what Roger called 'the pick of the litter,' a '45 Palmer, whose cork he was examining with the same eagerness and attention that our second bull terrier reserved for the south ends of unfamiliar canine interlopers who wandered into the neighborhood.

"Where on earth did he get this?" he asked, then went on and on about the best proportions among claret-style blends, how he'd never really been a fan of St. Emilions or Pomerols, and the curious way that the Margaux appellation can sustain the 'violets on the nose' for decades.

I asked him a question about the taste of violets and why that might be attractive but he was already off on the '90 Latour, which he called the jewel of the vintage. "A miracle, a miracle," he said.

"What's that?" I asked.

"The '90 vintage, of course, back to back with the '89. It's like heaven, followed by…"

"Heaven: the sequel?"

"Yes, exactly," he answered. "There will be very little spitting at this tasting."

"I should hope not," I said. He started to explain his comment but I told him I understood and that I hoped he wouldn't be disappointed. There was only one problem—the absence of Dickie and Deanne.

"Let's check the back," he said. "I feel like a man on a mission now." He looked longingly at the Palmer and Latour, as if he might break down and taste them straightaway, but then turned to me, with wincing eyes, and headed toward the back of the house.

What he took to be French doors at the back of the dining area were actually the doors to a shallow cabinet. "That's no help," he said. "Let's try the kitchen." The hallway continued beyond the dining area, with the kitchen to the right and living room on the left. The living room was done in a minimalist manner. The room was outlined in pinkish-cream marble with a center island of carpet that was flush with its marble outline. There were two couch arrangements and a center glass-topped table. The east boundary of the room was a fireplace which opened onto the kitchen area as well. The walls to the west had a center window that was nearly the size of Rhode Island. On either side were Diego Rivera originals.

"Look at this kitchen," Roger said. "Have you ever seen an Aga in an American house before?"

"Not that I can remember," I said, wondering how much Daryll and Daphne had paid for the Rivera paintings. I had to stop Roger from opening the door of their outsized SubZero refrigerator and reminded him that he wouldn't want strangers breathing into his cooking pots. After lifting one of Duane and Dinah's metal whisks he noted that one of the wires was bent and expressed the hope that they had taken better care of their white Burgundies and red Bordeaux.

At the east end of the kitchen was a bona fide set of French doors, which Roger approached. The pink and beige drapes that were stretched across the doors had filtered some of the sun, which dazzled Roger's eyes when he turned the handles and pulled. He stepped back and said, "Look at that glare from the pool."

We averted our glance slightly and walked onto the patio of rose marble that surrounded the pool and spa. "Perfect," Roger said, when he saw the curving row of cypress trees that outlined the back of the property and the olive groves at each corner. Beyond the pool there were gardens with gravel walkways between the parterres, extending to the length of the lot and linking the symmetrical groupings of olives. "Very smart," he said, noting that the gravel path ended in an expanse of grass beneath the trees. "Those trees are beautiful, but very dirty when the olives start to drop and rot and stain the stone. I wonder if he makes his own oil with them; he must…"

"Not anymore," I said.

"Oh?" Roger answered, turning toward me and then following the line of my extended arm and hand to the deep end of the pool. "Good God!" he said, seeing Dennis' head bobbing against the top of the pool. His ankles were secured by a heavy chain which was itself attached to a cinder block that rested at the bottom of the pool. His hands were tied behind his back, his eyes and mouth open.

"He looks like a large-mouth bass," I said.

"My God!" Roger answered.

"We should call someone," I said.

"Holy God!" Roger said.

"Don't touch anything," I said. "The police will want us to preserve the crime scene. Just use your cell phone."

"Jesus…" Roger said.

"Come along, Roger," I said, "and please don't touch anything."

"All right, all right," he said, approaching the French doors, but continuing to look over his shoulder. The doors were still open and I closed them gently with my foot. We walked through the kitchen, the dining area, and down the hallway to the front doors. I took a handkerchief out of my purse and handed it to Roger. He opened the door and stared into the eyes of a policeman aiming a pistol at his chest. His nametag read: Kelly.

"Good God!" Roger said.

"Removing your fingerprints?" the policeman asked?

"Preserving the crime scene," I answered.

The policeman smiled and then began to laugh. "Nice try," he said. "Where's the owner?"

"He's in the pool," I said. "We were just about to call you."

"Doesn't your husband talk?"

"Of course he talks. He's in shock. The owner was his friend."

"Yeah, right," the policeman said. "Let's head out to the pool. Don't touch anything."

When he saw Dennis' body in the pool the policeman made a call on his cell phone.

"Mr. Kelly…" I said.

"Chief Kelly," he answered.

"Sorry. Chief Kelly, how did you know that the man had been murdered? We didn't have the chance to call you."

"I don't think you understand, miss. I ask the questions; you and your silent husband do the answering."

"Well we certainly didn't kill him. Our clothes are perfectly dry. If we had thrown him into the pool there would have been a splash. We certainly wouldn't have waited to dry off; we would have left immediately."

"He called me."

"He?"

"Mr. Carberry. Dennis. He said that he was worried. He said that he feared for his life. I drove out immediately…and found the two of you here."

"How long ago was that?"

"Never mind," the chief said. "We'll have plenty of time later to talk about the details."

"Are you arresting us?" Roger blurted.

"Not just yet," Kelly answered. "We're taking you in for questioning."

"I want to call our lawyer," I said.

"Why do you need a lawyer? I thought you said you were innocent," the chief said.

"It's our right," I said. "We make it a practice to exercise our rights."

"You can call from the station," he said.

By the time we reached the driveway a second cruiser pulled up. "You come with me," Kelly said to Roger. "You (indicating me) ride with my deputy."

We arrived at the station on the north end of Sonoma in fifteen minutes. I was taken to a room and told to wait there. I told the deputy, whose name was Klassen, that I wanted to call my lawyer. "All in good time," he said, and locked the door behind him.

It was at least an hour and a half before the door opened. Kelly walked in and pulled out a chair. I immediately stood up. "First," I said, "I need to use the bathroom. Then I am going to call my lawyer."

"This won't take too long," he said.

"I don't care how long it takes. If you stop me I'll have you charged with battery."

He stared at me for a second and then said, "The toilet's down the hall on the left. Unisex. I hope that's no problem. The public phone's just across from it."

I went into the toilet, locked the door, and took out my cell phone. Deputy Klassen had searched me perfunctorily (I think he was a bit embarrassed to be doing it) and probably mistook my phone for a compact. I had to call Pasadena information for the number. Then I called Donald Fell.

Donald is a neighbor. I didn't know him well, but I had met him at a dinner one evening at the Athenaeum. His wife was able to reach him at a tennis shoe store in Old Town. He called me immediately (by then there were loud knocks at the bathroom door, which I had locked). He told me to say nothing until he arrived.

I left the bathroom and returned to the interrogation room. It was empty. I turned just as Chief Kelly was coming down the hall. "My attorney has instructed me to say nothing until he arrives. He will be here in approximately four and a half hours."

"That's fine," the Chief said. "In the meantime, you should know that you are under arrest for murder. You have a right to remain silent…"

When he finished, I told him that I certainly hoped that he had evidence. "We have excellent evidence," he said. "We've caught your husband red-handed." Then he laughed, walked me down the hall, and put me in a holding cell. Roger was nowhere in sight.

Donald arrived late in the afternoon. He had taken the shuttle from Burbank to San Francisco and driven straight to Sonoma. When he walked into the room containing my holding cell he seemed to fill it. One of the officers smart-mouthed him; he received a withering look and a threat of legal process that sounded like a death sentence from the Inquisition. Donald Fell is a prosecutor's nightmare; he's the lawyer who was called first by O.J. (and refused to take the case).

He talked to me for a few minutes, asked me what I knew about Dennis Carberry, told me to relax, and then went off to meet with Chief Kelly. An hour later he returned. "You'll have to stay in custody at least one night," he said. "They won't set bail until tomorrow. Hopefully I can finish this up before then."

"Finish it up?" I said, surprised.

"I've got some ideas. Let me check them out."

"What kind of ideas?" I asked.

"Laura, I really should get to work," he said. "Just relax. Remember, the world may be filled with irrational people, but the world itself is rational. There are explanations and the best way to find them is to do so as soon after the crime as possible. I'll be back as soon as I can."

"You think you'll be able to defend us successfully?"

"You're innocent. I'm certain of it."

"Thank you," I said.

He just smiled, nodded, and left. I suddenly felt very comforted, but the feeling began to fade as the daylight turned to darkness.

In the morning there was no word. I passed on breakfast. By 9:00 there was still nothing. Then 9:30. Then 9:45. I hadn't seen Roger for hours and was worried about him. He didn't do well under harsh circumstances.

When the deputy permitted me to use the bathroom I told him I wanted to speak with the chief. "That's not possible," he said.

"Why not?" I asked.

"I can't say," he answered.

"I want to speak with my attorney. Please bring me my cellular phone."

"I'm not permitted to do that," he answered. "You're only allowed the one call."

I returned to my cell, nervous and angry. "What about my husband?" I asked the deputy.

"He's been taken to another facility," he answered.

"What facility?"

"I'm not permitted to say," he answered.

At 11:53 the door opened and Donald entered. He was holding a large paper sack. There was another man with him, wearing a uniform. They spoke with Deputy Klassen, who was sitting at a desk near the door. The man in uniform handed him some papers. The deputy came over to my cell, unlocked the door, and told me I was free to go. "Where is my husband?" I asked.

"He's in the car, Laura. He's fine," Donald said. He then introduced me to the other man, whose name was Lang. We walked outside and I saw Roger in the back seat of the car. In the front passenger seat was a thin man who looked as if he needed a shave. Donald introduced him; his name was Bill Nevers. Officer Lang got into his own car. Donald thanked him and he drove off. Donald then drove to a motel in Agua Caliente, a few blocks south, and dropped off Mr. Nevers next to a dark blue sedan. "How about some lunch?" he said.

"Yes," Roger said. "That sounds wonderful."

"How about an explanation?" I asked.

"Of course," Donald said. He drove back to an upscale diner that was part of the Mission Inn complex and we settled into a booth overlooking the highway.

"How did you free us so quickly?" I asked

"Quickly?" Donald said. "I was about to apologize for taking so long. It took awhile for Bill to get here from the city; the 101 was clogged with traffic. It also took some time to work through the bureaucracy in Santa Rosa. Once Bill got here—he's an investigator by the way—and Chief Lang was on the case it was quite simple, as these things usually are. As a rule, criminals aren't intelligent, Laura. The explanations are not that difficult. Once we had a sympathetic ear in the Santa Rosa P.D. and access to their lab techs it was easy."

"So please tell us," I said. I looked at Roger, who was poring over the wine list on the back of the menu. The waitress came and we ordered club sandwiches. Donald and I ordered iced tea; Roger dithered for a second and then ordered a glass of Grgich Hills Chardonnay.

"As I said, it was quite simple. By the way, you're probably wondering why Mrs. Carberry escaped death."

"Yes, Dee Dee," I said, stretching out the vowels.

"Because there was no Mrs. Carberry," Donald said.

"No Dee Dee?"

"Yes, there was a Dee Dee, but not a Dee Dee Carberry."

"Roger?" I said.

"Yes, dear?" he answered, as he paused over his chardonnay.

"It's not polite to put your nose in the glass, Roger," I said.

"Certainly around here they would understand…"

"Go ahead and sniff then. But please tell us, who was Dee Dee?"

"Dee Dee Snyder. I picked her out of a lineup."

"A lineup?"

"Yes," Donald said. "It was quite simple, really. The first hint was that Carberry's wallet was missing, along with a set of sterling flatware. When thieves are caught in the act they don't respond by drowning people with chains and cinder blocks. It was obvious that the putative theft was a simpleminded diversion. There was a collection of wine in the house worth hundreds of thousands of dollars and the best bottles remained on their shelves."

"Perhaps a stupid thief…?" I asked.

"Yes, they're all generally stupid," Donald answered, "but in this case the ignorance was simply too exceptional to be believed. Most murderers introduce diversions to hide their true motives, which, in this case, was…"

"Revenge," Roger said. I was surprised that he was able to speak, since he had been gargling his chardonnay and rolling it around in his mouth.

"Yes," Donald said. "A crime of passion motivated by a desire for revenge. That usually means either a woman, several women, or money. We began with the first possibility. Bill compiled a quick list of those who might be suspects, checked their phone records, developed a list of their girl friends, found Ms. Snyder's number on all of Chief Kelly's bills from the past year, and added her to the lineup which Chief Lang was happy to arrange. Roger identified her immediately."

"So that…" I started to say.

"Yes, it's still the same old story," Donald said. "Dee Dee was Kelly's girl friend and Dennis was slipping her his best sauternes and petite syrah.

The chief found out about it and drowned him. She would have almost surely been next, once the dust had settled and Roger was in prison. Kelly probably would have made that look like an accident."

"But why Roger? Kelly said he caught him red-handed."

"Pure happenstance. When he went to confront Dennis he saw the dining room table set for a tasting. He knew someone else might be coming and he took the opportunity to frame whoever walked through the door."

"But how?"

"After securing Dennis' hands behind his back he got the rusty chain and cinder block from his car and rubbed the chain around the doorknob. As soon as he opened the door, Roger had the red dust imbedded in his fingers. Of course, it was clear that Roger was an oenophile, not a murderer. His fingerprints were all over one of the bottles on the tasting table and left a clear residue of red powder along with some finger prints. There was also powder on the kitchen utensils and a smear on the kitchen drape."

"Roger! What an ill-mannered guest," I said.

"Kelly outsmarted himself by wiping the doorknob clean when the four of you left the house. Every doorknob carries fingerprints. This one didn't, but it had some linen threads instead. All very amateurish, in my judgment. Plus the silly phone call."

"Ah yes," I said. "He called his own phone from the house, so that it would show up in the phone records and support his story that Dennis had called him, saying that he feared for his life."

"Yes, the phone record only shows the length of the call and numbers of the two phones."

"What a horrid man," I said.

"Perhaps he had cause," Roger said, swirling his chardonnay in his glass. You didn't meet Dee Dee."

"What was she like?"

"I'll tell you this," Roger said. "She appreciated the difference between the grapes of a dessert wine where the botrytis has been artificially introduced and one where it occurs naturally."

"Va-va-voom," I said.

"Va-va-va-voom," Roger said.

"So then, all that we've lost is the weekend and your fees, Donald," I said.

"I must admit to something," he said.

"Yes?" I answered.

"I thought that since Dennis was gone and was unable to thank us for finding his murderer and bringing him to justice, that I might somehow help him, after the fact as it were."

"Help him?" Roger said, suddenly curious.

"Yes, help him thank us."

"What's in that bag you've been carrying?" I asked.

"A small souvenir. Think of it as my retainer," he responded. "Don't overreact, Roger," he said, as he slipped out the magnum of Petrus. I tilted my head and read the date on the faded label. "Nineteen forty five," I said. "I know nothing about wine, but I know that that's the number you want to see."

"Holy God," Roger said. "And you'll share?"

"Of course," Donald said, "In a sense. Is that drool around the edges of your mouth, Roger?"

"It could be," he said. "You see now, don't you, Laura?"

"See what? Why he's the best?"

"Yes, and the most generous and considerate as well."

"Let's consider both the deceased and your thirsty spouse's actions as contributions to my retainer," Donald said. "I'll absorb the actual retainer and cover the costs of those who assisted me, as my contribution."

"I don't quite understand," I said.

"It's quite simple," Donald said. "I'll share it with Roger if and only if he consents to join us at our annual charity event for the underserved in Pasadena and Altadena. The collection was actually worth tens of millions and the magnum probably only $75,000 or so. Dennis Carberry's will specified that the entirety of his estate would go to charity, so I'm simply widening that reach. We'll auction the magnum by-the-drink and sweeten the Christmas for those who would usually go without."

"So my glass will cost something like $5,000," Roger said.

"Probably for a rather small glass I'm afraid," Donald said.

"So this is what they call pro bono?" Roger asked.

"I'm afraid so," Donald answered. "Christmas is approaching and we must be attentive to its true meaning."

"Jesus turned water into wine," Roger said, "and the early reports, though not particularly specific, suggested it was of very high quality."

"The '45 Petrus is approaching its peak," Donald said. "At a formal auction it would begin to slide in price and that auction could take years to happen. The Lord's wine would have been the pick of the vintage, perhaps the pick of all the vintages. I believe he would forgive my efforts to do a slight bit of good with an aging French competitor."

"Amen," I said. "Amen, indeed."

IX

—

WHAT I LEARNED

Back when we were still in grade school there was a guy downtown who rented a corner of a warehouse that used to be part of Miller's Dairy. The space had a walk-in freezer where the guy stored the ice cream which he sold in the neighborhoods from a converted van, with pictures on the side and a bell that could be heard at least a mile away. At night he worked out of the warehouse, selling ice balls to the kids and their parents willing to make the trip. At the center of each ice ball was a scoop of homemade vanilla ice cream. The ice was shaved in a large glass box that looked like it was designed to pop popcorn, then packed over the ice cream, and drizzled with fruit-flavored syrup that was somehow sweeter and fresher and more authentic than the stuff you get now that's all chemicals and cheap dyes.

In July and August, when the humidity matched the temperature and the temperature was just this side of hell's, he did enough ice cream and ice ball business to get him through the winter months, when he worked odd jobs for his customers' parents.

He was one of those local institutions, the kind of person you imagine in a grammar school picture book, operating a 'shop' and waving to the policeman and fireman on the other side of the page. His name was Bill and he insisted on being called that, regardless of the age of the individual customer. When I was in high school I found out that he had died. He was killed in a robbery, which happened early in the evening and probably netted less than fifty dollars. He was hit over the head and left to bleed to death behind his counter.

They never found the person who did it. One day Bill was there and the next day he was gone. I couldn't figure out why the police didn't do anything. My father called them and they told him that the case was 'still open,' but so is every other unsolved murder case. That doesn't mean that anybody works on them or that they ever get closed.

I wouldn't have minded so much if somebody had broken into the poor box at St. E's, since I figured the money was probably taken by the pastor anyway to buy gas for his Buick. If the money was for the poor it was likely that the thief was poor anyway, so he was just avoiding the middleman. At least nobody was hurt.

There was another guy I remember from around that time. His name was Molloy and he thought people were basically good, just misunderstood or temporarily stretched. He put up a box in a small town down on the river, right in the town square next to the brass statue of the civil war artilleryman. He put a five-dollar bill in the box. He said it was there for whoever needed it. All that he asked was that whoever took the bill should replace it as soon as he was able to. He hoped others might follow his lead and slip in a few dollars of their own. That way the people who needed it wouldn't have to beg for it and since people were basically OK, they'd appreciate the help, replace the money when they could and join the crusade when they were fully on their feet. The local paper interviewed him when his loss reached $125. When it rose to $250 he took down the box. Maybe he converted it to a bird house. I don't know, since we never saw it again.

I don't understand why some good people won't recognize that there are bad people out there. It seems so clear to me. For instance, I was at this church festival once—the kind where they set up rides that look like they're about to fall over--and a girl lost her glasses on the ferris wheel. She wasn't very pretty and that made it even sadder, but when she got off the ride, crying, her father asked her about her glasses and then slapped her across the face before she could finish her answer. My father told me that the man was poor and ignorant, but somehow that wasn't enough of an answer. Getting hit like that was the sort of thing she would never forget, especially when he hit her in front of people she wanted to be her friends.

At that moment I thought that I'd like to kill him. I didn't say anything about it to my father, because I thought he'd think I was as bad as the man was, but I kept thinking about the girl and the fact that nobody was standing up for her. He'd probably beat her again later after they got home.

Everybody 'minded their own business' while the girl was sobbing. There were no cops and no judges, just some son-of-a-bitch bully with a daughter who could have used some help and some comfort. He'd probably beat his wife too if she tried to say anything to him. What would it be like to live in a house like that, to feel that kind of anger and stupidity around you all the time?

I wondered how often that kind of thing happened and realized that if I really knew I'd probably have trouble dealing with it. For awhile I followed my father's advice and let it alone. He told me that the cops said that the worst kind of situation you could face was a domestic dispute. They'd go in, trying to calm everybody down, and suddenly they'd be catching hell from everybody. "One would be hitting the other and then suddenly they'd both be hitting you," they said.

It sounded right, at least at first. Nobody likes a stranger judging them or telling them what to do. On the other hand, nobody likes to get their face pounded into hamburger and not be able to go outside for weeks because people will know the kind of things that happen in their family. I figured the cops said what they said because they didn't want to know too much either. They want to be saviors and peacemakers. They want to shine their shoes and show their badges, not be forced to look into the human heart and find out that what you're likely to see inside can sometimes look and smell like a sewer.

The first time I decided I couldn't take it anymore was when I was seventeen. Some guy from the west side of town named Kress was giving this guy at the Creamy Whip a hard time. Kress was a local punk who liked to impress the slugs who hung around with him by hurting people who were smaller than he was. The guy at the Creamy Whip was actually an older man, maybe even thirty-five or forty, but he was real small and wore a white uniform and white paper hat in a kid's size. Kress cornered him in the parking lot when he got off of work and started to make fun of him. Then he started to push him, while everybody laughed. He pulled off his hat and spat in it and asked the guy what he was going to do about it. You could tell the man was afraid. First he asked Kress to please let him alone. Kress told him he'd have to beg. The guy refused and Kress hit him in the face twice. The second time he hit him he broke his nose.

The man crawled to his car and drove away. Kress yelled at him that he'd see him the next night. I was watching all this from the back seat of a car. We were in line, waiting for our orders at the drive-up window. Later that night I went home, picked up a turtle neck sweater and a ball bat and drove over to Kress's house. I looked in the side window of the living room and saw him watching a cartoon on television. Then I pulled the sweater up over my mouth and nose, just under my eyes, rang the doorbell and waited at the side of the door in the darkness.

Kress came out on the porch, looked around, and started to swear. Just as he caught a look at me from the corner of his eye I hit him in the face with the bat. I could hear his nose snap and see the blood gushing down his face. He was clutching at his nose and cheeks in shock and pain, but trying to lunge toward me at the same time. I hit him in the right shin with all the strength I had and he fell forward, screaming in pain while his body shook. He tried to get up on his feet and I hit the left shin, then the right again and then the left, until I was sure they were both broken.

By that time he had stopped reaching for me. He was choking on blood and snot and begged me to stop. "If you ever bully anybody again, I'll be back," I said, "and next time I won't stop."

He couldn't see very clearly by that point but I wanted him to know that the person who hit him was not the man from the Creamy Whip. "I saw what you did to that man," I said. "You ever touch him again or anybody else and I'll be going for your eyes and knees."

He was passed out by the time I left. I saw him briefly a few months later. He was on crutches, leaning and shuffling like he couldn't understand the concept behind them. The people who used to hang around him all the time were gone. He didn't look as if he'd be causing anyone any trouble. It was like he had been broken in half and put back together and something leaked out in the process. I didn't take any great pride in what I'd done. It was more of a sense that I had tipped the balance in the right direction for a moment or two. You never get rid of people like Kress. There's always more, but somehow it feels good to keep the numbers down.

The next time out came three years later. I was in college and there was a girl in one of my classes who had a boyfriend who hit her. We had become friends and she felt as if she could confide in me. I told her she didn't have to take that. She said she knew that she didn't, but that she cared about him. I asked her how she could care about somebody who treated her like that. "I don't know," she said. "I just do."

One day she came to class with her arm in a cast. I asked her over and over and finally she admitted that her boyfriend had done it. "Is it broken?" I asked. She said that it was, but that it wasn't a bad break. "Tell me what a good break would look like," I said, but she didn't answer. Finally she said that he had paid the deductible on her doctor's bill, as if that somehow made it right. I asked her if she had said anything about this to her father. She told me that her father was dead and that she didn't want to worry her mother.

I didn't want her to think of me in the same way that she thought of her boyfriend, so I told her that I was going home that weekend and that I would talk to her next Tuesday, after class. I didn't go home. I got out my turtle neck and a ball peen hammer.

Her boyfriend lived in a rooming house on the edge of campus. On Saturday night I waited in the backyard by the side of the garage where he parked. He drove in after midnight. When he got out of the car and was fumbling with his key and doorlock I walked out from behind a stand of evergreens and hit him in the ribs with the hammer. I could feel them split and watched as he gasped and fell down like a broken scarecrow. He started to beg right away. One thing I've learned is that these bullies are always cowards.

I told him that I worked for the insurance company that processed the doctor's claim form and that I knew right away that the injury wasn't the result of an accident. "By the way, you shouldn't pay with a credit card," I said. Then I stepped on his wrist, pinning his right hand on one of the paving stones, which led to the back porch. I hit it with the hammer until each bone in each finger was shattered. Then I did the left. "Tell her you're sorry," I said. "Tell her you're ashamed of how you acted and that you don't deserve her. Put it in writing. If you ever get close to her again and I find out, I'm coming to kill you. That's a promise and God help me, I'll keep it. Understood?"

By now he was crying and shaking uncontrollably. "I'll take that as a Yes," I said, and walked away. On Tuesday she told me she had tried to call him but that there was no answer. "You're probably well rid of him," I said. We never saw him again.

I learned a lot of things besides the fact that bullies are usually cowards. I learned that they need to bring other people down so that they can feel whole and important. I learned that a certain number always seem to be around, no matter how old they are, where they come from, or who their parents are. All you can really do is help cull the herd.

When I was in college we had a big discussion about this. The teacher told us about Rousseau and about how he believed that people are basically good but that society somehow makes them bad. If we could just let them be themselves they'd be fine. One of my classmates said that he didn't believe that. He said that life was more like that *Lord of the Flies* book. If you let them return to their natural state you find out how nasty they really are. Another kid in the class said that that was true, that people were basically selfish and mean and maybe even bloodthirsty and that you needed police and prisons and armies to keep them from doing what they'd otherwise do. The teacher didn't seem to like that. He was kind of a bully himself, so he probably gave the two of them a B-, which was the lowest grade he gave.

I didn't say anything myself, because it would have been a waste of time. I didn't agree with any of them. What I've learned, or at least what I think I've learned, is that in any group you've got your basic mix: some smart people and some morons, some good people and some thugs. Short and tall. Fat and skinny. More or less good and more or less bad. There's some bad in the good and some good in the bad, unless they're bad all the way through. I guess some people would want to experiment with the gene pool and try to change the mix, but I don't believe that genes are the whole answer, since you get these same kinds of mixes in families. You even get them with twins. So when I say 'cull' I don't mean kill them; I mean reduce their numbers by trying to somehow change them. Using touchy-feely methods would be nice if they'd work, but with bullies it's hard. If they think you're weak they just tighten the screws on you. At least that's what I've learned. I'm talking about real bullies now, not just rude people who might respond to something milder. The real bullies don't respond to that; that's what makes them real bullies rather than pretend bullies. The only way they can feel good is to inflict pain on other people, so you've got to teach them that the result of hurting other people is that they themselves get hurt. Except that they don't respond to raised eyebrows or pamphlets or holy water. You need something more serious, something that makes a lasting impression.

The worst of them—the truly evil--live in a different world. They have thoughts and fantasies that aren't like other peoples'. They see other people as something they can use. They don't care about how those people might feel. It's like they come from another place or they've been on the internet too long. They're like sex geeks or violence geeks, only they don't wear plastic pocket protectors or glasses with old tape between the eyepieces. What they are are predators.

That's why I became a psychologist. To help people understand these things. The only problem is that most of the other people in the clinic go for the touchy-feely manual rather than the revenge and justice manual. I figured somebody had to tell the truth, even if it left you out of synch with the rest of the people in the trade.

Like today. I've got a patient named Jennie. We're supposed to call them clients, not patients, but Jennie's not shopping for a used car or a textbook answer. Jennie's desperate. Her uncle's terrorizing her cousins and Jennie doesn't know what to do. That's why she came to me.

"I know you can help me, Dr. Moore," she said.

"I'll do my best, Jennie," I said. "You told me that the problem is with your uncle and what he's been doing to your cousins. What is he doing, specifically, that's bothering them?"

She stared at me, as if the words were caught in her throat.

"Go ahead, tell me," I said. "Anything you say stops here. It's protected."

"Everything. He yells at them. He hits them. He forces them to do things they don't want to do."

"What kind of things?"

"Physical…things."

"You mean sexual things?"

"Yes."

"How old are they?"

"Eight and eleven."

"What about your aunt?"

"She's afraid of him too. She doesn't' really do anything to stop him. Whenever I see her she looks like she's taken a lot of medication. Mostly she just tries to stay out of his way. He's hit her too. I've seen the marks."

Jennie is nineteen. This is her first personal encounter with evil.

"What about your father?"

"My father's dead," she said.

"Can you help me?" she asked. "I mean really help me."

"I can try," I said.

"That's not what I'm saying," she said, her eyes fixing on mine.

I tried not to reveal what I was thinking. I wondered if she knew something. There had been talk in the past, rumors, but I had always been successful in squelching them.

"We can talk to the police," I said.

"My aunt already did that. A year ago. And once before that. They'd come by once or twice, sometimes send out a social worker. It didn't really help. He wouldn't care anyway. If they took his wife and kids away he'd just find somebody else."

"Perhaps they should take him away," I said.

"That would be nice," she said.

Our time was up, but I promised we'd talk some more and figure out a way to deal with him. She thanked me and left. I knew that she felt lost and helpless, but I couldn't simply volunteer to go after him. Now she was seeing how little a psychologist could do and how little the law was likely to do. I felt like something much stronger, but I poured myself a cup of coffee and began to think. I couldn't just take out every person who hurt one of my patients, no matter how much I might want to. It would be too obvious. I'd end up in jail and the bullies and freaks would all still be on the street and in peoples' homes. On the other hand, I couldn't just stand by and watch this happen to somebody I cared about, somebody who was suffering unnecessarily, somebody who was looking to me for help, not just advice.

If I could just find some evidence I could get the justice system to grind a little faster and do a little good, but I didn't want to wait so long that this guy might kill somebody. They were probably scarred enough already, at least psychologically. This isn't a crime against property. It's a crime against people. Innocent people, who deserve better.

I checked my files and found the form Jennie had filled out when she first came to me as a patient. Jennie's last name was Wills and her father's name had been James. He was recently deceased. Her mother's name was Charlotte. I checked the phone book. There were three listings for the name Wills. C. S., Carl, and B. L. C. S. Wills was Charlotte; the address corresponded to Jennie's. I wrote down the addresses and numbers for Carl and B. L., then drove to a convenience store and called B. L. on a public phone. I didn't want any records of the call traced back to me. A woman answered. I apologized and told her I had the wrong number. A lot of time women use initials in their phone listings. I couldn't be sure that Carl was Jennie's uncle, but it was a reasonable place to start. He lived on the south side of town, a few miles from Jennie's address.

I've got an old sedan that I don't use very much. Most people associate me with the car I drive to work. I went home, had some soup and a sandwich, waited two hours for it to get dark, and then got out the sedan. It took me fifteen minutes to drive to Carl Wills's house.

It was a small house. The frame siding needed paint and there was grass growing in the joints of the sidewalk. I could see an old swing set in the backyard. In the faint light it looked as if it was broken. There was a sedan in the driveway and a van parked across the street. Its windows were dark.

I drove another half block, found a darkened house, checked the rearview mirror, and parked. Then I got out, slipped into the backyard and walked along the lot lines back to Carl Wills's house. The front had been dark except for a porch light, but there was a light on in what I figured was the kitchen. A window was open, so I walked carefully, trying not to make any noise.

I took off my glasses because I didn't want any reflections in the dark. I basically just use them for reading, so I could still see at a distance. The grass had been cut recently and the clippings were still there, softening my footsteps. It helps when you catch a break. Now I could get close to the kitchen without being heard. I stood behind a tree with my face between some of the lower limbs, trying to break up any silhouettes that might be visible from inside. I could see the top of a man's head. I reached up to the next set of limbs and slowly pulled myself up. My tennis shoe slipped a little on the bark of the tree and there was a slight scuffing sound but the head didn't turn. Finally I was high enough to get a clear view.

The man was sitting at a table with an oilcloth cover. I saw what looked like cigarette burn marks in the cloth. He was wearing dark pants and a white T-shirt. His hair was full and black and seemed to be slicked down in the back. There was a bottle of beer on the table and a small ashtray, filled to the edge. He was looking at a magazine and taking sips from the bottle. The kitchen light was reflecting off the pages of the magazine so that I couldn't see it clearly. A woman came into the kitchen briefly but then left right away. The man didn't look up. After a few minutes he got up and left the room. He didn't turn out the light. The woman came back in a few minutes and flipped the switch. A few moments later a light went on in a small window upstairs, probably a bathroom. I got down from the tree, figuring that everyone was turning in for the night, but suddenly I heard a car engine start.

The driveway was on the other side of the house. I saw the lights flash as the car backed into the street and turned. Then it drove right past me. I started moving as quickly as I could, so that I could get back to my car and follow. Then I heard another engine start. It was the van that was parked across the street from the Wills house. Whoever was driving it was following the first car. I didn't figure on the man going out this late; I should have been ready.

I ran through the backyards and hurried out to my car. By now all I could see was a distant set of taillights. The van was turning right. I got in my car, started the motor, and drove away from the curb, trying not to let the tires squeal. I turned at the same intersection as the van but when I made it around the corner there were no taillights visible in the distance. I drove from block to block, looking in each direction for some trace of red light. After four blocks the street ended in a T and I had to choose a direction. I turned right, drove for another six blocks and saw nothing. By now it was too late. Cruising the main streets would be a waste of time; the town was filled with nondescript sedans and suv's and I couldn't just knock on doors or enter restaurants or bars. All I had seen of Carl Wills was the back of his head and I didn't want him to see me.

The next day I had trouble working. My patients all seemed to have trivial problems and I was worried about Jennie. I was also thinking about the van parked across the street from her uncle's house. At first I thought that someone else might be following him. Then I realized that whoever was in the van might be a friend of Carl Wills, waiting to meet with him—someone he didn't want his family to meet. A girlfriend? A dealer?

That night I went out a little earlier, just at dusk. As I drove down Wills's street I saw the van parked on the opposite side of the street from Wills's house. It was a few car-lengths away from its previous night's spot, sitting under a pair of maple trees whose limbs were growing together. I stopped a half block away and turned off my lights. Knowing that I might be in for a long wait I had brought along a thermos of black coffee. I opened the thermos and poured some into an insulated cup. I waited for thirty minutes. Then another thirty. The van was still in place. There were lights on in several rooms of the Wills house, but I couldn't see any movement. I sat back and poured another cup of coffee.

Fifteen minutes later the door opened. Carl Wills came out, walked over to his car and started it up. The moment I saw the puff of smoke from his exhaust I could see that the driver of the van had started his engine also. Carl backed out and drove past the van, which waited for him to drive a block and a half before following him. I started my engine and pulled away from the curb. Suddenly we had a convoy.

Carl drove through the neighborhood streets for a mile and a half and stopped at a bar called the Clovernook. It had a large, crumbly asphalt parking lot that was dotted with giant foxtail and clumps of dandelions. There was a neon beer sign in the window of the bar that could have predated my father. It was sputtering and flickering. After Wills got out and went into the bar the van pulled up on the left side of his car and stopped. The driver didn't get out. I saw the hint of exhaust stop as the driver turned off the engine. I parked a row behind and to the left of the van, about twenty yards away, and waited.

It was at least an hour and a half before Carl Wills came out of the bar. He was alone and unsteady on his feet. He also seemed angry. He bumped into someone who was entering the bar and turned as if he was thinking about hitting him. He was about to return home in that condition and frame of mind.

He was halfway across the parking lot when I saw the exhaust puff of the van. When he was a few feet away the van lurched forward and came close to hitting him. He flew into a blind rage and started pounding the left front fender of the van with his right fist. Suddenly the van accelerated, turning sharply to the right. The left rear wheel ran over his feet and he howled in pain, falling to the asphalt. His body was convulsing, his hands reaching desperately in the general direction of his legs and feet. The van had pulled forward a few feet, remaining in the lot. I thought to myself that this was justice of a sort. At least he wouldn't be going home that night and assaulting his wife and kids.

Then the backup lights of the van came on and the driver backed over Carl Wills a second time, this time rolling slowly over his knees and shins. By now he was in shock, the pain blocking out everything around him. The van pulled forward, stopped, shifted into reverse, and drove back over his head. Then the backup lights went out, the driver shifted to a forward gear, and quietly drove out of the parking lot, and into the night.

I followed at a distance. The van drove down Hatton Boulevard and turned into a Shell station with a carwash in the rear. The driver drove past the pumps and into the carwash, emerging a few minutes later, with drops of water falling from the wheel wells. I continued to follow, as the van returned to the Boulevard, then turned right on Radley Street. After nine or ten blocks the van turned left on Carmine and then right on Simplon Boulevard, accelerating slightly toward a horizon of green lights.

From Simplon the van turned left onto Hensley Street and then right onto Prentice. The name sounded familiar. I hung back a little and watched the van turn into a driveway three doors from the intersection. The moon and the street lights provided a clear view as the door of the van opened and the driver got out. It was Jennie. She paused, removed a handkerchief from her pants pocket, and wiped off the fender at the point where her uncle had pounded it with his fist. Then she put the handkerchief back in her pocket and went into the house. If I hadn't been following her I might have thought she had simply run out for a loaf of bread or a quart of milk.

She skipped the next week's appointment, calling first and telling me that she had to go out of town, but the week after she was there and she looked as good as new. I asked her about the problem with her uncle.

"That's been solved," she said. "He died in a car accident."

"Really?" I asked.

"Yes. Things seem to have worked out perfectly. There was even some insurance money from his company."

"So how are you feeling?" I asked.

"Terrific," she said. "I don't think I'll need to come back, at least not for awhile. That was really weighing on me and suddenly I feel as if I've been let out of prison. It's sorta the same way I felt when my father died. He wasn't very nice either."

"Oh yes, I believe I saw that in your file. He hasn't been gone too long, has he?"

"No, not too long."

"What happened to him? He must have been a young man."

"It was a drowning accident. He and my mother were on vacation in the mountains. He must have been distracted or something, because he fell off of this rock and into a stream. By the time my mother could get to him it was too late."

"It's very sad that your family has seen so much violence," I said, "but one of the things I've learned is that when bad things are happening to good people, somehow or other something happens to set things right. I'm not saying that this is God intervening, but, I don't know, it just seems to happen."

"Maybe it's angels," Jennie said.

Maybe so, I thought. Pretty to think that, at least. The only thing that I knew for sure was that Jennie had learned what I already knew. It wasn't what you would call a nice lesson, but it was a very important one: when those you think should help you can't or won't, your only choice is to either live with your problem or solve it yourself.

X

THE BISHOP'S GAMBIT

"There is no one else for whom I would do this," he said to himself, as he made his way through the grit and muck of the barely-lit streets. The moon was clouded and blocked by moist layers of smoke and fog, but an occasional house lamp was lit and the light from a handful of candles glowed against sooty windows and cast faint gleams through the effluvia. He coughed, wiped his mouth with his now-soiled handkerchief, and continued to walk.

Thirty minutes earlier, when his coach had arrived in Holborn at the Lion and Sparrow, the smells of its stable had assaulted his already weakened senses. His eyes had nearly rattled from their sockets in the ruts of the west country roads and his kidney was bruised from the constant jostling against the coach frame. The sickness of an infant had contributed to the general discomfort of his fellow passengers and the curses of those men clinging to the top of the coach had removed any hope of sleep, even when the hard roads were temporarily cushioned by a soft coat of mud.

The coachman, whose name was Porter, had sawn his remaining teeth to form a space that would accommodate the handle of his whip. The resulting spectacle had received the unanimous approbation of the inn boys and 'prentices along the route. At least they had been spared the greetings of any highwaymen, who had, perhaps, been discouraged by the wind and rain that had blanketed and whipped the Thames valley.

He had proceeded down Fetter Lane from Holborn, remembering for a moment that the great Dryden had once taken lodgings there. At Fleet Street he could see the corner of St. Dunstan's but the heads of the '45 rebels piked above Temple Bar were lost in the mist and the telescope operator who offered better looks for a penny had retreated with his likely customers to a warmer, drier, and more comfortable corner.

The Fleet Street kennel was clogged with the remains of long-dead cats, the stench relieved somewhat by the steadily flowing rivulets of dark water that found their way around the lumps of matted, mottled fur. An elm water main had given way beneath the street and created springs that burst through the cobbles and added to the general flow heading toward Fleet Ditch. At least the wind from the west had increased and carried with it the smells of butchers' and tanners' offal.

At the entrance to Johnson's Court stood a woman, blowing warm breath over the blackened fingertips that projected from torn gloves. He walked past her, down the alleyway, praying that he not meet with any footpads. A minute later he stood at the southwest corner of Gough Square, looking for the number 17 beside the door of the house that loomed above him.

Next to the building, on the south, was a small garden and necessary house. As the moonlight broke through the clouds he could see the remains of summer blooms, now dried and cold, moving to and fro in the heavy air. Their colors now gone, they had become little more than gray stalks. From the east, toward the ditch, came the sounds of cats, fighting over mice, mates or shelter.

There was the slight glow of a candle in the northeast window of the top floor of the house. It seemed to shift and move, as if the wind had penetrated the brick facing and threatened to extinguish it. He gathered his courage and his strength, put his handkerchief over his face, so that he might take in a breath free of black seacoal smoke, stepped up to the door and then grasped the brass knocker. Hesitating for a moment, he raised it higher and then released it.

The sound echoed down the square and he caught the gleam of small eyes retreating into the darkness. He knocked twice more and then stood there, waiting.

Three minutes later the door opened, the silhouette of a large man stood between him and the faint light within. "What is your business at this hour, sir?" the figure asked.

"My name is Hodder, James Hodder."

"There is a writer of sermons with that name," the figure answered. "Are you that same man?"

"I am, sir," Hodder answered, "and I have come to seek your help."

"Come in then. Come in," the figure said. "Will you take tea?"

"I will indeed, sir, but I do not wish to put you to any trouble."

"It is no trouble," the figure answered, ringing a bell on a small table. The figure directed Hodder to sit in an adjoining room. He paused for a moment, looking at the woodwork.

"American pine," the figure said. "Used as ballast on English ships. Are you a student of the domestic arts?"

"Not really, sir," Hodder said. "I was simply admiring the workmanship."

"I don't own the house," the figure said. "I let it several years ago to be near my bookseller."

"He is printing your dictionary," Hodder said.

"Yes, and doing much more. He is my banker, my friend…many things. Now, sir, how can I serve you?"

Before Hodder could speak, a young woman entered the room, carrying a pot of tea, spoons, cups, and saucers. Hodder was surprised. "She knows my wants," the other man said, "and she heard your knock at the door. There is nothing else for which I would call but tea. Have you eaten?"

"I brought something with me and ate it as the coach approached the city."

"That was wise of you. I have cheese and bread and some boiled ham…"

"You are too kind, sir. The tea will do very well."

"Tell me if you choose otherwise. Now…your problem?"

"My daughter, sir. She is lost."

"Lost? Is she ill? Was she taken by someone?"

"I pray that she is well, but I have received no word from her in six days."

"Your daughter lives in London?"

"No, sir. She came as my representative. The moment she arrived she wrote to me. She told me that she would leave further word at the coach stop in Holborn…"

"The Lion and Sparrow?"

"Yes, sir, but when I arrived today there were no messages for me."

"Perhaps there was an intermediate letter, one sent to your home."

"No, sir. She was very explicit when we parted. Any further communications would be left for me in Holborn. We wished to avoid any possible confusions. Now there is confusion indeed. I simply do not know what I shall do if I lose one so dear to me. That is why I have come to you, sir. There is no one whose work and knowledge of the city I respect more."

"You do me a great deal of honor, sir, but I fear that you have exaggerated my knowledge and my abilities."

"I knew that if you were unable to help me you could direct me to someone who might."

"That I could do," the man answered, "but let us take our tea and talk more. Here, allow me to pour."

"I am in your debt, sir."

"Now in what way was your daughter representing you?"

"A new collection of my sermons is being printed by Mr. Winn…"

"In Bride Lane."

"Yes, sir. My daughter assists me in their preparation. Mr. Winn had a number of questions and Elisabeth—that is her name, sir—agreed to come ahead and work with Mr. Winn. My dear wife has been ill with a fever and I could not leave her until the fever had passed."

"Which it did?"

"Yes, sir. We are all grateful for that."

Hodder noticed that the man uttered something under his breath. His fingers were moving across the arm of his chair as if he were searching for something.

"So your daughter arrived approximately one week ago and she has now vanished."

"Yes, sir."

"Perhaps she is with Mr. Winn."

"She would have left a message for me, sir. She is the most thoughtful and accomplished of young women."

"Mr. Winn will be in his shop early tomorrow morning. You should begin there. Your daughter may have attempted to contact him. At the very least he should know of your situation."

"You are very kind, sir. May I return and solicit more help from you if it proves necessary?"

"Where are you going, Mr. Hodder? You will sleep here tonight and we will go together to Mr. Winn."

"I fear I may be imposing upon you, sir."

"Nonsense. I will be pleased to accompany you."

Suddenly there was movement in the room as a cat leaped upon the man's lap, startling Hodder. The man cuddled the cat, scratching it behind its right ear and kissing the back of its head. "We will find Mr. Hodder's daughter, will we not?" he said, as the cat purred gently.

Winn was standing in his window as the two men approached, arranging books for passers-by to inspect. He said something, which could not be heard through the thick window, after which a young man appeared behind him and promptly opened the door. Winn approached them immediately.

"Mr. Hodder and Mr. Johnson. Good morning."

"Good morning, sir," Hodder said, "pray, have you had any communication from my daughter?"

"Why no, sir, though I have been expecting to see her since you wrote. Is anything wrong?"

"She is missing," Hodder said.

"There must be some explanation. She came by coach?"

"By post coach, actually. I wanted to provide for her safety in every possible way. Mr. Johnson has generously volunteered his help."

"There is no one better," Winn said. "I pray that all will be well."

"We cannot spare any lost time," Johnson said. "Good day, Mr. Winn. We shall find Miss Hodder presently, so that you can continue with your printing of her father's sermons."

"Thank you, sir. I am in your debt."

"Come," Johnson said, placing his left hand against Hodder's back. As they walked west on Fleet Street Johnson gripped his cane tightly in his right hand, sometimes tapping it against the posts separating the street from the pedestrian walkway, sometimes using it for leverage and balance, and sometimes brandishing it in the air as if it were a sword or cudgel.

"I pray that she has not been the victim of some miscreant," Hodder said, his voice wavering at the thought.

"That is unlikely," Johnson said. "Young women may be the prey of miscreants, but such individuals are more likely to seek to exploit their youth and beauty than destroy it."

"I have heard stories, of course…"

"Yes. Poor young women come to the city seeking positions, often in domestic service. They are met at the coach stop by criminals—women as well as men—who fill their heads with promises of grand clothes and lodgings. Their heads swimming with false hope and their imaginations fed with wine as well as lies, they soon find themselves prostituted by those who had pledged to seek only their welfare."

"Elisabeth would be wary of such blandishments and falsehoods. Our papers have reprinted stories of such individuals. Just last month there was an account of a woman named Keane."

"Yes," Johnson said. "Her accomplice was a man named Edward Diver. Both ended their lives in the pillory. His ears were nailed to the frame. She was spared that, but each was pelted with bricks and bottles. The people of London do not countenance such crime and the justice they mete out is swift and violent."

"Once the criminals are taken."

"Yes," Johnson said, "that is the difficult part. The Charlies are often aged men who can do little and the magistrates receive no regular pay. Hence their susceptibility to bribes. The evidence must be overwhelming and there must be public pressure as well. I am sometimes amazed at how well we do, considering the resources at our disposal. But let us not think of that. Let us think only of your daughter and let us do all in our power to find her and reunite her with those who love her."

"Indeed," Hodder said. "Shall we go first to the Lion and Sparrow."

"Yes, sir," Johnson said. "I know a man there who might be of service to us."

The man's name was Harrison, a smith who saw to the horses at the coach stop. "I found his daughter in the Strand, sick with fever," Johnson said. She had been sold into whoredom at a very tender age. She had come from a village near my own in Staffordshire. As she regained her health I contacted her father, who was overwhelmed with grief at her loss. He came to London, rejoiced that his daughter had survived, and found work here."

Harrison was away for the moment, so Johnson and Hodder went into the Angel tavern and breakfasted on bread, cheese, and tea. Johnson sent the tavern boy to check on Harrison, but he had still not returned.

He then spoke to Hodder of his sermons, trying his best to put him at ease and take his mind from his fears concerning his daughter. Ten minutes later the tavern boy checked again and informed them that Mr. Harrison had returned. Johnson pressed a copper coin in his hand, saying, "There's a good boy, Ned."

Harrison greeted Johnson warmly and told him that his daughter was now in service to an elderly widow who valued and rewarded her. Johnson introduced him to Hodder and then inquired concerning the events of the last week.

"There has been nothing beyond the ordinary, sir, at least nothing that I have seen. The coaches come and go. The rains have created problems, but they have always done so. The footpads have been about, but fewer in Putney, I'm told, so that has been a blessing. The only thing that I might mention is the boy."

"The boy, James?" Johnson asked.

"Yes, Mr. Johnson, the boy. A very young boy. Dirty. Almost like a sweep. He appears in alleys and doorways, like a cat on the alert."

"Here by the Lion and Sparrow?"

"Yes, sir. He comes several times a day."

"Have you seen him yet today?"

"No, Mr. Johnson, not so far."

"Have you spoken to him, James?"

"I tried to, Mr. Johnson, but he ran away, as if he feared me. All that I sought to do was offer him some food."

"Why should he fear you when you are here every day and an honest craftsman?" Hodder asked.

"I don't know, sir," Harrison answered.

"Perhaps he has been so instructed," Johnson said. "He should not fear a curate, Mr. Hodder. Let us return again and see if he will reveal himself. How old is he, James?"

"I shouldn't think more than ten or twelve years, Mr. Johnson."

"And how is he dressed?"

"Nearly in rags, sir, but he does have leather shoes. His hair is dark brown, his eyes blue."

"Thank you, James. We will seek him out. Please convey my best wishes to your Sophie."

"I shall do that, sir," Harrison answered.

They returned at 2:00, at 3:00, and again at 4:00, just as the coach was arriving from Bath. The travellers were angry, as their trip had taken three days, a full day longer than expected. One wheel had required repair in Salisbury and another had required replacement as they crossed into Hampshire. The deep ruts from the autumn rains had thrown the outside passengers from the top of the coach and resulted in constant sickness among those inside. The horses were tired and hungry; only the coachman seemed at ease and he was flicking his whip from right to left, holding his expression in the face of the travellers' complaints.

Johnson and Hodder came out of the Lion and Sparrow and walked into the street from behind the coach, as if they had been passengers. "There," Johnson said, "in the doorway just across the street. Do you see his eyes?"

"Yes," Hodder said.

"Don't stare at him. We'll cross the street, but once there we'll walk away for a moment and see what he does."

As they stepped out of the roadway and onto the footpath the young man stepped forward. "Mr. Hodder?" he said.

"Why yes," Hodder answered.

"Meet me on the river side of Temple Bar after the sun sets."

"Why not speak to me now?" Hodder said, but the boy turned away as if he had made a mistake and hurried off through the stands and smoke of street vendors.

"This is very odd," Hodder said.

"Not at all," Johnson answered. "He has been seeking you. Surely he has word from your daughter."

"When will it be dark, sir? I fear I cannot wait any longer for information."

"In an hour or so," Johnson answered. "Let us take some tea."

"I cannot think of tea, sir, not now."

"There is nothing else you can do," Johnson said. "Sustenance will not harm you. I know just the place."

They walked to a coffee house in Chancery Lane owned by a man named Green. Johnson ordered small cakes and tea. He again tried to distract Hodder by speaking of the thoughts of theologians. "For example," he said, "consider Mr. Clarke…" but Hodder's attention was elsewhere, his eyes focused upon the windows and the diminishing light that filtered through the smudged glass.

"You must excuse me," he said. "My mind is on my daughter and her safety."

"I understand fully," Johnson said. "The sun is setting. We will meet with the boy presently."

Temple Bar was snarled with coach traffic on either side. Johnson and Hodder stood in a shopkeeper's doorway a few steps to the south and east, watching and waiting. A group of link boys hurried by, carrying bright yellow torches which cast moving shadows as they passed. As if from nowhere the young boy appeared, standing at Hodder's side. "Follow me," he said.

A few moments later they were standing along the river. The cries of rowers could be heard in the distance. There was an altercation over a passenger's choice of oarsmen. "This is Mr. Johnson," Hodder said. The boy bowed, then turned to Hodder. "I bring news of your daughter," he said.

"Is she well?" Hodder asked, insistently.

"Yes, sir. She is now."

"What do you mean, now?"

"There isn't time, Mr. Hodder. She is safe, but she dares not stir abroad."

"Where is she?"

"You must be very careful, Mr. Hodder. If she is seen on the streets her life will be in grave danger."

"What is your name?" Johnson asked.

"Nathaniel," he answered.

"My brother's name," Johnson said. "Nathaniel, it is clear that you have Miss Hodder's trust. Please believe me when I tell you that we will do all in our power to protect her. We will reunite her with her loving father and take her some place where she will be even safer than she is now. You may join us in our efforts, if you choose. I give you every assurance…"

"It would not be safe for me to be seen there, Mr. Johnson. She is in Ropemaker Alley; she is protected by a woman named Mrs. Lewis."

"Can you get word to her?" Johnson asked.

"Yes, sir."

"Tell her that someone will come for her tomorrow, just after dark. Trust me; we will take every precaution."

"I will get word to her, sir."

"Thank you, Nathaniel," Johnson said, handing him two shillings.

"That is unnecessary, sir," he said.

"Take it, Nathaniel. You are a brave boy. We will see you again after this business is completed."

Nathaniel took the stairs to the river, walking along the shore and into the darkness. "I fear I cannot wait so long to see my Elisabeth," Hodder said.

"We will require the protection of the darkness. We will also require time to make our arrangements," Johnson answered.

"What will you do?" Hodder asked.

"We will remove her under the pretense that she has died. Her body will be covered when she is carried from the house."

"And send in a physician first to ascertain the degree of her illness?"

"Physicians would prove too dear for the residents of Ropemaker Alley, Mr. Hodder. We will send in an apothecary. He will secure a porter and a wagon. We shall be nearby. When it is clear that the wagon has not been followed we will join her and bring her to Gough Square. Can you fire a pistol, Mr. Hodder?"

"A pistol, sir? Why, no."

"I know a retired soldier who mans the Barbican roundhouse. I will enlist him in our enterprise; he and I will provide protection for your daughter."

The apothecary was named Wilson; the watch's name was Howard. Howard suggested a porter named Digges, who had served with him at the battle of Blenheim. Each of them still carried its scars. Both still strong and vigorous, they provided every reassurance to Hodder. When they reached Little Britain they stopped; they checked until they were satisfied that no one was following them. Johnson handed his pistol to Howard and replaced the white sheet that encircled Elisabeth's head with a hooded coat. Hodder was anxious to speak with her and assure himself that she was well, but Johnson urged him to wait and remain silent until they were safely inside his house. They arrived there in fifteen minutes, being careful to stay in darkened storefronts and alleyways whenever possible. When they got inside and Elisabeth Hodder removed her coat her father was shocked to see her face in the light.

Her left cheek was badly bruised and her eye was red and swollen.

When she brushed her hair away from her face he could see similar bruise marks along her left hand and forearm.

"Who has done this to you, my dear?" he asked.

"All in good time, father," she said, kissing him on the cheek and then turning to Johnson to thank him. Johnson rang for tea and they sat comfortably, away from the window on the square. When Johnson saw how she supped and realized how hungry she must have been he sent his manservant Frank to secure some bread, cheese, and cooked beef from the Mitre.

"I know that I have caused you great pain, father…" Elisabeth said.

"Nonsense, my child. Your welfare is my only concern…"

"You see," she said, "I was unable to meet you because I feared for my life. I sent Nathaniel to watch for you and was thus so very relieved to hear that he had found you."

"What has happened to cause you this fear, my dear?"

"It is really quite simple, father. I arrived by the post coach and began to proceed directly to Mr. Winn's shop. I used the map which you had given me and was walking past Black Horse Alley when I heard a sound. A boy was screaming in pain. I walked into the Alley and saw a large man, standing with the boy. He had an implement in his hand that he was shoving in the boy's mouth. The boy was crying and gagging. He must have seen me because he turned his head toward me. Suddenly the man saw me as well and ran after me. He grabbed me and attempted to strike me with the iron tool that he still held in his hand. I believe he was truly attempting to kill me…"

"Horrible, horrible," Hodder said, "my poor dear girl…"

"I was able to block the blow with my wrist, though the head of the instrument still struck my face. I did all that I could to prevent his hurting me and used the fingers of my right hand to poke at his eyes…"

"Well done," Johnson said.

"I also cried out. A porter entered the alley, the man threw me against the wall, and ran toward the south end of the passageway. The porter gave chase and I went to see after the boy. When I got to him he was choking on something. I tried to help him, but it was hopeless and he died in my arms. Just then, Nathaniel entered the alley and he took me to safety, lest the man return and see that I had witnessed a murder. Nathaniel was the boy's brother. They were to meet next to the Ditch; Nathaniel was late and his brother had been abducted. He took me to Mrs. Lewis' house; she is the mother of his late cousin."

"Would you remember this man if you were to see him again?" Johnson asked.

"I could never forget him," she answered. "I still remember his smell and the look he carried in his eyes."

"What must have happened to the boy, to Nathaniel's brother?" Hodder asked.

"Such men as this who attacked your daughter prey upon the young," Johnson said. "He was doubtless attempting to steal the boy's teeth and sell them to a rich client. Forgive me, my dear," he said, turning to Miss Hodder, but she said, "Go ahead, sir. I have seen him. That is as bad as any account you might give of his actions."

Johnson tilted his head toward her, in recognition. "Such men have no qualms about the pain they inflict and give no thought to precision or delicacy. He was doubtless removing as many teeth as he could, without regard to the actual needs of the customer who would purchase them. Perhaps the boy swallowed one or more of the teeth in the process and began to choke."

"That is truly horrible, sir," Hodder said.

"Indeed it is, sir. Regrettably, the practice is not as uncommon as one might wish."

"So what is to be done?" Hodder asked.

"Why, sir, justice is to be done," Johnson said. "I have no intention of allowing this man to walk about the streets of our city."

"But how, sir? The boy is dead and the only witness is my dear daughter. It would be her word against his and if he is not found guilty and executed she would likely be his next victim. That cannot happen."

"No, it cannot, sir, but neither can we allow this man to escape the sentence for which his crime calls."

"But how, sir? How can this be done?"

"Let us first see to Miss Elisabeth," Johnson said. "Then we shall see to her attacker."

Early the next morning Elisabeth described her attacker expertly. He was a tall man, nearly as tall as Mr. Johnson, though not as heavy. He had piercing green eyes and though he wore an ill-fitting wig and had recently shaved his head she could see that his eyebrows and the stubble at the edge of the wig were red. His chest was thick, like a barrel, and his hands were small but strong, his fingers stubby. She made particular note of his forehead, which was heavily lined, as if he were angry and impatient. She estimated his age at no more than 45 years and stated that his speech was slurred with drink and his language low and vulgar.

"And what of his clothing, my dear?" Johnson asked.

"A simple cloth coat, dark brown, with matching waistcoat and breeches. Unfortunately I do not remember his hose and shoes."

"You have done very well, very well indeed," Johnson said. "I will make some inquiries while you and your dear father rest."

He left promptly with his manservant. Each wore coats against the light rain and each carried a cane for balance on the rain-slicked stones. As they walked into Fleet Street the kennel was clogged with dead cats and puppies, the water finding new channels. "You know, Frank," Johnson said, "a child may be purchased in this city, and it will cost the purchaser as much as a young terrier. What does that say about us, pray?"

"I don't know, sir," his manservant responded, "but some purchase terriers to protect their children and their houses from rats. They continue to value their children."

"True enough," Johnson said. "We seek a different sort, a man who looks upon children as vehicles to support his own greed."

"Where will you begin, sir?"

"With Thomas."

"Very good, sir."

Thomas Crisp wiped and polished shoes behind St. Clement Danes, where Johnson sometimes worshiped. He served many of the attorneys of Chancery Lane and the Temple and sometimes the criminals of Alsatia. Johnson approached him and asked him about the red-haired man. Thomas focused his eyes on Johnson's shoes, wiping them carefully, and speaking quickly. He knew of such men as this, he said, but he did not know of a particular man of this description. He promised to make discreet inquiries and get word to Mr. Johnson as soon as he learned anything.

The next morning there was a knock on Johnson's door. The housemaid answered and informed Johnson that there was a young boy to see him. "He is not particularly clean," she said. "I will have him wait outside."

"Nonsense," Johnson said, "bring him in and offer him something to eat."

As the boy drank a cup of chocolate Johnson entered the room, with Hodder behind him. It was not Thomas.

"My name is Lawrence Crisp, sir," the boy said. "I am Thomas' brother. He has sent me with a message for you."

"Very good, Lawrence. What is it?"

"It is very simple, sir."

"Yes?"

"The message is: at the Crow and Grapes, Jack Somers."

"Thank you very much, Lawrence," Johnson said, handing him two shillings. "The second is for your brother," he said. "I appreciate such fast work."

As the boy left and the heavy lock fell into place Hodder turned to

Johnson. "What will you do, sir? Will you confront the man? Will you bring in Mr. Howard?"

"I will certainly bring in Mr. Howard, but not right away. A criminal will be wary of a member of the watch. I like that fellow Digges. He will help me secure our Mr. Somers."

"Then you intend to arrest him yourself, sir?"

"Why, yes, I do."

"But on what grounds and with what evidence?"

"Mr. Hodder, you simply must relax and be patient. With regard to crime, this city is an open kennel. We deal with such matters regularly. Now, see to your daughter, put your trust in me and my friends, and we will arrest this fellow presently."

"I certainly hope that you will enlist the aid that you require, Mr. Johnson."

"Why yes, sir. I intend to enlist the aid of my favorite bishop."

"A bishop…?"

"As I said, be patient, sir."

Three days hence they prepared to go to the Crow and Grapes. Hodder was anxious because Johnson had been away for the previous two days, making arrangements. "You must realize," Johnson said, "that we may need to be there for quite some time before he appears. The readiness is all."

"Yes, sir."

"Mr. Howard will stay here with Miss Elisabeth; she will be quite safe. You shall dress in as nondescript fashion as possible. I do not want you to draw attention. I shall be dressed as a porter; you and I will act the roles of employer and potential employee."

"A porter?"

"Why yes, sir. When I first came to London to make my way as a writer, a fellow looked at me, saw my size, and advised me to obtain a porter's knot. I now have one."

Johnson removed his wig, put on simple, old clothes, and asked his manservant to bring in his knot, which he did promptly. They then walked to the Crow and Grapes, a dark tavern within the liberties of the Fleet. When they entered, the tapster nodded to Johnson, who led Hodder to a corner table, near the door. Hodder noted the presence of a woman in a distant corner. Slumped over her tea she ran her finger up and down the side of the cup. He could also see Mr. Digges, who sat at a table closer to their own. He was drinking a mug of small beer and eating a piece of bread with cheese. A few minutes later Johnson's manservant Frank entered. He was dressed in his best clothes, wearing a tight, white wig and carrying a small cane.

"Now we wait," Johnson said.

After three and one-half hours Hodder became restive. "Do you think he will come today?" he asked Johnson.

"If not today, tomorrow," Johnson replied. "Did you think that catching this criminal would be an adventure? I assure you, sir, more patience and planning are required than strength or courage."

"So I see," Hodder answered. "Fortunately you possess patience as well as courage."

"I believe that strength will be more necessary than courage. You see, sir, this man who preys upon children is little more than a common bully. Such men are generally cowards. Wait…look there."

The smoky, yellow light from the alley glimmered in the doorway and silhouetted a tall man who walked directly to the tapster and ordered a mug of porter. Before he turned he took a deep drink. The tavern candles were bright enough to reveal the red hair along his neck. As he turned Johnson saw his brows and forehead. "Our man," he said.

"What now, sir?"

"Patience," Johnson said, as his manservant approached the man and invited him to his table.

"What is Frank doing?" Hodder whispered.

"He is telling Somers that he is in the employ of a wealthy gentleman, a gentleman in need of the services that Somers is able to provide. Somers will ask him how he knew that he could provide such services and Frank will tell him that he bribed the magistrate. He will also tell him that the magistrate informed him of the recent occurrence that resulted in a boy's death. He will tell Somers that his employer—a baronet, by the way--will never tolerate an association that brings with it such results. When Somers finishes the protestations which provide enough evidence to implicate him in the act, Frank will signal that he is finished. Mr. Digges and I will then place the fellow under arrest."

"But it will be his word against Frank's. There is no other witness and a black fellow like Frank will be at a considerable disadvantage before the magistrate."

Johnson looked at him and Hodder said, "I know, sir. Patience."

Johnson smiled. Just then Frank stood and walked toward the tapster. "That is the signal," Johnson said. "He is offering to buy Somers a drink, to seal their arrangement." As Johnson rose so did Digges. They walked directly to Frank's table and confronted Somers.

"I am placing you under arrest for murder," Johnson said. Digges stood next to him, his hands on his hips.

"Are you now?" Somers responded. "And without any evidence?"

"We have ample evidence," Johnson said.

"Whatever your informant might say about any murder will be a lie," Somers said, "and the magistrate will see it as such."

"Ah, but we have a witness," Johnson said, "a witness who has heard your every word and will testify to it."

Suddenly Somers picked up his mug and swung it against Digges's face. Then he reached inside his coat for his pistol. Before he could remove it Johnson brought the handle of his oak cane across Somers' right hand and wrist. Somers momentarily released the hand from his pistol and Johnson swung it again, this time striking him across the bridge of his nose. The nose snapped like a twig and the blood began to pour across his mouth and chin. By now Digges was on top of him and removed the pistol from his breeches. Somers hurled insults at both of them, using the foulest of language. Johnson then struck him again, this time across the mouth, and he struck so violently that Somers' teeth were cracked and loosened. "Save your words for the Tyburn cart, Mr. Somers," Johnson said. "You will have chance enough to share your thoughts then."

Frank had sent the tavern boy to Gough Square to get Sergeant Howard, who arrived a few minutes later and took Somers to Newgate with the help of Mr. Digges.

"I did not expect you to strike him the third time," Hodder said to Johnson.

"I was tiring of his voice and his words," Johnson said.

"So was I," Hodder said. "Well done, sir. Now you must tell me how you have obtained your witness. My patience is gone, sir."

"Come," Johnson said, and ordered fresh tea, bread, cheese, and even some fruit in celebration. He took Hodder to the remote table where the lone woman was sitting, sipping her tea. "Miss Williams, Mr. Hodder. Mr. Hodder, Miss Anna Williams," Johnson said.

"Miss Williams…" Hodder said, still not comprehending, particularly when he saw that Miss Williams was blind.

"Miss Williams is a dear friend of mine," Johnson said. "Her father is laboring to solve the longitude problem and I am attempting to be of assistance to him. Miss Williams has had the distinction of assisting Mr. Grey in his electrical experiments. She is most accomplished. While cataracts have deprived her of vision her hearing is exquisite. She can identify voices with the utmost precision and will so demonstrate when she is called to testify."

"But, sir, she was sitting at least thirty feet away from Frank and Somers."

"Indeed she was, sir. If she was close to them Somers would not have spoken freely."

"But how could she hear him, sir?"

"Quite simply, Mr. Hodder. We have installed a tube that ran from Frank's table to hers."

"Underneath the flooring?"

"Yes, that is why I needed some time--to prepare our trap. Surely you know of Bishop Wilkins' talking statue."

"Cromwell's brother-in-law, the Warden of Wadham College."

"Why yes, sir. He had a statue installed in the gardens of Wadham and ran a tube beneath the soil back to his lodgings. When the puritans passed he provided them with special revelations from the talking statue. I love Wilkins. He never lost his good humor, even in perilous times. You know that he is responsible in good part for the Royal Society itself."

"I did not know that, sir."

"Why yes, sir. He brought men of science together, without regard to their religious or political associations. Such men help create what little civilization we have. You should read his *Mathematical Magick*, sir. It is quite remarkable."

"I shall, sir, the moment I complete my work with Mr. Winn and return to Wiltshire with my daughter."

"And you will stay in touch, sir? It is my hope to make a new friend every day."

"You have made two for life, sir."

"I pray that I have," Johnson said. "Now, let us finish our food and join Miss Elisabeth. You have not yet had the time to see our city. It can be very comfortable when the air clears and the sun appears. It has its bad elements, of course, but its good as well and you shall see the latter now that you have fully experienced the former. I will join you. We will take a walk along the river and enjoy the afternoon sun. There is much of it today. The residents of the city call these 'golden days'. Like justice, they are not as rare as we sometimes think."

XI

______

LARRY AND THE PIRATES

"So what the hell are you supposed to be?"

"What do you mean what am I supposed to be? Are you referring to my hand?"

"Now why would I do that? Every day I see guys wearing plastic hooks that they got from Disneyland for a dollar eighty-nine."

"They're eight ninety-nine now. Do you want to loan me the actual money or not?"

"No, as a matter of fact, I don't. When I loan money I want to have some assurance that I'm gonna get it back. Lookin' at you I doubt that you could make the vig for two weeks running. What do you want it for anyway?"

"What do you think? I want to buy a hand."

"What happened to the first one?"

"I got it caught in a machine."

"And the new one is how much?"

"Bargain basement: eight grand."

"That's a lotta money. Can't you get one cheaper?"

"Yeah, but it won't have the little gizmos and the sensors like the top-of-the-line models do. Like…if you're holding something and you start to drop it, the hand somehow knows and this little motor inside tells the thumb to move and then the hand sort of tightens around whatever it is you were about to drop and you don't drop it."

"No shit?"

"No shit."

"And what did you say your name was?"

"I didn't. I don't want to get personal until we get some kind of deal here."

The shy looks at Captain Hook, smiles, and stares at him as if he's thinking it over and trying to figure out if he's worth the risk of eight large, but inside he's thinking that the captain reminds him a lot of this other guy who used to hang around the garage and watch the mechanics eat their lunch. The guy was always scratching himself in places where even a flea would feel uncomfortable. One day he's looking at this one guy pouring some soup out of a widemouth thermos and another guy pouring some ice tea out of a narrow neck and suddenly he reaches around, scratches his ass, and starts getting philosophical about the thermos. He says to the two guys, "It's amazing, isn't it? It keeps the hot things hot and the cold things cold."

One of the guys looks at him and says, "Yeah…so?"

And the guy scratches his ass again, this time a little harder and deeper, and says, "Yeah, so how does it know?"

"Son-of-a-bitch," the guy says to nobody in particular. "I coulda made the vig, no problem. What it is is fucking discrimination. I get my hand caught in a milling machine and now I'm like disabled and nobody'll lend me money."

Two of the guys at the bar look in the other direction but the guy keeps talking anyway.

"I mean, it ain't as if I'm the first guy something like this has happened to."

The bartender responds to him out of a sense of duty and says, "You know somebody else had the same thing happen?"

"I sure as hell do. In fact, he'll be here any minute."

"That's nice," the bartender answers. "We can always use another customer."

Ten minutes later the other guy walks in. He's also wearing a plastic hook, but he's missing his left hand, not his right. He looks at the bartender, looks at the beer in front of the other guy and then nods as if to say, "I want one of those too." Instead of answering, the bartender points at the Miller tap, then the Miller Lite tap, then the Michelob tap, and looks at the guy quizzically. The guy looks at his friend's beer and then looks back at the bartender, who points his finger at the Miller Lite tap, whereupon the new guy shakes his head no and tilts his head to the left. The bartender puts his hand on the Miller tap and the guy nods yes.

The guy sits down, the bartender slides a Miller draft in front of him, which he acknowledges with a semi-twitch, and the guy turns to his friend and asks, "So what happened?"

"He turned me down, he flat out turned me down. So don't bother asking. I didn't say anything to him about you. There wasn't any point."

"So what do we do now?"

"Just sit tight and enjoy your beer. It's gonna be OK. I got a plan."

"Jesus, Sarge, your eyes look like freeway maps," the patrolman said.

"We lost power for five hours last night and the bedroom turned into a swamp. I couldn't sleep, so I came in early and caught a full night's worth by noon. I'm getting too old for this."

"What happened?"

"Just more of the usual. Purse snatchers, rental car boosters, weenie waggers, half the drivers on blow, the other half on meth…oh yeah, and a real special. This one little precious number gets a haircut from Tony Silva over at the Breakers this morning. Tony tells him it's forty-five bucks and the guy tells him he'll have to go back to his room to get that kind of money. Tony asks him his room number, the guy futzes around in his pocket, says that his wife must have the key, and tells Tony he's gonna go look for her. Tony follows him out the door and sees the guy running south. He calls security and the one guy available catches up to haircut boy, just as he's standing in the shade of a clump of palms, taking a leak on the beach. A couple of honeymooners from Westchester start complaining to the security guy and the perp runs away, jerking at his zipper and trying not to get himself caught in it.

"Later we figure out that he was getting a new haircut to change his appearance a little, since his real plan was to hold up a store on Worth."

"And did he?"

"Not exactly. Two of our uniforms caught up to him in a gallery. The new one, 'Valerie's Gallery'. While they're reading him his rights he picks up a can of garbage on the floor and throws it at them. Valerie goes jungle shit because the garbage can was actually what she claimed was a piece of sculpture, part of something she called an 'installation.' She says it's worth twelve thousand bucks. One of our guys says, 'Christ, to who?' The three of them get in a pissing contest and the perp escapes again. Next we hear he's in a restaurant demanding a free lunch because he says he's seen a roach on the floor. He points under the table, where the waiter and maître d' can't see, and then says, 'There he goes again. He just went under the toe stripping.' The waiter says to him, 'How do you know it was a he?' and the guy says (louder now), 'It's a figure of speech. They're always he's. What did you expect me to say--he must have been a he because he lifted a couple of his legs and took a piss on the table leg?'

"Anyway, the long and the short of it is that everybody else in the place hears him and starts demanding free lunches also. I sent Flaherty down to referee. Oh yeah, and the lieutenant is pissed at the officer in the gallery for saying 'Christ' to the owner."

"You know what, Sarge...?"

"What?"

"Tony gives a pretty good haircut."

"Don't say that; you can't afford one of those haircuts and I don't want anyone thinkin' you're taking something on the side."

"He never charges me that much. I think he likes having cops on the premises."

"So what do you mean you got a plan?"

"I've got a plan; it will work; trust me."

They realized that the bartender was standing in front of them, staring at the plastic hooks on their hands.

"Yeah?" the first guy said.

"I'll give you each a free beer if you tell me about the hooks."

"Throw in a shot too? For each of us."

"Yeah, OK."

"Don't put the shots in the beer."

"I'll put them on the side."

"There's nothing to tell," the first guy said, after throwing back the shot and taking a deep drink of the cold beer. "We were hurt in what you would call an industrial accident."

"So you actually lost your hands?"

"Of course. What did you think we were doing, wearing the hooks just for the hell of it?"

"I wasn't sure; that's why I asked."

The second guy was shaking his head in disbelief. The bartender said, "So is it like wedged on or something?"

"It's glued on," the first guy said. "And it's not as simple as it sounds. We started with Elmer's but the stump sweats and then the glue doesn't hold. Crazy Glue and epoxy are too strong. They irritate the stump and sometimes you can't get the hook off."

"So what are you using?" the bartender asked.

"That stuff they use in school, with the rubber tip and the slit through it."

"Mucilage?"

"Yeah, professor. Mucilage."

"I hated that stuff," the bartender said. "I mean, it worked OK and everything, but the stuff always got hard around the slit and then it got flaky and you'd have to break it loose before you could use it again and sooner or later you'd end up with a bunch of it all over your fingers. Then when you tried to work with it you'd find out that your fingers were sticking to the paper and everything would get all fucked up."

The second guy looked at the first as if to say, "Welcome to the twilight zone."

"You're really the expert on that shit, aren't you?" the first guy said.

"No," the bartender answered. "I just think it's kind of interesting to see two guys with plastic hooks glued onto their wrists. I was curious about how they worked."

"Well if you want us to poke you and stick you with them so you can find out it'll cost you another two beers and two shots," the first guy said.

"I think I'll pass," the bartender answered.

"So they finally caught the guy, eh Sarge?"

"Yep. He said his name was Randolph Kingston. He called his daddy, who called a lawyer. They keep calling him 'Ducky' instead of 'Randolph.'"

"I can see why he wouldn't want to be called Randy, but I wonder how he got a nickname like Ducky."

"I don't know, Jerry. I'll check with the lawyer and get back to you with a full report."

"I wasn't trying to mouth off or anything, Sarge."

"I know. Forget it. It's been a long day. Now the wife's pissed. She was hacking at this banana plant that's been trying to take over the side of our porch and something brown that was living in it jumped out. Scared the hell out of her. I told her she had evicted it and it was simply looking for a new place to live. She said she didn't think that was very funny. I told her to put whatever she was using on the banana plant away and lock up the tool shed before I came home. I'm done for the day. She didn't think that was very 'empathetic'. God, my feet are killing me."

"What's wrong with your feet?"

"My orthotic cracked, the one in my left shoe. I had to take it out for awhile. I also took out the right one, since I didn't want to hobble around like somebody wearing one high heel."

"So did you fix it?"

"I epoxied it. It wasn't split all the way through so I got a good seal. It'll be OK in awhile. Meanwhile I just can't go anyplace unless I can go there barefoot."

"Shit, Sarge. You know what you need?"

"What's that?"

"A little down time. Just a little."

"You got that right, Jerry, but I'm not holding my breath."

"Oh, Sarge…"

"What?"

"My brother-in-law's got a machete if you want to borrow it, you know, for the banana plant."

"I don't want Lois to see it; it could give her ideas."

"OK. If you change your mind, let me know."

"It's a nursing home," the first guy said.

"You want to knock over a nursing home?"

"Not knock it over, just light-finger a few things. Like, they got these beautiful candle holders…"

"Candle holders?"

"Yeah, the kind with the arms for seven different candles. They look like they're made of gold or something."

"Menorahs?"

"Yeah, whatever. And rare pictures all over the place. With the artists' signatures and everything."

"Those may not be worth that much."

"Well, besides the stuff that they own they got cash up the ying-yang. And it's just sitting there in their nightstands."

"Are you telling me that you want to knock over a Jewish nursing home?"

"Are you listening to me? I said we'd just take a few things. We'd be selective."

"And you think they'll let you just walk in and take their stuff?"

"Don't be ridiculous. Of course not. We'd have to create some kind of diversion. I mean, it's not like they're all sitting there guarding their stuff all day long. A lot of them are asleep and those that aren't asleep hang out around the nursing station and watch the nurses work. It's kind of like going to the movies or something. It entertains them, gives them something to occupy their attention. They line up around the station and spill out down the hallways. It's a big deal. Meanwhile there's nobody back in their rooms. It'll be a pushover."

"I'm not so sure about that. When did you find out about this nursing home?"

"A week ago. I know this guy who makes sheet and towel deliveries, mostly to hospitals but also to nursing homes. He let me ride with him and check out the place. He's full of ideas for scams; the problem is he's just not too quick."

"What do you mean?"

"Well, like, he told me I should steal Tylenol from the hospitals. He said that they don't guard them the way they do all the other drugs. I told him they're not worth anything and he said, "The hell they're not. Have you ever seen a hospital bill? They're a couple bucks apiece, not like the kind you buy in the grocery store."

"Jesus," the second guy said.

"Yeah, I know. I told him how they jack up the prices on that stuff and rip off the insurance companies. He said, "Oh yeah? Check these out." He reached into his glove compartment and came out with a handful of those little cups they use to give the patients their pills. They were all squished together at the top so the Tylenol wouldn't fall out. "This is the good stuff," he said. He told me he'd sell a couple to me for fifty cents apiece."

"Don't tell me you bought them?"

"Of course not. The next time he made a delivery I took one from the glove compartment."

"And how did it work?"

"I don't know yet; I'm saving it."

"Hi Larry, how you doing?"

"Good, lieutenant. I was just about to pack it in for the day."

"What's with the socks?"

"I cracked one of my orthotics; I've been waiting for the glue to dry."

"How do those things work, Larry?"

"Pretty well, lieutenant. Once you start wearing them you can't walk without them. That's the only problem. But then you couldn't walk without them before. That's why you got them in the first place."

"Let's go get a beer, Larry--celebrate the end of a long day."

"You're on, lieutenant."

"I got the whole thing scoped out. It's called the Mar Vista Nursing Home."

"Can you see the ocean from it?"

"No, why?"

"Never mind."

"OK. Anyway, it's got about a hundred and thirty-five rooms. Big place. Almost like a hotel, except all the hallways lead to the nursing station instead of just to the end of the hall. It's very pricey. I heard this social worker talking to these people who were thinking about putting their mother in there. She said the bottom line is that after the Medicare runs out the room costs sixty eight hundred a month. That's more than eighty large, before taxes."

"Yeah, I figured that out."

"What's more they don't promise you anything after you run out of money. The state won't pay their usual rate and they don't want to eat the difference. You got to go to the cheapie places for that. At this place they expect to get top dollar until you keel over. That means you got to come from a family that's got eighty large a year that they don't know what to do with. That means you can afford the finer things and it's the finer things I plan on taking."

"And you also plan on not getting caught."

"Of course. This is gonna be sweet and easy. Think about it as our right."

"Our *right?*"

"Yeah. We went to work for that cheapass company that didn't pay for proper health benefits, so now we'll get the artificial hands that we should have gotten anyway. It's not like we're looking for luxuries, just for hands, like everybody else has. Then we won't look so weird. And we can lead normal lives…meet women, drink in a bar without everybody staring at our hooks…stop worrying about glue and shit."

"How do we get in without drawing any attention?"

"Easy. We dress up like we're delivering sheets and towels. We put the stuff that we take in the bottom of the bin, underneath the dirty laundry. Then we just roll it outside and into the van and we're out of there. They won't know that anything's missing until they're sitting down to eat their afternoon jello."

"But we don't have a van."

"I'll get one."

"And what about the diversion?"

"I'm still working on that. I want it to be something good."

"You did a nice job on the banana plant, Lois. Really nice. It's all trimmed back and the porch looks just the way it used to. Maybe even better."

She put the dinner on the table without speaking.

"That smells great," he said.

She put glasses of iced tea at each of their places.

"That looks good," he said. "I'm thirsty and there's nothing quite like iced tea when you're thirsty. How was your day?"

She sat down, paused, looked him in the eye, and said, "I've just got one question; why did we move to Florida?"

"Because..." he said, searching for an answer.

"That's what I thought."

"The sunshine is nice."

"It keeps the rats and roaches warm."

"Palmetto bugs," Larry said.

"Call them what you like..."

"I hear you."

"Death is natural, Larry. Here it only happens to humans and to whatever happens to wander across the interstate. I rinsed out a coke bottle four times yesterday before I put it in the garage. Three minutes later there was a line of ants crawling toward it that looked as if it could have stretched all the way to Sarasota."

"The manatees are nice."

"They're great if you swim underwater all day and get to know them."

"OK, how about the everglades?"

"Wonderful, but does a road called Alligator Alley really sound as inviting as one called the Pacific Coast Highway or the Chicago Skyway? Be honest and think about it. The thing is, Larry, I've just seen one too many scruffy people walking on our street, one too many nervous German tourists looking over their shoulders, one too many palm fronds on the top of the car, one too many people who hate me but don't speak English, and one too many things with a lot of legs crawling up our drapes. Frogs are something I expect to see on Sesame Street, Larry, not in my bathroom."

"I understand."

"How many days until you can finally retire?"

"Twenty three, if nothing happens in the meantime to screw it up."

"Then we can move to a place where the ground freezes at least once a year?"

"I promise."

"A place where people don't buy things with cash stuffed in brown paper bags?"

"I promise."

"The diversion will be simple."

"Yeah? What have you got in mind?"

"Well, I thought about turning loose some mice."

"Are you crazy? The old ladies will start jockeying their wheelchairs and the hallways will be gridlocked. Plus they'll be screaming and going nuts."

"I said I thought about doing that. I wasn't going to do it back by the old ladies anyway; I was going to do it in the cafeteria. That way all the supervisors and security people would be running toward the cafeteria, away from us."

"That's crazy. You think you can control mice? What were you going to do, put little antennas up their asses and run them around with a remote control? Mice aren't smart like cats or dogs. If everybody ran toward them they'd run toward us."

"For the third time, I thought about the fucking mice. I've got a much better idea than that now."

"Which is?"

"Something dead in the ductwork. The smell will start to work its way through the system. They'll all be talking about it and asking questions and we'll just go about our business, picking up their goodies and their cash."

"Where are you going to get something like that?"

"Off the highway, where else?"

"I'm not going to touch it."

"You won't have to touch it. I'll get some tongs or something. I'll slip it into a plastic bag and we'll put extra twist ties around it."

"A pancake turner might be better than tongs."

"Good idea."

"OK, how are you going to get it into the ductwork—ask somebody if you can borrow a ladder and then climb up into a crawl space carrying a plastic bag full of roadkill?"

"No, numbnuts, I'll go into the basement, find the air conditioning unit, walk around, look for the basement vent that's closest to the nursing station, pop off the two screws on the vent cover, remove it, stick the dead thing inside the ductwork, put the cover back on, close the little vent thingies, and let the smell work its way upstairs."

"It could work…"

"Fucking 'A. I know it will work."

"When did you plan to do this?"

"As soon as I can borrow Billy's van, steal a laundry bin from a motel, and get some towels from Wal-Mart."

"Shit, you mean like tomorrow?"

"Why not? The sooner we make the score the sooner we get our hands."

"Give me a kiss, Lois. I'm leaving for the station."

"How is your orthotic working? Is that glue holding?"

"So far so good."

"Maybe you'll have a good day today. I'll make pot roast tonight. We'll have a little celebration."

"That sounds great. I'll look forward to it. We're due for a little break in the action. We extradited that rapist to Alabama on Tuesday and we finished testifying on that arsonist from Louisiana yesterday afternoon."

"What about the guy who peed on the beach and then ran through the galleries on Worth?"

"He gets arraigned this morning. Pete's going; I don't have to."

"Good. Maybe this'll be an easy one."

"What is that noise?"

"The laundry bin. I didn't have time to secure it, so it's rolling around in the back."

"Where'd you get it?"

"At the Ramada."

"Does it have Ramada written on it?"

"Yes, Mr. Question Man, but I covered it up with some white chalk."

"Chalk?"

"Yes, it worked fine; stop worrying."

"How about the roadkill?"

"Yeah, I got something. I'm not sure what it is. Probably a cat."

"Would you do me a favor?"

"What's that?"

"Would you drive with your good hand and not try to hold on to the wheel with that hook?"

"OK. Does this make you feel better?"

"Much better. I don't want to get in an accident and have to explain that shit in the back of the van. Did you get the towels from Wal-Mart?"

"There's a little problem there, but, yes, I got them."

"What kind of problem?"

"They're not exactly white."

"Oh shit, don't tell me you tried to save money and got old beach towels or something."

"Of course not, they're just not white. They'll be fine. They're sort of beige."

"Beige towels in a nursing home?"

"It's not that big a deal; besides, they'll be thinking about that smell and not paying attention to the towels. If anybody asks I'll tell them that the company changed its policy."

"They should like them better actually. If they have to clean up piss you wouldn't notice it as much on a beige towel as on a white one. Using beige would be more…I don't know…sensitive."

"That's a good idea. I'll tell them that if anybody asks."

"Except don't say 'piss'; say 'urine'."

"Good thought."

They drove another six blocks and suddenly the guy in the passenger seat pointed with his plastic hook and said, "There it is, right behind the wooden sign."

"I know where it is; don't worry."

"Park around back; we'll check out the basement."

"Shit, there is no basement."

"The unit must be on the roof. Look, no problem, there's the fire escape ladder."

"Who's going up?"

"I am. Check this out," he said, as he removed his white shirt and revealed a tee shirt that read West Palm Heating and Cuuling.

"Very clever, but that's not the way they spell *cooling*."

"Shit. I knew I shouldn't have trusted that asswipe at the mall. Look in the glove compartment and see if there's a pencil or magic marker or something. We can turn those u's into o's."

"There's a red ballpoint; I don't think that will work."

"Shit. I'll wrinkle up the shirt so people will think the two o's are in one of the folds."

"Why don't you put it on backwards and put your arm in front of the two u's if you see anybody?"

"Good idea."

"Did you get it in there?"

"It worked like a charm."

"There was a vent on the ductwork?"

"Not exactly. I had to punch a hole with the screwdriver and cut a little with the tin snips, but the air conditioner was operating, so I'm sure no one heard anything. I dropped Mr. Stinky into the hole, bent the sheet metal back in place, and got out without anybody seeing me."

"Mr. Stinky?"

"What would you call it?"

"Sarge…"

"Yeah, what's up, Benny?"

"It's the nursing home up on Crescent."

"What do they want?"

"They say they heard somebody on the roof."

"Probably a repairman, Benny."

"No, they hadn't called any repairman."

"Maybe a city guy trimming some overhanging trees or something."

"No, they didn't hear any chain saws, just some hammering."

"Well, it wouldn't have been a meter reader or anything. You want to go check it out?"

"I gotta pick up my kid in an hour, Sarge. Do you think you could…"

"OK. I'll go."

"Stop whistling."

"Those delivery-type guys always whistle."

"We don't need any extra attention. Do you smell it yet?"

"I smell something, but it doesn't smell dead. It smells curdled or spoiled or something."

"Probably their lunch. It's coming from over there, toward the cafeteria."

"Here, take some of the towels. Hold them under your arm like you're real busy and then write something down on the sheet of paper on that clipboard. Those delivery guys are always writing things down. I'll check out this first room and see what they've got."

As the second guy doodled on the sheet and checked his watch the first guy came out of the room quickly. "Jackpot. Already," he said.

"What'd you get?"

"Sh-h-h-h," he said, as he slid something into the bottom of the bin and dropped a used towel on top of it.

"Well what is it?"

"It's an original oil painting, one by that 'painter of light' guy."

"I don't know what you're talking about."

"That's because you don't pay any attention to art and shit. You'd rather stay ignorant. Here, let's check out the next one. Keep playing around with that clipboard. Chew on the edge of the pencil every now and then."

A few minutes later he returned.

"What did you get?"

"Nothing great, a few dollars in change, a bottle of perfume, and a hair dryer."

"A full bottle?"

"Almost full."

"Shit, that isn't worth anything."

"I'll add some water and make it look full. Keep writing."

Ten minutes later they heard a voice from beyond the nurses' station: "Phew. That smells terrible. What is that?" Suddenly the wheelchairs were turning in different directions.

"It smells like the casserole that my daughter-in-law makes. I told my David that I don't understand how he eats the food she puts on their table, but that's his problem, not mine."

"It smells like a dead muskrat."

"How would you know what a dead muskrat smells like? Besides, everything dead smells alike."

"We had muskrats in our yard on the island. I should know what they smell like."

"My daughter-in-law makes something that smells bad too, only with her it's the curry. Always the curry. I say to her, 'So are you turning your house into Calcutta or something?' and she tells me that they like curry and that her husband Arnold likes curry even more than she does, as if I never fixed it for him and should somehow feel guilty now."

"My Harry liked curry, may he rest in peace."

"Your Harry would have eaten muskrat; he liked everything."

"How can you say that about him? He didn't like coconut."

"He would eat coconut. He just didn't prefer coconut."

"OK, Mrs. Expert. Let me tell you; he ate coconut at your house because he didn't want to starve and die. If you had put out anything else he would have eaten it instead."

"He asked me to cook it. I think he liked the way I fixed it. Not everybody can fix everything to somebody's liking."

"So now you're saying that my husband Harry didn't like the food I cooked for him?"

"Aey-a-a-a-a-a-a-a-a-a-a-!" The voice came from the end of the hallway.

"I think that's Selma. That sounds like her scream," a voice said. The wheelchairs turned and the three closest headed toward the sound, with a second group of three following just behind them, like the second row of cars at the Indy 500. A few seconds later the wheelchair on the left side of the first row nearly collided with a wheelchair emerging from a room on the left, just as a man walked into the hallway and felt the wheel of one of the chairs roll over his foot.

He started to say "shit," but held it back, winced, and asked about the reports that some unidentified person was pounding on the roof.

"Never mind that," the woman who had emerged from the room said. "Somebody's stolen my Thomas Kinkade! And it was beautiful! And my son gave it to me! And it was the picture of the cottage at the end of the little English village, the one with the light in the windows and the snow on the roof and the cows and the sheep and the church and the lighthouse and the people dressed up for Christmas."

"So Selma, why are you celebrating Christmas?"

"It's not about religion. It's about the scarves and the mittens and the man carrying the goose and the children playing in the field and the old man feeding the birds. That Christmas."

By then the administrator appeared, along with the receptionist and an unarmed security guard. "I'm Sergeant Hollis," Larry said. "There was a report that somebody was making noise up on your roof. Now this woman says that someone stole a painting from her room."

"An original oil painting and my name is Mrs. Green."

"We'll check on it Selma, don't worry," the administrator said. "I'm Jane Gibson," she said, "and this is Mrs. Heninger and Mr. Schneider."

"How do you do," Larry said. "Has anyone seen any strangers in the building today?"

"Strangers?" one voice said. "You mean like my son and my two daughters?"

"No. People you don't know," Larry said.

"I know what you mean, sonny. I was making a point."

"Yes, ma'am," Larry said.

"There were the pirates," one voice said.

"The pirates?" Larry answered, incredulously.

"Delivering towels. Two men with hooks instead of hands."

"When was this?" Larry asked.

"Five minutes ago."

"Check the hallways," Larry said to Mr. Schneider, "but don't try to do anything without backup. I'm going to check the parking lot." When he got to the door he took out his service revolver and two of the women cheered. "Go get 'em," one said.

A few minutes later he found the van parked at the rear of the building. The rear doors were open but there was no one in the passenger seats. He popped the hood, removed the spark plug wires, and returned to the building. "See anybody?" he asked Mr. Schneider.

"Not a one," he answered.

"Call 911; they'll connect you with the station; tell them we've got a theft in progress and that they should send as many people as they can spare."

"You got it, Captain," Mr. Schneider said.

"Sergeant," Larry answered, "but don't worry about it."

"I can't breathe in here."

"Shut up, unless you want to get us both caught."

"What's that smell?"

"Somebody's turned on the furnace. It's the heat and dust and the dead thing. They haven't been able to find us, so they figure we went up in the ductwork or something. They're flushing us out."

"Well, it's working."

"Put a towel over your nose; it won't smell so bad then."

"Then I won't be able to breathe at all."

"Stop whining."

"Shit…"

"What?"

"The only towels left are the used ones we got from their rooms; they smell worse than the dead thing. They're all mildewed or moldy or something."

"For the last time, shut the hell up. We'll wait here until the middle of the night. They'll figure we got away. Then we'll slip out."

"How long will that be?"

"I don't know, fifteen hours or so."

"I'm not going to last that long."

"I don't think that heat is going to work, Sergeant," Mrs. Gibson said. "I don't want to frustrate your plan, but the clients are starting to complain. We closed the vents so the heat wouldn't go into their rooms, but without air conditioning it's beginning to get stuffy."

"I understand," Larry said. "Their van's disabled and I've got officers stationed at all of their possible exit points. Patrolman Vesey and I will go from room to room until we find them."

They started in the areas closest to the nurses' station and then branched out, checking under every bed, checking every bathroom, every closet, every common storage area, and every cabinet large enough to hold a body. Thirty-five minutes later they were working their way down the corridor of the rehabilitation section. The rooms—which were undivided--were clear but there was a closet in the far corner. The door was closed. "What's in there?" Vesey asked.

"Probably weights and flotation stuff," Larry said.

"Listen," Vesey said. "What is that?"

They each got closer to the jamb. "It sounds like somebody snoring."

They each stood back and Vesey whispered, "You did it, Sarge.

The heat relaxed them and now the air conditioning is making them comfortable."

"Stand back," Larry said, reaching for the knob. Suddenly he threw open the door, aiming his revolver at the center of the small room. He heard movement, turned on the light, and saw the two men lying like spoons in the bottom of the laundry bin.

"Oh shit," one of them said. As Vesey pulled the bin from the closet a hook came out, its point thrust into the back of his hand. The rubber point bent upon impact and Vesey said, "Ouch. What the hell are you doing?"

Suddenly both of the men tried to leap from the bin at the same time. It tipped from side to side, then fell to the left. They rolled out and each stood up, brandishing a rubber hook. Before Larry could comment, the shorter one leaped toward him, swinging wildly with his hook. The second looked at Vesey with some apprehension. Before he could make a move Vesey hit him across the bridge of his nose with the side of his hand. "Goddamnit," the man said, as the blood began to stream over his chin and onto his white uniform.

His partner kept swinging at Larry, striking him occasionally with glancing blows. Larry kept his left eye closed and threw a punch at the man's stomach. That slowed him, so Larry threw a second, then an uppercut to the chin which finished him off. He immediately realized that he had broken a finger in the process. "Damn!" he said, and then "Sorry…" when he saw Mrs. Gibson behind him.

As Mrs. Heninger brought a towel with some ice Larry and Patrolman Vesey cuffed the two robbers. "All right, mateys," Larry said, "you have the right to remain silent…"

As he finished Mirandizing them, a row of wheelchairs appeared at the door. "Selma, I don't think you should come in here just yet," Mrs. Gibson said.

"I want my Kinkade," she answered. "If he doesn't have it you should torture them until they tell you where they put it."

"Torture?" the first man said. "Are you out of your mind? We want a lawyer."

"It's right here," Vesey said, "though I think they might have cracked the frame." He moved the dirty towels aside and picked up the painting. He noticed the smell of perfume in the bin and around the frame and saw the wet mark on the bottom of the bin. "Don't worry. We'll make sure he makes it right, ma'am," Vesey said.

Selma rolled forward in her wheelchair, stared into the eyes of the two robbers, and said, "You're cruel men, to do something low like that to a helpless widow."

"Give us a break, lady," the second man said. "At least you've got both your hands."

"So what are you, a victim already? I'll show you a victim," she said and started kicking at his shins until Larry pulled back her chair with his good hand.

When he got back in his car his cell phone rang. It was his wife. "I've found the place for us. Wyoming. No people there, just antelopes and moose and sheep and a bear every now and then. There's 97,914 square miles of it. The state mammal is the bison; the state bird is the meadowlark; the state flower is the Indian paintbrush; the state tree is the plains cottonwood; the state gemstone is jade; the state fish is the cutthroat trout; the state reptile is the horned toad (that doesn't sound too bad); did you know that they had a state fossil and a state dinosaur?"

"No, I didn't," he said. "What about sunshine?"

"You want sunshine? The first line of the chorus of the state song is "Wyoming, Wyoming! Land of the sunlight clear!"

"How about pirates?"

"Pirates?"

"Yes, pirates."

"None at all as far as I can see. Why would they have pirates?"

"Start packing."

XII

—

SANDMAN

The exact details aren't all that important, but suffice to say that when Norbie took his '56 Bel Air ("pea-green and baby-shit yellow, with continental kit," he always said then) to Little John Rannert to be bored and stroked he made a very big mistake. When Little John wasn't joyriding in his customers' cars he was drinking beer and telling stories to the ever present collection of hangers-on who congregated at his Fairmount speed shop. When he was completing his work on Norbie's Chevy his tongue was almost surely loose, his brain clouded and his mind elsewhere. In retrospect the most plausible diagnosis was that he neglected to blow out the crank journals before he reassembled the engine. The problem wasn't apparent until Norbie started to run seriously against the clock. When he did, the metal filings which Little John had left behind reduced the lubrication just when the engine was most in need of it and the assembled masterpiece of chrome and hardened steel simply burned up.

Rannert pleaded innocent, said that these things happen and that all racers take the same risk. Norbie's insurance man offered him open palms, told him there was nothing he could really do, and that without putting too fine a point on it, Norbie was basically screwed. When the numbers were totaled he was out nearly a thousand bucks and that at a time when you could buy a good car for fifteen hundred and most high school kids were working heavy-duty construction for $1.25 an hour.

Norbie finally sold off some of the remaining parts and scraped together the money to get his car running again. The machine that resulted was little more than upscale transportation, not the flying chariot of his faded dreams. I thought he took it very well under the circumstances. While I didn't think about it this way at the time, he probably took it as well as he did because he had experienced much worse.

He was one of those guys you consider to be endlessly and effortlessly popular, but who you later learn are lonely and without any real friends. When Norbie's car had slowed to a dead halt the people who had always stood around it, gaping, drifted off toward other people and other places. Cars were everything then, especially to those who didn't own one themselves. They huddled around those who did, like the entourage behind the high roller, cheering loudly until his luck goes south and the action suddenly disappears.

Norbie and I didn't meet until my junior year in high school. Though we were in the same class he was a year older and as a result always treated me like a younger brother. I had had some work done on my own car that hadn't quite worked out the way I expected and Norbie offered to make it all whole again. He removed the twin-carb manifold, replaced it with the original (with a fresh gasket), installed the carb, set the linkage, told me to turn the key, and watched the look of wonder appear on my face when the engine turned over and the smoke billowed from the exhaust. He adjusted the mixture, reduced the smoke, and suddenly we were in business. We drove into town, grabbed some dinner and cold drinks, and enjoyed the moment. He had offered a little free help, but to me it felt like salvation.

And his touch was always so light and so sure. He always selected a wrench carefully, not casting around in confused impatience. When he handled a screwdriver he lifted it as if it were a scalpel and replaced it in the tool tray as if it were a sleeping child. There was a certainty about him, a reassuring aura of skill and craft. "I wouldn't have let Little John near the Bel Air," he said, "if I had had the necessary tools to do the job myself."

Norbie was one of the fringe kids. He didn't live where we did, he didn't drive what we drove, he worked more than the rest of us, dated experienced girls, and always somehow seemed much older. When he smoked he turned the cigarettes between his fingers, rolling them slowly, handling them like sticks or rods. He never smoked to excess and never carried the smell of tobacco on his clothes or breath. He drank the local beer and blended whiskeys but always in moderation. When we'd find a bar that would serve us we were careful not to get drunk or even tipsy. We were playing at being adults or at least I was; Norbie was already there.

I saw the depth of his loneliness when he joined high school clubs that were really of little interest to him. He later brought me into his car club, but that was much more of a social affair than anything to do with speed or racing, its meetings consisting mostly of 3.2 beer drinking and talk about girls and adolescent sex.

He was full of unique expressions. When he went to confession he said that he "had gotten right with the man in the box." He had a special relationship with our high school's vice principal, the man who collected demerit slips at the end of the day and impaled us with his stare. A tall man, at least 6'6", he gazed down at us, projecting a feeling of suppressed anger and supreme disappointment. He never spoke, except to Norbie, who was chronically late for school because of problems at home. The vice principal attributed the problem to Norbie's love of his car and the distractions it presented. "Norbert," he would say, "ride the big yellow job. Be here at eight and you'll never be late." It was one of those strange and almost-silly expressions, the kind that were repeated endlessly in hallways and locker rooms.

There was a student in our class who fancied himself a mechanic and was fond of intimidating freshmen and sophomores with his prowess in the garage. Curiously, his parents had a breakfast show on a local radio station. Their faces adorned the sides of city buses and their abundant on-air cheerfulness and educated speech contrasted with the hard case image projected by their son Bill. Whenever he worked on a car and was confronted with a problem his response was the same. He'd reach for a torch or an awl or a hammer and chisel and say, "I'm afraid we're going to have to cut…" For Norbie this became the opportunity to give birth to a new verb. "Whatever you do," he'd say, "do it right, don't Bill Case it."

Norbie's girl friend was a brunette named Linda Worley. As fast as his Chevy in its prime, she had come close to marrying at least three people by the time she was seventeen. With Norbie she was somehow different, less sexual, more mature, almost tired and blasé. Linda was the type of girl Norbie was expected to attract, but she was quickly changed by his presence and company into a world-weary twentysomething who seemed to have been working half of her life.

Norbie was slight in stature, no more than 5'9", but he never attracted violence or the kind of envy that often preceded it. In part it was the coolness which he projected through every pore, but in part, I think, it was also the aura of sadness and the sense that he had moved beyond such things years before.

I never heard all of the details because Norbie kept them private, but there were a few things that came out over the years: his father had died when he was very young and after a period of struggle his mother had remarried. The second relationship was nothing like the first. We didn't have the word then, but Norbie considered it abusive and tried to persuade his mother to leave or move or somehow change her situation. When she wouldn't or couldn't he retreated into himself, lived like a lodger in his mother's home, spent the majority of his time at work, school, or in his car, and took on the role of an overlooked adult rather than that of a neglected child. He never cried or gave in. Even today, decades later, it's difficult for me to say just how much I admired and respected him for it.

It wasn't as if we dwelt on such things. We were young and the summers were long. Every night was an adventure, as we drove through and around the city, the windows of our cars open against the lingering heat and the air heavy with the humidity that was one of the few constants in our lives. The city was still rural in attitude if not in economy and the conversion of a favorite farm to a new subdivision was still seen as an invasion and an affront.

Parks and party rooms still carried the suffix "-farm," a sign of the fervor with which we clung to the past and the old ways. The smells of honeysuckle, mint, and wildflowers gave way to those of fresh asphalt, frycook's grease, and the scent of chopped onions, grated cheese and cinnamon-laced chili. Pancake and waffle houses displaced fruit and vegetable stands and ribbons of highway covered the ground, linking chain stores and strip malls with service stations, groceries and four-apartments.

Farm ponds became pay lakes, with moderate prices and pungent outhouses. Greenhouses appeared in the corners of fields as farmers became florists and fields became nurseries. Blue spruce, pin oaks, and red maples were coveted and contrasted with suburban scrub pine and dusty city sycamores. The country was shaped and demarcated, hills were levelled and the landscape humanized. Hedges and fences appeared, cement driveways, and screened porches, bondstone, metal siding, and brick veneer.

One evening Norbie and I drove across the north side of the city, with Linda Worley and a girl named Mary Lenhardt. Snaking through the curves of Dailey Farm Road we drove into the purest sunset, holding each other's knees for balance in those days before seatbelts and finally coming to rest on the top of Grove Hill, where we drank beer in longnecks from an icy cooler and ate chips from a jumbo bag lined with foil and pretzels from a two-foot metal can with swinging handles on the sides. We toasted the sunset, spread out on a blanket, and stared up at the night sky dotted with stars, and though the sky and sun and stars were there for us every evening this one somehow seemed to be special and perfect in its simplicity.

I went off to college and to life and Norbie and I quickly lost touch. Then, in the mid-nineties, I received notice of his death. Everybody dies, but not this young, and most of them were less important to me than Norbie. A few years later when most of the grieving had passed and I had enough free time to find answers to my questions I drove off to discover just what had happened.

My wife was skeptical, but she told me to take the most reliable car and call her whenever I could. I drove north, into the edge of the sunrise, across the fields of summer wheat, and into the midwest of my youth. At first it seemed as if I was too late. I checked the telephone directory for familiar names and most of them were gone. My class scribe, who has spent a good part of her life keeping up with such things, told me that Jimmy Gels and Pat Murphy had each died years earlier, as had Ted Baker and Donny Ford. Three of their wives were gone as well. I asked her about Norbie and she drew a blank.

"He left the city years ago," she said. "His death was reported directly to the high school; I didn't know it had happened until they told me."

"Did they tell you about the circumstances?" I asked.

"No. I asked but they told me they didn't have any additional information."

"Who contacted you?" I asked.

"Gerry," she said.

"Gerry…?"

"The administrative assistant in the office. She may have something in the file; she didn't volunteer anything when I asked her for further information."

Geraldine Hanmer was the only person in the office when I arrived the next morning. She seemed uncomfortable that she was alone there and talked about the summer schedule and about some recent budget cuts. I told her

I was trying to find out some additional information on a classmate who had died.

"We don't keep files," she said. "We just maintain a data base; it won't say anything once the person's dead. We take out the address and phone number and all that sort of thing. All that's there is the name, with a cross in front of it, the date of graduation and the date of death. What was your classmate's name?"

I told her. She said she thought she remembered receiving the notification from his son. She couldn't remember his name, but the more she thought about it the more she felt that she was right; it was the son who notified them.

"Where was he writing from? Do you remember?" I asked.

"Someplace out east," she said.

"New York? New England?"

She shook her head. "It's really important," I said.

"Let me ask Brother Larry," she said. "He may remember."

"Our Vice Principal?"

"Yes, he was Vice Principal for awhile," she said. "He's not well, but at least he's still alive."

I expected her to pick up the phone, but she didn't. She asked me where I was staying, told me that she'd do her best to contact him, and promised to call me with any information he might have. I gave her my cell phone number as well as the number at the hotel, and left.

That afternoon and evening I drove through the old streets. Some had been blocked by new development; some had been expanded; some looked pretty much the same as they always had, except for some tattered edges.

After driving for several hours I settled in at a bar on the north side of town, a place that Norbie and I had spent some hours in. The clientele had changed; the blue collars had been replaced by barflies who began and ended their days on the same stools. The bartender's name was Sid; he looked as if he'd rather be someplace else, anyplace else.

The next morning I waited for the call that never came. At 1:00 I called the school and asked for Geraldine. "I'm just about to call him," she said. "Don't worry; I'll call you back if he knows anything."

"I'd appreciate it if you'd call me either way," I said.

"All right," she answered.

She didn't call until 4:00. "He was busy," she said. "He just now called me back. He said that the son lived in New York. Albany, he thought. He said he also thought that the son's name was Carl."

"Thanks very much," I said. "I'll let you know whatever I learn."

"OK," she answered. There wasn't a great deal of enthusiasm or curiosity in her voice.

I got the son's name and phone number from the internet and called. A woman answered. Her voice sounded impatient, as if she was expecting me to try to sell her something. I asked to talk to Carl and she told me he was out. I asked about her father-in-law and she told me he had died of cancer in a hospital in Chicago. She also told me that he had been a policeman. That surprised me, at least initially. I was also concerned that Norbie and his son might have been estranged, but I figured that I was little more to his daughter-in-law than a voice in the dark and that she was just being guarded, not uncaring. What she told me was all public information, but she had saved me a lot of time. I gave her my name, address, and cell phone number to reassure her that I wasn't some nut and that she could check on me if she wanted to. She then told me that she and her husband were about to leave for an important trip and that I could call back in a couple of weeks if I wanted to talk to him. "He doesn't like to talk about it," she said, "but he'd probably talk to one of his father's friends."

I was surprised by her statement, but didn't pursue it. I just thanked her again, checked out of the hotel, and got back on the road. I paid less attention to the scenery and our old haunts. The answers I sought were elsewhere now.

I drove for six and a half hours, found a motel on Sheridan Road with a vacancy sign, and turned in for the night. The next morning I started calling desk sergeants. The first two told me that I'd have to come in and submit a formal request for any information on former members of the department; the third paused after I gave him Norbie's name, called him a son-of-a-bitch, and hung up. I called a fourth and was told that Norbie had left the department two years before he died and that he was working for a security company on the north shore. "Evanston?" I asked and the man answered, "Wilmette, I think."

There was only one security company in the telephone directory with a Wilmette address, an organization called SecuriCorp. I phoned them and my call was bounced from office to office. Finally I reached the personnel division, which told me they had no record of an employee by that name. I asked if there were any other security companies in Wilmette and was told that there was one, but it had closed the previous year. The personnel officer remembered the name, North Shore Security, but didn't know the name of the company's owner.

I thanked her and got back on the internet, checking court cases involving North Shore Security. There were no names of any owners or directors of the company listed, but the company's attorneys of record were Kent, Armstrong, and Pulley, a downtown firm. I called, talked to a receptionist, was forwarded to an associate, and then to another associate. I gave him my name, address, email address, phone number, and cell phone number, inviting him to check on me and verify that I was who I said I was. I told him that an old friend of mine had died and that he was working for North Shore Security just before his death. He volunteered to call someone who had been with the company and ask that person if he was willing to contact me. I thanked him and requested that he himself call back if the person was unwilling to do so. "I don't want to bother you," I said. "I just want to know if I have to pursue some other course." In passing I mentioned Norbie's name and there was silence at the other end of the phone.

"Are you still there?" I asked.

"Yes, I'm here. Your friend…he was a good man. At least I thought he was."

"You knew him?" I asked.

"Not personally."

"What can you tell me about him?" I asked.

"The man at North Shore can tell you more. I'll do what I can to persuade him to call you."

"Thanks," I said.

I hung up the phone and got on my laptop, searching for information on Norbie. The problem was that his surname was too common. Even though I had typed in '+ Chicago' after his name I got over a thousand hits. Scanning the first batch it was clear that the search engine was not pulling the surname, given name and location together as neatly as I might have wished. I was working my way through the first page of entries when the phone rang.

The man identified himself as James Allen. He told me that he had been associated with North Shore Security and that he was familiar with my friend. I asked him if we could meet and he agreed to have lunch with me.

"Today?"

"OK," he said.

He told me to meet him at the Orrington Hotel in Evanston. When I got there at 11:45 the dining room was deserted except for a single individual, sitting at a distant table next to the window. He was drinking a martini. I was struck by the fact that he was young, no more than 35.

"Mr. Allen?" I said.

"Jim," he said, shaking my hand. "Would you like one of these?"

"It's a little early," I said, taking the chair next to his.

"You may need it," he said, pausing before he continued.

"Norb was a good man," he said. "Not everybody believed that, but he was."

"I know," I said.

"It was all too early," he said. "No one was prepared to face it."

"I don't know what you mean," I said.

"You don't know what happened?"

"No, I don't. All I know is that he worked for the police department and then for the security company."

"He was a policeman for nineteen years. He lost his pension over it. I hired him at North Shore. At the time no one else would."

"What happened?" I asked.

"There was a boy named Richards. Danny Richards. Norb was investigating the case. He believed Danny, even after Danny hung himself. Especially after he hung himself."

"What was the nature of the case?" I asked.

"Years earlier the boy had been molested. It was ugly. It wasn't just some movie theatre grope or a bathroom peeper. He had been raped so severely that he required hospitalization. Not just for the trauma but for the physical injury. He was very young at the time."

"And Norbie…Norb was looking for the perpetrator."

"Danny told him the identity of the perpetrator. The problem was that a lot of time had elapsed. The person was older. He was established, respected, and very well represented."

"He had good lawyers."

"Yes. He had the best. There were problems with the case anyway. The boy had bled so much that the emergency room staff thought it might have been a stab wound of some sort. The boy was hysterical and the parents knew nothing except for the fact that their son was screaming with pain, desperately trying to catch his breath, and bleeding profusely. The attending resident cleansed the wound and removed any possible physical evidence in the process.

The boy wouldn't talk about what actually happened for years. Eventually his father died. A year and a half later his mother died. Finally he decided to report the crime and called the department. From what he told them they thought that the rape had just occurred; Norb was sent immediately to investigate. He listened to the boy's story, made some other enquiries, chased down the old medical records, checked as best he could for motive and opportunity and then eventually made an arrest. He went through all the right steps. He studied the case for weeks and talked to as many people as he could before he made his move."

"But he lost in court."

"Yes."

"That happens, unfortunately," I said.

"Yes, but not quite like this."

"Who was the perpetrator?"

"A man named Boyle. Charles Boyle. Monsignor Charles Boyle."

"And the diocese refused to settle?"

"There was never any thought of a settlement. Their immediate impulse was to counterattack; they made phone calls, starting with the mayor's office. Then they called the department. Threats were made, budgetary support could be withdrawn and officials embarrassed; there were promises of public relations nightmares. As crazy as this may sound, they even threatened to keep the department from marching in the Holy Name parade."

"That's not crazy; I know how important that kind of thing is in Chicago."

"The department asked Norb to pull back. He respectfully refused. They ratcheted up the pressure; he continued to refuse. The district attorney was up for reelection; he punted the case to a subordinate. The hospital to which the boy had been taken was controlled by the diocese. They all but refused to cooperate."

He finished his martini and ordered a second. He looked at me and I nodded yes. "It's amazing, isn't it?" he said. "You would think that the Trib or Sun-Times would have smelled the coverup and blown the story all over the front page, but they didn't. Boyle had been all but canonized and painted as the victim of a horrendous fabrication perpetrated by a liar seeking a lucrative settlement who was aided and abetted by a gullible policeman. When the plaintiff and policeman didn't cave in they were characterized as willful and stubborn. Suggestions were made of anti-catholicism; the fact that the plaintiff had left the church was used against him rather than seen as the result of his reaction to the church's bad faith.

"When they went to trial the assistant D.A. sat on his hands while the jury was selected. They later deliberated for thirty minutes before bringing in a Not Guilty verdict.

"Norb was in tears when the verdict was read. Three months later the young man hung himself. This was spun as evidence of his guilt for telling such lies about a respected and faithful member of the clergy. Norb was dismissed from the force. Several people urged him to contest the action, but he refused, even though it was obvious that the city was scapegoating him in an effort to throw a sop to the diocese.

"Instead he put together every penny he had and brought a civil action."

"What happened?" I asked.

"It was dismissed on the grounds that he lacked standing. By then the cancer which had started in his chest cavity had spread throughout his body. He did everything he could, but the end came quickly."

"Is he buried on the north shore?"

"That's a good question. When he brought the civil action the diocese was outraged. There were some discussions and a decision was made to formally excommunicate him. I know, that hardly ever happens, but it happened this time. The diocese claimed that his action was malicious and that in taking that position he was, in effect, setting himself outside the church. He had chosen his own excommunication.

"As a result, they denied his son the opportunity to bury his father in hallowed ground."

Jim Allen paused again. "We should get something to eat," he said. "I'd like another drink first. How about you?"

"Yes, thanks," I said.

Eventually we ordered club sandwiches and some soup, but neither of us were very hungry. We put our plates aside and ordered coffee. After finishing a third cup Jim Allen asked me about my relationship with Norbie. I told him that except for my wife he had been my best friend and that I felt terrible about not being there for him when he was going through all of this. "He did just what I thought he'd do. He was always a standup guy." I took a drink of my coffee and then continued. "I want to thank you for helping him and for believing he was right in what he did."

"I knew he was right," Jim said. "It didn't take any leap of faith or intuition. I knew it."

"How so?"

"Because Charles Boyle molested me also. I didn't have the courage that Danny did. I should have come forward. At the time I figured it wouldn't have helped. I knew how powerful the church was. Danny and I were classmates and friends. They would have said that I was lying on his behalf. Before I had the chance to change my mind Danny was dead and Norb was dying. So I carry this with me now.

"It's gotten easier though. Boyle was finally indicted last week. Already the archbishop is back-pedaling. He's not going to be able to pull this one out. The press smells the blood on the water now that public attitudes have changed. People are coming forward. Boyle's going to do hard time."

"Like you said earlier, Norb was too early with this case. People weren't ready to see what had been going on for years. This is a vindication. Not perfect, but good. You know, I'm glad you and I were both his friend."

"I think about this all the time," Jim said. "I hardly think of anything else. I read something recently; it made a lot of sense to me…

happenstance reading…strange, like someone had intended that I should read it."

"What's that?" I asked.

"You sure you want to hear?"

"Yes, I do."

"OK then. I was reading about some movie they were thinking about making, but couldn't raise the money for. It was too abstract, somebody said. Not enough action. Too…what did they call it—*cerebral.* No box office possibilities. Anyway…years ago they buried the ancient heroes and kings of East Anglia in mounds above the river Deben in modern day Suffolk. When they later started to excavate the site they found jewelry made of solid gold; they also found spears, helmets, bowls--rare items from throughout the Mediterranean. The heroes were buried in working ships that they brought up the river. The ends of the ships originally projected from the mounds. This was the real deal; one ship was ninety feet in length. These were seafaring people and that was the way they wanted to be buried.

"When the archaeologists excavated further they found something else, something no one expected. In between the burial mounds were what remained of the bodies of people who had been executed. In some cases you could detect that their necks had been broken or severed. The sand there is so acidic that the bodies had disappeared completely, but the images of the individuals who were buried there remain in the sand, almost as if they were printed there. The best guess is that when Christianity came, those in authority buried whoever committed crimes or, perhaps, opposed them, next to the old mounds as a form of additional punishment. This was pagan ground, unhallowed. That was the worse thing they could do—condemn them to sleep for eternity in pagan soil.

"But now we know what these bishops and cardinals and popes could be like, don't we? They might have had Jesus' message, but they didn't always follow it. Sometimes they betrayed it, the sons-a-bitches, and then betrayed us when we didn't do their bidding. When the betrayal comes from those you should be able to trust most it tears your heart out. Rape is one thing, but rape with a Roman collar is another. But the final question is easy to answer…"

"What's that?" I asked.

"Where would you rather be buried—next to the betrayers with the little white and red caps, the people who demanded that you kiss their rings and follow their orders? Or would you rather lay in the ground next to the heroes and kings?"

I lifted up my coffee cup; it may not have been the best thing to use for a toast, but it was all I had and the action seemed right. As I drove home I kept turning these thoughts in my mind. I wanted to strike at something, to take some physical vengeance. My imagination ran to thoughts of bloodied faces and broken limbs, but at the end of the day that never really works. What works is the change that is finally irreversible. It comes slowly, too slowly, but in the end history has a long memory. We tinker with its judgments and massage them around the edges, but if the evil is real the basic picture is fixed in our personal memories and there's not much going back on it. The simple truth is that there's not enough holy water to cleanse away all of that blood and not enough lies and legal maneuvers to change the basic equations and facts. You put a black hat with a red pom pom on the head of a rapist and he's still a rapist.

As I drove farther south I began to see the shiny leaves of magnolias, their white flowers spreading over their limbs. The azaleas and the dogwoods were no longer in bloom, but the cherry trees were dotted with red fruit and the birds were feasting. The willows had taken on that polished summer look which gives them a special prominence, setting them against the oaks and maples and ashes and bringing a special feeling of languor and peace. The boxwood was lush and dark and clusters of pink, white, red, and purple impatiens were gathered at the corners of houses and in the baskets that hung from porch roofs.

An occasional cloud passed overhead, dotting my windshield and the surrounding earth with heavy raindrops, but bright sun followed quickly and the skies slipped and drifted overhead, drawing me forward even as they receded into an unseen distance.

There are still times when I think of Norbie and the fact that I will never hear his voice again or feel his presence, but those who leave with such beauty and grace are never far from us and those whose style is matched with something more solid and more lasting are sleeping among the heroes of our hearts and wait for us in the distance with silent smiles and outstretched hands.